CORNIS

BUTTERFL

Copyright © David Lenderyou 2020

First Printed in United Kingdom 2020

ISBN – 978-1-9996559-83

Email   davidlenderyoubooks@gmail.com

Author – Publisher

David Lenderyou

CORNISH MIST TRILOGY

Cornish Mist (1) – Pebbles & Stones
Cornish Mist (2) – Butterfly & Nettles
Cornish Mist (3) – Ladybirds & Hawks

AUTHOR

David Lenderyou direct lineage dates back to the year 1318 from the Lynderiowe family in Mylor Village near Falmouth. Many of his descendants were Yeoman, Tin Miners, Pikemen, Paupers and Butchers. David was raised in Cornwall with his Father being from Falmouth and his Mum from Palmers Green, bless her, who met one another in Trafalgar Square just after the War. David laughs at the time he had to dance in the Hal an Tow on Floral day, 8th May 1971 in Helston, and having to wear his Mums tights with his mate Denis Bagnall. Life has many ups and downs and so keeping that Cornish spirit will help you on the path.

PREFACE

CORNISH MIST (2) BUTTERFLY & NETTLES

In the year 1708, the niece of Count Philip de Albret and the begotten son of King Louis XIV, want revenge, no matter what. Their arrogance holds no bounds and anyone who gets in their way will be silenced. They alone will decide how it will happen and that the Love of the Cornish way is just a myth. Joshua, and the love of a beautiful strange lady, who cannot be named or spoken of, must use their means to keep the Cornish safe.

....

SOUTHERN FRANCE 1708

''Catch me, catch me,'' she shouted excitedly and then ran quickly away from the cottage doorway. Jon was sitting inside with coffee in hand and laughing aloud at her girly behaviour but he was so in love with Zoe, and she with him, he played the game she liked They had once been childhood sweethearts until that nasty Philip de Albret had taken her away so many years ago. But now they were back together and together they will stay, forever. ''I will catch you,'' Jon said aloud, ''And when I do, I will spank your bottom.'' He heard her giggle and then ran out after her.

The man, secretly known as 'Snipe' had lay silently for two nights dug in at the forest edge waiting patiently for this very moment. It was about six hundred metres but with his experience, iced cold steady eye, and his new technology long range scope, he was confident. Without taking his eye away from the lens he ever so gently adjusted for drift. Then holding his breath one last time he slowly, ever so slowly, squeezed the trigger.

Chapter 1

It had been six months since the success of the operation to uncover the fiendish plot by the French in poisoning the good people of Mousehole before an all-out attack. It also had given great reward to rescue Jeanne who had been held captive in the dungeons of a Chateau in France, once owned by the very nasty Philip de Albret, Count of Morlaix.

George Kernow, the man in charge of that operation, was alone in his grubby little office preparing a full and detailed report for his superiors. They expect every minute detail to be covered and nothing could be left out, nothing. He was contemplating where things went right versus things that went wrong and, where things could have been improved on. George Kernow was Chief of operations for the South West region incorporating all the land from Cornwall to Bristol. He has ten teams to control but in his heart knew the Cornish team, of the very South West, lay most fondly.

His mind drifted to the deadly seriousness of the beautiful but the ever so secretive world of the 'Butterfly Witch' and, how people would laugh at him at the very mention of her name. He, however, knew different and so did the Cornish. This woman knew everything and will protect the Cornish people and their land with deadly devotion. The thought of writing anything about her in his report would be seen as utter madness but, he knew the very instigation and success of the whole operation was made by this powerful recluse. They just would not believe it and that was fine by him. He had also sworn an oath to her upon his own death that he would not mention or even think of her in any way shape or form. A cold icy shudder then went straight through his body and so shook his head and shoulders to quickly get her out of his thoughts as she may be listening, somewhere or somehow.

Moving his thoughts to the vital part he played in the operation, he was particularly proud of how he managed and manipulated the French spies, especially their leader on the ground called Jacques. However, all that was history now and hopefully his team which incorporates Joshua and Rebecca had recuperated and rested from their experience.

He again went over in detail what had happened, and again a dark feeling came over him. He tried to pinpoint why this keeps happening and knew that something was not right. Something inside kept niggling at him about something or someone but he just couldn't reason it out what it was.

He knew his bosses will be particularly interested in what concessions he had given, if any, in order to achieve his success. Hmmm, he thought, this was a little tricky but, he had to be truthful, and truthful he would be.

Jeanne had been given Mr and Mrs Wards Farm to live in which was located at Sennen. Both the Wards had been found guilty of Treason and so had been hanged by the neck at Bodmin Jail. Jacques, the French turncoat, had been given a full pardon for his help in the success of the operation. Zoe, Jacque's French compatriot, was given a full amnesty and as agreed returned to her native France. It appeared that Jacques and Jeanne, in their covert working for their Countries, and both from two very different walks of life, had secret liaisons with each other for nearly fifteen years. No one in England knew a single thing about this until it was uncovered during the operation and used as a pivot of emotion to rescue her. George Kernow knew this was the main reason why the operation was a success. He had used Jacque's dying loyalty of love for Jeanne to turn him for his own gain. He would tell that also.

One thing that was clear that pleased him was he had kept his promises to all, which included Zoe, Joshua and Jacques. Hopefully, they would respect and honour their promises to him, as he had respected theirs. He was confident they would, but he must be alert.

Henry Hosking, his Cornish lieutenant then came into his mind. Why did he now start to feel uncomfortable? Why did he feel something in his tummy, a gut feeling? He had worked with Henry for many years so why; he thought. He tried to dismiss his unease but the niggle inside him just would not go away.

He decided that was enough and his brain was aching and time was pushing on but he needed to go over once again and amend the report. He was assigned to start his report to the highest board in the land first thing in the morning. He decided he would work just one more hour but that was it. He looked down at the wine jug, poured himself another large glass and drank it down in one.

Chapter 2

''So, my crinkly old physician, you do have the potions I asked?'' ''Yes, my Prince, and I can assure you they will fill you with manly passion.'' ''They had better work this time or I will have you guillotined on the morning.''

The Physician tried to smile but knew this spoilt brat of a Prince was serious. He bowed his head in acceptance and handed over two small capsules he had made especially. They were a mixture of herbs, spices and ground animal bones. ''You are to drink the first one this afternoon, then take the second thirty minutes before you are ready to do the deed.'' ''Yes, I understand, now leave me and wait downstairs as I may have other duties for you to perform.'' The Physician bowed his head, turned and left the room without a word. The Prince sat back in his comfortable chair looking at the two capsules with utter delight.

The Prince was a Prince but really only in name as he was one of many illegitimate children from his Father, King Louis X1V. He had influence but again in name only. He also had property but not the kind to impress anyone of real high status such as other real Princes. He would change that and show everyone he had the King's blood, albeit from a prostituted Mother. He was now touching forty years of age and he was tired of being just a middle class, no one.

The Killings of Philip de Albret, the Count of Morlaix, and Pierre Bouchier were excellent news as they had given him a great opportunity to fulfil his ambitions. He just needed to work things out carefully in his favour.

He knew what Albret and Bouchier were up to as he had heard things in court and so made it his duty to secretly find out what exactly they were up to. As he got to know more and more of their plan through covert means, his plan for his own self good was taking shape, just in case, things didn't go the way they wished. However, both now being dead it obviously hadn't. He chuckled aloud at the very thought of their failure and deaths as their downfall would be his success.

However, it was the chemical thing to pre-kill the Cornish inhabitants before the French Fleet sailed that intrigued the Prince most. What a brilliant idea he thought. Who would have believed that Philip de Albret could create and devise such a devious plan? And so it was this line of enquiry that the Prince tenaciously and quietly pursued.

Whilst still sitting looking at the two capsules given by his Physician, he casually took his left hand and felt the inner lining of the right pocket of his silk jacket. He then very carefully pulled out a small glass tube filled with the said Chemical. He had got it from a little quiet Monk whom he had found and manipulated from the Abbey at Landerneau, where the Chemical had been made and where he had seen Philip de Albret visiting many times.

The little old Monk, thinking he was helping, had paid most dearly in secretly dealing with this nasty Prince that of his very own life. Once he had given all the information he had him drowned and weighted in a deep lake on a dark night, never to be seen again and carried out by the Prince's thugs.

With a cruel smirk on his face, the Prince relaxed back in the chair and stretched his legs out saying to himself, 'thank you, you stupid old Monk. This little tube of chemical will be the start of the process to bring about the success that he should most rightfully have and, it will start tonight.' He then glanced back at the other two capsules held in his right hand and said laughingly aloud, 'but not before I use you two lovelies.'

Meanwhile, as the Prince was enjoying his thoughts of the coming night with Antoinette, twenty miles away in a posh town house in Rennes, a man named Samuel pleaded again to his wife, ''Please don't go Antoinette, I just need to finish this work and then we can go and have a drink together.'' Antoinette couldn't think of anything worse, she hated him with a vengeance. They had been married now for over ten years after her Uncle, Philip de Albret, introduced them to each other at a party he was hosting.

However, that was when she thought he had money and prestige. She then found out, after they were married, that he was limp in bed and had no muscles as a real man should and, all the money he said he had was loaned out to him by his rich Father. He also, couldn't produce her any children which she now believes was an absolute blessing.

Her life was a total sham but the Prince had got word to her saying to meet him at his seaside retreat at St Malo. He had plans to sort all this out and so that's exactly where she was heading.

Then Samuel again pleaded, ''Please don't go Antoinette, my Father said he wanted to talk with me tonight and I don't know if I have the strength to speak with him alone.'' ''I thought, you just said once you have finished work we would go for a drink together." "Well, I did mean that at first then I forgot about my Father coming over. Maybe, we could go tomorrow." Antoinette, sick of his pitiful speech and weakness said, "I simply cannot cancel Samuel, what with all that has gone on and with my Uncles unsolved death at Morlaix, I need to get away and have some time with my loving cousin Caroline at her beach house in St Malo. You well know that we have had this planned for over a week now and I simply cannot and will not let her down. Now the coach is ready, and I am all packed." "Will you at least kiss me with your love before you leave?" Antoinette moved toward Samuel feeling utter hatred and dread. However, she had to play the game of appearing she loved him but hopefully, not for much longer.

She kissed him quickly on the cheek and said, "There, are you happy now." "And when will you return my loving beautiful wife?" "I believe the coach will return Monday afternoon." "O good, then I will make everything ready and maybe then we can have a drink together. We could afterwards enter the bed chamber together and I will show you how much your dear husband loves you." With an immediate thought of an angry reply, that in no way would she ever want this, she calmed herself and politely said, "Thank you my husband, you are most very kind I will look forward to seeing it."

The carriage seemed to take an age to get to her. However, as soon as it arrived, she quickly got on board while the driver's assistant loaded her luggage. Once all were safely aboard, they were off. At last, she thought to herself, what a relief. While simply letting the carriage take the road she looked out at the passing scenery and smiled at the thought of the evening to come with the

Prince. She then sat back, took off her wedding ring and adjusted her blouse to reveal more of her cleavage.

The ride to St Malo took just under three hours with no stops. On arrival, three of the Prince's men were there to meet her. One of the men stepped forward and opened the door offering his hand to help her down. ''Thank you, she said.'' ''My pleasure Mademoiselle, I am also to escort you to your room, please follow me.''

The Prince's seaside retreat was a fine three storey building set in a very posh promenade in the most expensive part of the seaside town.

Antoinette's quarters were to be on the second floor which overlooked the sea with splendid views. Her escort showed her around the big apartment which included a bath and a fireplace with beautiful tapestry adorning the walls.

''The Prince has asked you to be in his quarters on the third floor at seven this evening. Dinner will be served at seven thirty, I trust this is acceptable Mademoiselle?'' That leaves her just over an hour to get ready. ''Yes, that is acceptable, thank you, but could you please get some hot water for a bath?'' ''It is being done as we talk Mademoiselle, the maids will also assist you in laying out your things and getting your ladyship prepared and ready for the evening.''

When the escort had left, Antoinette looked around and could not help but notice the opulence. She headed for the decanter of wine which was on the table and poured a large red one.

At seven o clock, she was outside the Prince's apartment and noticed that the door was ajar. She peaked her head around the door but saw no one so she entered and then heard a voice say, "Antoinette, I am here in the bedroom, could you close the front door and bolt it." Antoinette did as advised then quickly went to the large mirror to check herself over. Going into the bed chamber she saw the Prince already on the bed lying naked and his passion alive. He had taken the second capsule of passion given to him by his physician at six thirty. She was simply taken aback at what she was seeing and stood motionless. "Antoinette, my beauty, take your clothes off and come to me now, dinner can wait,"

At eleven thirty that evening dinner was at last allowed in. He had shouted at them twice to come back later and twice they had, only to be turned away each time. However, this time he unlocked the door whilst in his bath robe and told them to lay things out on the veranda.

When they were once again on their own sitting around the luscious filled table the Prince poured two large glasses of red wine. The moon was up and the stars were out in the clear night sky. "Here is to us and together we will have what we each deserve." Antoinette was completely lost for words with this confident man in front of her, who had completely satisfied her women's needs, he was a real man.

He went on to discuss the plan of action and gently handed over the lethal chemical tube. She looked at the little tube in awe, smiled and slowly slipped it between her breasts.

They agreed that on her return home on Monday she was to pour the chemical of death into Samuel's wine glass before they got into bed. In the morning when the deed had been done and all the staff was in a state of shock, she would cry out loud but somehow find the courage and get word to the Prince. He would then come dashing to her rescue.

With the death of her husband being very alike in strategy to that of her uncle Albret and his man Bouchier, the Prince would then request a meeting and plea to his Father, King Louis X1V. He would then inform him that the killing of Antoinette's husband is a further conspiracy on and above that of Count Philip de Albret and would appear that it was spreading. He would also put across that with the King's approval and sufficient funds given, he could stop it and find the ultimate person or persons responsible. One thing he did know is that the killers were English. This particular point would be put across more strongly as he knew the King hated the English what with their constant and lofty attitude that they were superior to him and his good French countrymen.

Although Antoinette was spellbound by this man's cavalier plan, she was aware enough to remind him to consider her own reward. She cared absolutely nothing for Samuel, her husband. In fact, she was actually quite looking forward to carrying out his imminent death by the chemical poisoning. So she said, ''My Prince, what about me and my new status in being the Countess of Morlaix and the taking over of my uncles Chateau in its entirety?''

''That's exactly what you shall have Antoinette when the plan has been fulfilled, but what we need first is my

Fathers authority and his money. Once we get that we can do anything we want and to anyone we want. The Chateau and its title will be yours forever and I will have real power and the prestige that I deserve."

The Prince continued, "Now my little Countess minx, let us retire to bed as I am again in need of your body." "But my Prince, we have only just come from the bed chamber and we haven't finished dinner." "Dinner can wait, my passion cannot."

Chapter 3

"I swear those English pigs will pay for this and don't care how much, who does it or how long it takes," Antoinette said aloud. "Be careful my lady, be careful," the man who was sitting opposite replied.

"What do you take me for a fool, I know full well that people around here have washed their hands of the whole affair and put the word about that Philip de Albret, my uncle, was working alone, but I know differently and will have none of it." She then carried on in the same outrageous voice, "The King of France has given his full backing for this mission to uncover who has done these awful deeds. I will have my revenge for my dear uncle and my lovely darling husband's similar untimely deaths."

As soon as she spoke these words about her husband's untimely death, she started to sob and cry out loud. The two men didn't know what to do so they just remained still with silent courtesy and graciously gave her the space and time she needed for her sobs of deep hurt to subside. Antoinette, with a silk handkerchief in hand, kept wiping away the false tears. She then looked down at the wet handkerchief in between her hands and with deep thought, drifted her mind back to the very night she had joyously killed him. Samuel had indeed been very happy and bright at seeing his wife's return from visiting her friend at St Malo. He had been all over her like a baby to his mother. Antoinette went along with it all and was all smiles and laughter. When all the staff saw how happy they were they too became happy for them both. However, Antoinette had other ideas and couldn't wait to get to the bedroom to carry out her and the Prince's plan of death.

Antoinette remembered back on how meekly and with utter sweetness she asked if she could go first to the bedroom as she wanted to be fully ready and prepared for her darling husband. Samuel laughed with happiness and chuckled at their new romance saying, "Of course my beautiful wife, I will come upon the hour and then kiss you all over as young lovers do." Antoinette chuckled like a shy lady and bowed her head sweetly acting coy like an awaiting bride.

As Samuel entered the bedroom at the appropriate time he had already undressed himself leaving only his pants on. Antoinette looked at him and thought how repulsive and skinny he was. He then moved over towards her and stood proudly by the bed and with his legs apart and hands on his hips he smiled at her. Antoinette smiled lovingly back and pointed to the full crystal wine glass by the side. She said, "O my beautiful handsome husband, I have made a wine especially for you and our new love, please accept it as a token of my new freshness for you." "Thank you my sweet dear wife," he replied. "Have you locked the door Samuel, we don't want anyone disturbing us this very night." "I have my love, now let me take the wine you have made and receive it with the knowledge of our newness of love together.

When Samuel drank the wine down in one he got into the bed and warmed his body towards her. She had no idea when the poison would start to work and its time frame to kill. However, the Prince had said that it was very virulent and attacked the throat and lungs without fault. Whilst being mauled by her disgusting husband's hands and tongue she waited with bated silence. Then, without any warning, he started to shake and cough and his hands went to his throat in a vain attempt to clear whatever had gone in. She pushed his body off of her and jumped out of the bed while all the time watching him with inner excitement. His eyes bulged widely as he reached out to her for help. His speech had gone and his body was thrusting up and down. She just stood there looking at him and grinning at his pathetic attempts to live. Once he had breathed his last he slowly and casually walked around the bed and poured herself a clean delicious red wine to celebrate her victory. In the morning, as planned, she frantically informed the staff of her husband's sudden death and all were in total shock. All this happened just over two weeks ago.

Samuels then Father, on learning of his son's demise, had quickly taken over the responsibility of his son's estate. He sold the house and everything else he could lay his hands on to pay off the massive loans and debts Samuel had got into. Antoinette, whom he totally disliked from the start, and she him, had kicked her out of the Rennes house. So she, with the King's permission, gained from her devoted and loving Prince, was living temporarily in her uncle's Chateau at Morlaix.

Once her thoughts had passed of her husband's death she gave one last sigh and sob. She then patted her face lightly and raised her head. Gently, as a lady would, she cleared her throat from the showiness of her distress and looked directly at the two men in front of her. Both men, as good gentlemen do, had given the lady the time to get over her distress and waited for her to resume the conversation. The three of them were sitting in the secret room of her now deceased Uncle's Chateau. Antoinette had much noticed that these men in front of her were in complete contrast to her timid, weak dead husband. Both were very capable, strong willed and knowledgeable in the field of spying and killing and, they knew many, many people.

Feeling now that the lady had indeed shed her last tears of misery, the Frenchman, named Peter spoke, "We are very sorry for your loss Mademoiselle and can only imagine what grief you are now feeling, what do you want of us and how can we be of service to you?" "You can start by bloody interrogating all the staff of this bloody Chateau; someone here must know something or someone. As I said before, my uncle was alive and well two months ago and now he is dead, found naked in his bed, asphyxiated. My husband also, God bless him, lay in the same way only two weeks ago"

"And what of Pierre Bouchier's death," they asked. "I don't give two hoops for that overrated so called thing of a man, I never liked or trusted him." "But he was found in his room under this same roof in a very similar way your uncle had died the very same morning." "Alright, I understand that, but my main concern is finding who done this awful, awful deed. Also, if you feel Bouchier was linked in any way then do what you must." Antoinette continued, "Now, I must go as I am so very upset and must meet someone who is waiting for me and am running late so may I thank you both kindly for coming here.

Why don't you both go away and consider what has been said and think about what is needed but could you please come back to me within two weeks with your actions plans to achieve what I want." "And what we want my lady," Peter retorted boldly. "Well of course, this is a two-way thing,'' she replied. The two men got up, bowed their heads and walked out.

Once the two men were out of the room and the door closed behind them, Antoinette got up and walked to the unseen side panel door and entered the library. Sitting in one of the chairs was a man who slowly and delicately put his arm out. Antoinette went to him, curtsied and kissed his hand.

''Well, did they fall for it,'' he asked. ''Yes, my Prince, hook line and sinker.'' ''Good,'' he replied, ''My Father Louis will be well pleased with you my little devil. Just think my dear, when we have what we want this Chateau will be all yours with the new title, 'Countess of Morlaix.''

''Thank you my Prince,'' she replied gracefully. The Prince continued, ''Now, as it is getting late in the day I have ordered my staff to lay out my clothes in your late Uncle's bedroom. I am just too tired to travel to Paris this evening and so will now go in the morning after breakfast. I will leave the bedroom door open and tell my servants that you will visit me later tonight for my comfort.'' ''Yes of course my Prince and thank you.''

Chapter 4

Rebecca and Joshua had decided they were getting married and were in good spirits. After all they had been through, deep down they knew that one day they would be together. They were in their little gig travelling to Sennen to see and tell Jeanne, Rebecca's Mother, of their wedding intent. They had left Little George and Christine to look after the two little Jack Russells at the cottage in Marazion.

Little George and his sister Christine, Joshua thought, what fine young children and the resilience and loyalty they both show, he greatly admired.

Jeanne, Rebecca's Mother, was now nearly recovered from her ordeal under the French, being captured, imprisoned in the dungeons in the Chateau at Morlaix and maltreated by the nasty Philip de Albret. On a previous mission linked to Jeanne's initial capture, Joshua's Father was not so lucky and had been killed or, looking at it from a different angle, maybe he was the lucky one. Henry Hosking, also involved with that failed mission, had very luckily escaped onto the Galleon completely unscathed.

However, that was over three years ago and after two years of capture, a new mission under the leadership of George Kernow, Rebecca and Joshua and others, had stopped the French chemical operation aimed at the Cornish and at the same time freed Jeanne from the dungeons and brought her home.

The only needle in the haystack from the entire mission is Jeanne's, new partner, Jacques. He was the front man of the French chemical operation based in Cornwall and no one knew of his relationship with our Jeanne. How they kept it secret no one knew but, someone did know.

It is true to say though that if it wasn't for Jacques, Jeanne would not be here. However, saying that, if it wasn't for Kernow's leadership and intelligence, Jacques wouldn't be here either. What a game they all played, in the sphere of their undercover workings.

Joshua pondered on his thoughts while Rebecca was sitting beside him in the buggy. He was admiring the coastal views and feeling comfortable with the ease of speed with which they were travelling. Joshua wanted to directly ask Jacques what his intentions are and had they changed since getting the amnesty to live with Jeanne on Cornish soil from George Kernow. It had been granted to Jacques for his services of loyalty in the success of the mission and the subsequent rescuing of Jeanne.

Funny thing, Joshua thought, only a few weeks ago before Jacques was eventually turned from a major player on the French side into helping the Cornish, Joshua was going to kill him. How very different things turn out.

On nearing their destination Joshua turned the gig into the front gate of the Sennen Farm and then slowed down to a snail's pace. This gave the horses a little rest bit and also allowed the humps and bumps of the hard ground to be gentler on their bottoms.

This Farm at Sennen had once been the property of the Wards. However, on the finding that this family of just two persons were both active traitors to our Good Queen Anne and the true Faith, they were jailed in Bodmin and then moved to London and hanged until they were dead. When George Kernow makes his mind up, he is ruthless. Saying that he also knows when to give and when to bend as Jacques is well aware.

Joshua tied the gig on the railing and patted his horse Harry and then helped Rebecca down. Jeanne had by now come to the front door and was waiting to welcome her Daughter with open arms and a big loving cuddle.

Rebecca was touching thirty-two years of age but she never tired of her mother's openness of love. Joshua also got a loving and friendly kiss on the cheek but no cuddles.

On entering, they could smell the roasting beef being prepared for their dinner. The Farm house in which Joshua knew from the past, when the Wards had owned and lived, had changed dramatically. Gone were the crosses, religious artefacts and the drab cold atmosphere. Now the place felt peaceful and loving with a lovely calmness about it.

Jeanne sat them both down by the fire place and suggested that dinner would be in about an hour. "Where is Jacques," Joshua asked. "He is in the barn chopping wood," Jeanne replied. "Would it be alright if I went to see him please?" "Yes, of course Joshua." As Joshua got up, Jeanne spoke again but this time it was in a different tone. "Joshua, I know you have orders from above to keep an eye on him." Joshua tried to interrupt her but she carried on. "Joshua, I have been in your line of work for many years and it's exactly what I would ask people to do if I was in Kernow's position. But please listen to me, Jacques is a good man and will honour his agreement with

Kernow. I also love him very much and if I didn't know this to be true, I would never want to be with him." "I understand Jeanne and I thank you for that, but really that isn't my intention, I just thought he may need some company."

Joshua did in fact have orders to keep an eye on this man, just in case. However, Jeanne just smiled and said nothing more and turned her attention towards her daughter who had kept quiet throughout.

With Joshua now out of the way, Rebecca, with a big smile on her face took her Mums hands in hers and asked in a loving tone if she would be happy if she and Joshua were to be married. "Has Joshua asked you my darling?" "Yes, he has Mother and I have said yes but only if you were happy with it." "O my beautiful Rebecca of course I am happy for you. Joshua is a good man but as you well know the job he is in is not for the faint hearted. Have you discussed this also?" "We have Mother and it's the life you and Father chose, and Joshua's parents too. It is also the life where we first met each other and it's the life we choose to continue with including all its humps and bumps."

Just as Jeanne leaned forward to hug Rebecca on the good news, the back door flew open and in walked Jacques and Joshua laughing aloud. Jeanne and Rebecca quickly turned their heads towards both of them whilst hearing Jacques say, "Brandy Joshua?" "Not brandy my dear friend how about a Cognac?" "A Cognac it is Joshua and a large one at that to celebrate this good news." All four of them laughed together with the happiness at the forthcoming wedding.

They then all went to the large kitchen area and sat around the table. With glasses filled and as Jacques announced the word 'cheers' of matrimony and happiness, they drank.

Rebecca proceeded to discuss the arrangements that both Joshua and she had made."Where will it be held," Jeanne asked. "At Gunwalloe in the Church on the rocks," Joshua replied, ''We have asked the vicar and he has suggested the Saturday after the last 'Banns' have been read." "So that's a month from now," said Rebecca. Jeanne looked at Jacques with soft loving eyes at the thought of her daughter being married and Jacques, understanding her thoughts, lovingly reached out his hands to hold her hands.

"Also," Rebecca continued, "We would very much like Little George and Christine to be page boy and bridesmaid." They all expected a cheer of joy; however, they all got something very different that surprised them all. Jeanne, on hearing the names of the two children, dipped and turned her head away so no one could see her expression as tears started to fall. Jeanne then got up and ran out of the house.

Rebecca looked at Joshua in complete confusion which led Joshua to look at Jacques. Jacques knew why this had happened but was forbidden to say anything, it would be too disturbing. Instead, Jacques rose from his chair and calmly said, "I think your Mother is so happy she is crying with love for you both. I will go and comfort her and bring her back." "Thank you, Jacques," Rebecca replied and then looked at Joshua for help. Joshua held her hands and said, "Love is a funny thing my lovely."

Jacques found Jeanne at the side of the house in tears and went straight to her to cuddle her tight. He whispered, "I know my love, I know." She cuddled him back tighter and said, "What are we to do Jacques?" "We must tell them, that is what we must do." "I know we must, but we cannot, not yet, the timing is wrong.

Everything about telling anyone is wrong, it doesn't feel right. We would put them in danger."

After agreeing to keep their secret, Jacque wiped away her tears. They then kissed and held hands and went back into the house to celebrate her daughters and future son in law's life together.

Chapter 5

"What will it be gentleman," the barman asked. "A bottle of your best Cognac and two glasses, we will be sitting over there by the window." The two men had just come from the Chateau of Morlaix and needed to discuss plans on how to achieve Antoinette's wants and wishes.

They initially discussed their thoughts on Antoinette who seemed to think that anger and brute force were the things that were needed, but they knew different. If that's indeed how she wished to proceed then they are not the men for the job. In fact, they needn't tell her at all as they could just drink up and leave. However, there was something that made them stay and that was money, loads of it. If they could get the plan right and succeed, they would be rich men, never having to work or take orders from anyone, ever again. So, this they thought was a golden opportunity to achieve their own life's goal and, at the very least, it needed to be discussed, before agreeing to do it, or not do it.

The two men were from the same background of poverty but from two different Countries being one from Spain and one from France. What they had in common was much more as they had both fought many times as mercenaries against the Dutch and the English and, they both spoke good English. They had learned their skills well and were much sought after in the hierarchy of governments. If somebody wanted something secretly done, these guys were it. Antoinette, or as she wants to be known after the success of this operation, 'The Countess of Morlaix' had money and was living in the high society of life, so she fitted exactly to their right kind of employer.

With the Cognac now poured they both sat forward and talked about what they knew and what they didn't know. The latter being much of the conversation and this was a worry to them whether to take the job or not. They both knew that good intelligence was the very key to success. Assumptions and supposes sounded very well on paper but in their game of high stakes, it was a no, no. They needed more, and they knew it. The information they had so far was sparse and not verified. They would take Antoinette's initial direction of speaking to all servants and workers at the Chateau. They would also scour the town and markets. They needed more information before any decisions could be made.

They also discussed the art of caution and the reason why this has kept them alive. Fighting hand to hand needed up front physical strength and bravery. Their bravery needed up front double dealing, cunning and brains. They both laughed at this way of working and poured more Brandy.

In the morning they would start their questioning. They would do this for as long as it takes, probably two to three weeks, subject to the answers gained and their solution to it. This then would define if a mission was feasible to achieve success. The first thing they needed was the total authority to use any means, as they see fit, to gain the intelligence from any person without hindrance. This they wanted in writing so they drafted a letter there and then and, once sealed, asked the barman to call for a courier to dispatch it to the Chateau at once and order him or her to await a written reply.

Once the letter was given to the courier they drank another Cognac and waited. It was only a fifteen to twenty-minute ride to the Chateau so expected a reply within a couple of hours or so, giving Antoinette plenty of time to scribe.

The Butler at the Chateau answered the door and told the boy to wait. He knew Antoinette was with her guest in her uncle's bedroom and it would be more than his life's worth should he enter. When nearing the bedroom, the Princes guards stood tall and challenged him. Explaining about the letter and the boy courier waiting outside, he was asked to hand over the letter and they will deal with it. He did as was ordered and then told to wait downstairs.

The guards did their duty and examined the letter and its seal for any abnormalities and seeing that all looked correct they knocked. They then heard the Prince shout, "Come in."

He and Antoinette were in the bed together but the guard remained straight face as he had seen this situation many times before and, not only with ladies.

Handing the letter across he was told to wait outside. The Prince asked Antoinette to keep massaging his chest while he read the letter aloud. They were both tipsy and through many giggles, he completed reading the letter. "Hmmm," he mumbled aloud, "so in essence, they want total authority to interrogate." "So, what do you think my Prince?" "I think it's a perfectly reasonable request. Fetch your letter headed paper and your family seal and I shall dictate while you scribe, this is such fun."

Doing as asked, Antoinette jumped off the bed and sat down at the Bureau. With ink and quill pen in hand and letterhead at the ready, the Prince started to dictate the reply giving them the full authority to do what was necessary but cleverly never mentioning his name. Instead, he always used the 'House of Morlaix' as the main factor of authority. Antoinette, being the dubious double character she is, noted this and was very tempted to add an addendum to the letter mentioning the name of the Prince and the King. However, she had a feeling of caution as the Prince may just want to see the finished article after she had written it. She thought about it again to protect herself but just couldn't take the chance. It read...

Gentlemen,
You are to do what you are to do and have my Authority as the soon to be Countess of Morlaix.
When you have found the person ultimately responsible for my Uncles death you must inform me immediately and then without failure personally lead me to them.
Only then can I take revenge for my Family's honour by severing their body, as they have severed my life, and stop any wider plot to hurt our most Gracious King& Country.

Signed by the hand...........................
STB Countess of Morlaix

When she had finished and signed it and then just about to fold and seal it she heard the Prince say, "Before you seal it my dear bring it over to me so I can read it."Getting up from the bureau she walked to the bed and handed it over and waited. "That's very good my dear, very good indeed."

It was now nearing two hours since the two men in the Inn had dispatched the letter and were getting a little anxious. Then out of the blue, the young lad came in and walked up to their table with the sealed, 'House of Morlaix' reply in his hand. Peter the Frenchman put his hand out to receive the letter. The young boy explained why he had waited so long at the Chateau. Both men nodded in acceptance and tipped him favourably for a job well done.

Looking at each other in anticipation the Spaniard poured the drinks while Peter opened the letter and read it silently. On completion, he said nothing but handed it over to the Spaniard who again read it in silence. When both had read the letter they looked at each other straight in the eyes and without saying a word, lifted their full glasses of Brandy and drunk them down really slowly in one. This they knew was their acceptance and the beginning of the initial phase of the mission and that the interrogation was on. They then slammed the glasses down on the table in complete unison.

Chapter 6

With his razor sharp fangs deep into the creature's throat, he laid silent but breathing heavily. His then eyes of gold with jet black irises slowly closed. He needed to rest.

Deep in the reeds of the cold boggy marsh in the bleakness of the midnight hour, he lay deadly still. He knew this to be wise as this once live animal of venison meat, now a lifeless corpse, lying dead in his powerful clutches, would need to feed not only his family across the moors of Bodmin but Zelahnor, their protector. He would need all his stealth and strength to deliver the food before the daylight hour.

After ten silent cold minutes had passed without moving a muscle, he felt her through the breeze. This made him stir inside and so slowly opened his beautiful black eyelids.

Seven miles away south, south west, isolated and asleep in the dark pits of the moor, Zelahnor awoke. Her beautiful crystal green eyes stared at the stars in the dark clear night. 'So, they are coming,' she felt herself say quietly. She must protect the children first at all costs and then deal with the threat as it would emerge. She knew they were dangerous, especially the female.'

Her bed was a nest of straw and reeds made previously by her animals across the moor. She loved and respected them all and treated them like new born babies, no matter how large or fearsome. They in turn adored and loved her like a mother and protected her, no matter what.

On her calling, a beautiful jet black moorland pony came up to her. "Thank you, my darling," she said and threw herself on his back. She needed to get to her shack in which she had lived all her moorland life.

Riding fast across the moor Zelahnor's blonde hair flowed freely with the wind. She wore only a flowing black silk see through shawl and was naked underneath. Whether it be cold or hot made no difference. She was just beautiful with a full body and blood red lips. A man could only dream of such a being.

Zelahnor knew things and felt things no one else could no matter where it be. If it affected the Cornish, be it animal, fish or human, she knew. They also knew of her but were not allowed to say her name in case she killed them or turned them into a toad. So they called her the 'Butterfly Witch,' which made her laugh like a young school girl.

The pony stopped and once she was down on the ground, patted his neck and kissed him on the nose. He shook his head up and down as in his love for her and galloped off. Zelahnor would walk to her shack from there as the terrain had now become rocky and too dangerous for the pony.

After three hundred yards and now deep into the crevices of the rocks unseen by the human eye, day or night, she was close. The shack's entrance faced due south allowing all the warmth through the day. Being also surrounded by rocks, the wind and cold breezes were blocked. The main body of the shack lay hidden inside the natural rocks contours and was built of old wood and mud.

Even before she reached the entrance the butterflies, moths and frogs went to her. She smiled with love for them all.

At the shack entrance area, she found a ripped hind leg of a deer lying on the ground. It was fresh and so must have only been delivered a short while ago. Standing still and looking up towards the night sky she whispered, 'Thank you my little darling, now go to your family and feed them, your little cubs miss you.'' The powerful and massive black beast with gold eyes was watching her. When he heard what she said he purred with an affection of love and took off silently with the remaining part of the carcass held in his jaws.

Taking the fresh meat in doors and closing the door behind her, every living creature came alive as if in anticipation of a newness of love. Butterflies and moths were everywhere and numbered in their thousands. They clustered to the walls and roof and when Zelahnor stoked the small fire they all fluttered their bodies and wings with the increase in warmth. She smiled and giggled at their love for her.

After making herself a nice tea of nettles she sat down and thought. She would need to send notice to the children's mother and would need to do it quickly as she lived over sixty miles away in Sennen. Zelahnor then lifted her head and looked all around at the butterflies and creatures in her wait. ''Now all you beautiful beings,'' she said, ''Which two of you can fly sixty miles and inform Jeanne that I need to speak with her?'' Nothing happened except an increase in buzzing noises and creatures fidgeting as if they were all talking with themselves at the question Zelahnor asked.

After a minute or so, two beautiful green butterflies flew up and landed on her hand. "Thank you my darlings, now you both be very careful and fly straight and swift." Bringing her hand up to her mouth she kissed them both very gently then let them go.

Chapter 7

''So my Dear woman, exactly where were you at the time we ask?'' The two men had taken over one of the dungeons to start their questioning and were going through in minute detail what exactly went on, who was involved, and why?

The young scullery maid knew nothing but that cut no ice with these ruthless men. They wanted information and lots of it. Once they have the raw ingredients of intelligence, they can then put it all together to find out exactly what they are dealing with. Then, and only then can they devise a plan of action, if it was deemed feasible. These guys had learnt well. They knew all about heroics and bravery but without the required intelligence and necessary skills to complete things versus the feasibility odds of failure, most of the hero's they knew were dead ones.

''We understand that you, your Mother and your Father are very poor, is that correct.'' 'Yes, Messieurs,'' that is correct, we have very little and they rely on me and my wages for all their food and clothing.'' ''There is nothing to be ashamed of with that Mademoiselle; our good King Louis is doing all he can for his people. She looked at them in total disbelief but kept quiet. Now tell us all you know about your work here at the Chateau.'' The young girl was petrified but she told them everything. The men continued until they also had everything. When they had finished, they thanked her for her support and loyalty and she was now free to go but not leave the Château until they told her she could. The notes they were taking were very extremely detailed as they needed to build this enigma and put it together.

Antoinette was still in the building but letting the two men get on with it. She had given then carte blanche to achieve what she wanted and, she would get it, irrespective of her Château staff's feelings of dislike or hatred. One by one the staff workers were questioned and ever so slowly a picture started to emerge. The two men were in no rush as patience was the overriding factor in this phase of the operation.

As the days ticked by most of the staff were asked to come back time after time. When a particular question was not answered with pure clarity they stopped. Vagueness was not an option, only precise answers whether good bad or ugly were needed. So over and over they went until they got what they needed.

The main guard to the dungeons was of much interest to them. He came across as loyal but weak. He mentioned the prisoner, as they all had but it was on his watch that she had escaped. The name of the prisoner was an English lady called Jeanne and she had been Philip de Albret's captive for nearly two years. She had been caught whilst escaping from the French coast after successfully assassinating a very important mole. It became very clear that Philip Albret had treated her with awful disdain and starved her when he felt the need and fed her only at his whim. She had no visitors and was basically left to rot.

They went over and over on what exactly happened at the time of her escape and, the very same night that Philip de Albret lost his life, as well as Pierre Bouchier, his right-hand man.

It also became clear that two men and a boy were involved. The guard knew the boy as a young lackey, who worked at the Château and did things he was told to do and be quick about it but he had never before seen the two men. The guard was further grilled as this was a really important part of what had happened. Again, they took copious notes.

One thing the two men didn't tell anyone was that once they had the information they wanted they would identify and kill the people who knew too much. It was brutal but necessary. The guard was asked to leave but stay around as he may be needed again.

The next day the butler was to be questioned. This they both knew to be important and so they wanted their full wits. Therefore they went steady on the brandy the night before and got an early night at the Morlaix Inn.

This man was different to the others as he knew everything that went on that night and, most importantly, the lead up to all that went on before Albert's death. He came across as very discreet and proper so they treated him more carefully whilst continuously grooming his status of 'Mr know all' by mentioning his excellent loyalty to doing a great job for the Count. They were preening his ego for intelligence and it was working. Going over the very night of the killings, the information was constant with that of an assassination, but why, why were Philip de Albret and Pierre Bouchier killed.

Jacques was a name they wrote down more than once and in fact, highlighted several times. Who was this man? The butler had escorted him several times into the secret room at the Château to talk with Pierre Bouchier. The butler was asked to describe him in every detail. Knowing this man was an important key to the mystery they had an artist brought in to draw him, based on the butler's description. When completed and the butler agreed that the image was exactly right the Spanish man drew a deep breath and said, "I have seen this man also but for the life of me I cannot remember, it's his cold icy blue eyes that I recognise."

Another name they had highlighted was 'Zoe.' The butler had taken a message from a courier that fateful night. He had handed the sealed message to his master Philip Albret in the library who was relaxing with a young maiden and, Bouchier was in there also.

The Butler continued his story. Soon after receiving this letter, Pierre Bouchier took his horse and rode away. On leaving, Bouchier advised him that my master was going to bed early and was not to be disturbed as he was taking the young maiden with him. The butler also said, 'they were all in very good spirits, except maybe the young girl.' "Have you the letter," they asked. The butler hesitated at this ask as it was his job to handle his master's requirements with total discretion in every detail. Philip de Albret, in his haste to bed the young girl, had left the note on the sofa after he passed it to Bouchier for his reading It was only when the butler was clearing up for the night that he noticed it. "Yes, I do have it." "Fetch it now," they demanded and sat back to await his return.

The butler came back down to the dungeon with the said letter in hand and was asked to take a seat as the two men silently read its contents.

It Read:-

My Love Pierre,
I write in favour that the mission has been a success and praise yours and Count Morlaix planning.
I am in wait at the Inn at Morlaix with my passion being aroused for you and your strong hands touching me.
You may find this letter a little naughty but please come quickly and release me from these chains of wait.
Zoe. Xxx

When they had finished they put the letter down along with the other information obtained. They said nothing except one thing, "What of this Zoe person tell us all you know of her?"The Butler did as asked and told all. He knew the men in front of him had the authority to do whatever they wanted with no questions asked. If he held back in any way and they found out, he would be dead.

After three hours the butler's interrogation ended. "Thank you, you have been very forthcoming," they said. ''Now my dear man please lead us to your once master's bedroom, we are finished here for today."

Once they had completed the inspection of Philip Albret's room they moved on to Pierre Boucher's quarters. When that was finished they headed away from the Chateau to the Inn for their debriefing. These guys were efficient and were leaving nothing to chance. They knew their job well.

On their return to the Inn, they stabled both horses and walked slowly into the building whilst quietly talking with each other. The message they had taken from the Butler, written by Zoe, highlighted that Pierre Bouchier had ridden to this very Inn the night he died.

They wanted to expand this line of enquiry and agreed they needed to speak with the owner this very moment and in private. However, then again, if the owner got wind of what they were about at this stage of the plan then it would only produce unnecessary risk and exposure to their well-being. So with that in mind, they agreed not to broach the subject with the Inns owner, for now at least. The information that was coming from the Château was steady and formulated a pretty good picture of what exactly had happened. Yes, they would leave the Inns owner for now but not let him off the hook. O no, it would only be a postponement until it best suited them.

Their incessant questioning was producing the results they needed such as people's names like Zoe, Jacques and Jeanne and place names such as Morlaix Inn and the Monastery at Landerneau. It was all beginning to take shape. The puzzle was appearing to be some sort of plan and secret operation against the English. The monastery was very interesting as it had a dark side of conniving with the French nobility. The monks were well trained and known in the art of alchemy for experiments. The Abbot himself was also known for taking back hander's which he justified as being just good business. They would need to visit this place also.

Antoinette was getting restless and impatient with the two men. They had been around now for three weeks and she couldn't understand why it was taking so long. She wanted to know whether they would do the operation or not and, if they did, how much did they want. They assured her their investigations were nearly complete and hopefully by next Monday week she would have their answer. ''Monday it is gentlemen, no later, I shall make beds ready for your stay the Sunday prior and have breakfast ready for us all." The day was Thursday so they had three days to decide.

On that Sunday they were satisfied they had most of what they wanted, not all, but enough. They had also visited the monastery and, as they were not staying at the Inn as of today decided to question the landlord that afternoon. He confirmed what they already knew except to add that two unknown men were with Zoe that night and two adjoining rooms were booked in her name. They left on good terms and feeling comfortable that the Landlord was of good character said they would come back in a few days.

Monday morning Antoinette came down from her bedroom and entered the breakfast room waking straight to the head of the table. The maid pushed the seat in as Antoinette sat down and then poured her some coffee. After a few quiet seconds had passed Antoinette looked up and said, "Good morning gentlemen, have you found what you wanted, and if so, what is your conclusion." They waited for the maid to leave and as she did, the Frenchman spoke for them both. "Yes, mademoiselle we have." "Then what is it?"

"It would appear that your good uncle Philip de Albret had set in motion an operation to invade England. We think it was via Cornwall, not confirmed, and that this was spoiled by someone who somehow turned defence into attack. It was then they killed your good uncle and Pierre Bouchier. However, we are unsure as to why your late husband got mixed up in all this and are struggling to find a connection. Maybe he was in communication with Albret and knew of things, we are not sure." He continued, "However, to take on your mission would be dangerous but given the time and resources we believe it to be achievable subject only to an agreed price." "And what may that be?" "Five thousand Guinea's plus expenses." "And how long will you need?" "We will have what you want no later than next spring, early summer." "Are you saying you need eight months." "Yes, that's exactly what we are saying and, we need two other people to join us whom we will pay out of our salary." Antoinette went silent and sipped her coffee. She started to think about the cost which she could easily afford with the luxuries, power and the new aristocratic lifestyle the success of the mission would give. The room was silent waiting for her reply.

After another silent sip of her coffee, she looked up at them both and said, "Agreed, but I must be there to finish it off, you understand." "We fully understand my lady."

Chapter 8

Jeanne was up early getting ready the coffee and bacon for herself and Jacques who was still in bed. It had been just over a week since her darling daughter Rebecca had visited announcing her betrothal of marriage to Joshua.

After her mini breakdown, due to her emotional hearing of the names of the children, Little George and Christine, all four went on to have a lovely evening getting merrily tipsy.

The wedding has been planned for two weeks' time on the Saturday at two o clock in the Church at Gunwalloe Cove. It was to be a quiet affair with only a few friends and maybe some colleagues present.

Whilst all were getting tipsy the night turned into morning and so Jeanne suggested they stay overnight and have breakfast in the morning after a good sleep. They could then set off to Rebecca's 'house at Marazion which Jeanne knew well as it had been her marital home and was where Rebecca was born. However, Jeanne's husband, Rebecca's Father, had been killed nearly seventeen years ago in the playing the same dangerous game that she herself had been lured into after his death.

It was only after Jeanne's disappearance and belief that she too had been killed that the house was then bequeathed to Rebecca. The house is an asset which one gets offered, if appropriate when a next of kin dies. It always happens when you work for the people they do. Don't get too over sentimental Jeanne, she thought, the house is also of great value to the Defence Services as they are all sited for use of surveillance and defence.

Jeanne had also asked her daughter again that night if she was going to carry on with her line of work after marrying Joshua. Rebecca, knowing first hand of the dangers of their line of work, having been injured herself only six months ago, was adamant she was. She also said she was proud of her Mother, Father and fore Fathers who had also worked this covert way to protect the Cornish. Jeanne, on hearing her daughter's confident response knew when to back off, as like Mother, like Daughter.

Although she was now only half way through cooking the breakfast Jeanne decided to go outside and get some fresh air and sit quietly for a while. For some reason, she felt the need for some inner peace and tranquillity. The bacon can wait for now. So taking the pan off the fire and with coffee in hand she went outside and sat down by the oak tree to gaze at the sea. What a beautiful morning she thought, just lovely.

The two butterflies were resting in the bushes not far away as they had flown all night to get there. They saw Jeanne walk out of the cottage and sit down by the oak tree. They decided to wait a little longer until they were both happy that she was on her own and at ease. When they saw that she was they flew off together.

Jeanne saw both of them come into her line of sight and somehow had a feeling they were heading straight for her. However, she didn't move or blink an eyelid. This couldn't be she thought but they kept coming straight. Then without fear or hesitation, they landed on her nose and Jeanne froze. The butterflies were beautiful and so very gentle that was true but it was the message they brought that feared her. The butterflies were now still with wings closed. She then talked with them as if they were like little children. "Good morning," she said, "have you brought me a message?" The butterflies quickly started to flap their shiny wings. "Then I will come." On hearing those words, the butterflies flew away as if answering her promise and their job was done.

Jeanne was struck dumb for words and sat there thinking of 'The Old Cornish Witches Tale.'

One on the Hand
Nothing to Fret
Two on the nose
The Moors you must get

The next full moon
You must be there
If not you come
Then Fate you stare

Jeanne had heard this tale many times from her loving late grandmother and also from other people in Cornwall. She had to go it was as simple as that. You do not cross or mess with Zelahnor of the Moor or, the Witch of Bodmin Moor as some people call her. Jacques simply wouldn't believe her that was for sure and would probably laugh at the sheer stupidity of it all. But that was his problem, he was French, she and the Cornish knew better.

What did Zelahnor want with little old me, she thought? Jeanne wasn't afraid and didn't feel at all uneasy about going to the Moor. She felt comfortable like going to see a friend. She had heard over the years that should you get two butterflies you must go to the place called 'Bolventor Inn' on the Bodmin Moorland and wait. However, there has been much talk that due to this place having so much booty of rum from the Caribbean and other miss goings on, that it is changing its name to the Jamaica Inn. Well if it happens it happens she thought, but for now, she must be brave and get going as the next full moon is tomorrow. Funny she knew that as only yesterday she was thinking of it. She would leave a note for Jacques to say she loves him very much and do not worry as Rebecca has asked her over to help arrange the wedding details and would be back in a few days. She lied.

Chapter 9

The Bolventor Inn was a spooky place and gave Jeanne the creeps. It lay deep in the centre of her beloved Cornwall, sitting just off the main highway. It was also again exactly half way inland from the North and South coast lying deep in the vast open moor of Bodmin. It was surrounded by entire marshes, fields, woods and rivers for miles on end. It was simply ideal for every type of piracy you could name with the exchanging of goods and money. It was also known for its brawling of drunkards and it did not take any prisoners. The police knew about it all but always turned a blind eye which fuelled its reputation.

Jeanne was in her small gig being pulled by her trusted horse. She quickly thought of the note she had left Jacques thinking she was with her Daughter and not in this isolated place she found herself in. He would be absolutely stressed out if he knew she was on her own. The full moon was up and shining as it glowed against the night which made the moors look even more ghostly. She had travelled this way many times when working in Plymouth and always remembered that when she got to this particular part of the Moor she would push the horses on as fast as she could, just in case. The Bolventor Inn was now just over the brow of the next hill so she reined the horse into a still and took stock. 'Be brave Jeanne, be brave,' she told herself.

Once she had calmed and got a grip of herself, she clicked the reins and rode forward slowly which she maintained and no faster. Around fifty yards before the Inn, she saw a lantern swinging gently back and forth. It was as though it was her guide and so carried on towards it. Twenty yards from the light she noticed it was a little girl holding a lamp.

Reaching just in front of the little girl, she stopped the gig. "What is your name please?" the little girl asked. "My name is Jeanne.'' "That is right, thank you, if you look over to the barn door there is a beautiful black pony. Please could you jump on his back as he will take you to where you are to go and I will look after your lovely horse and trap while you are gone?" "Thank you little lady," Jeanne replied politely and then asked, "What is your name." "I am not allowed to say but thank you for asking."

Jeanne did as was asked by the little girl. The pony was indeed beautiful and once on its back immediately walked off away from the Inn out onto the dark still of the moor.

Jeanne had only hearsay of what the moors were like at night. It was an extremely eerie feeling and she felt very lonely and vulnerable. The pony was taking her in a North by North West direction, that she knew by where the Sun had a set an hour ago. The pace of the pony was slow and methodical so up and down and around they went. There was no saddle, so she only had the mane to hold onto but the pony was well balanced and didn't rush things. Going through into another deep valley they then turned a tight bend when a small wooded area appeared in front of them. The pony then came to halt and so Jeanne looked about but saw nothing. They both waited but still, nothing happened.

Zelahnor was waiting inside the small woods out of sight but was watching Jeanne. She was waiting for reassurances that they had not been followed and so stayed quietly out of Jeanne's vision.

After a long eerie silence of two or three minutes, a massive cougar type beast crept to Zelahnor's side and rubbed his head on her side. "Thank you my darling," she whispered then bent down and kissed his nose. He purred quietly with love. "I won't be long with Jeanne," she said to him and with that he silently crept away but not too far. He was the brother of the largest cougar whose wife had just had cubs. He also had one other brother and one sister and all were constables of the moor and utterly loyal to Zelahnor.

Once the animal had left, Zelahnor walked forward to the inside edge of the trees and then sat down and crossed her legs. She then let out all the fire flies under her black shawl which created a luminous blue florescent light all around her body.

On seeing the lights appear the pony flicked his ears up and inched forward a little further and then stopped. Jeanne being now only yards away from the Witch got down and stayed still.

"Hello Jeanne, thank you so much for coming to see me, you do know who I am?" Jeanne was a little scared that was true but the voice before her was so reassuringly calming. Jeanne could see that a lady was in the sitting position but couldn't work out how she glistened with light as the dark of the night was all around."Yes, you are Zelahnor." "And do they call me anything else?" Jeanne was unsure whether she should answer that one so stayed quiet. "I take your silence as a yes they do, but we shall leave that as it is for now, shall we."

Zelahnor continued. "Jeanne, I have asked you here this day to inform you of something extremely important but before I do, let me ask you one question if I may, what do you know I do?" "You protect the Cornish People and the land they live in." "That is true Jeanne. I live and breathe to do just that and therefore you must also know that if I protect my people, they must protect me. With this being the truth means you may never disclose knowledge of my existence or mention my name to anyone, ever." "Yes, I understand my lady,'' Jeanne replied.

"Jeanne, your children Little George and Christine by your long time love Jacques are in extreme danger. Whoever the enemy are they are coming soon and they want blood. On hearing her children's names mentioned startled her as she had always kept this secret for nearly fifteen years. "Yes Jeanne, it may surprise you that I know but I know all that goes on here and these beautiful innocent children, born of a Cornish woman in Cornwall, must be protected no matter what, do you understand that?"

"What do want me to do?" "What I would like you to do is take Little George far away to Bristol, out of harm's way. An apprenticeship at the Bristol docks would be good for him. Joshua, as you know has the right connections and introductions.'' "I understand, and Christine, what of her?" "Christine, O little Christine, I have waited twelve years since she was born. I would like her to join me here and for me to show her the way of love and affection. She will be safe, well looked after and loved. She will have a good life and an option every ten years until she is forty years of age whether to stay on the moors or go away and live a normal life and to have children." Jeanne started to cry and asked, "Would I be able to see her?" "That is up to

Christine, but I would say yes but Jeanne, you may never talk of it." "Can I tell Jacques, their Father?" "No, that cannot be at this time, due to his French connections of his past work." Then there was silence between them. Zelahnor was feeling Jeanne's pain and her conscience of love swing one way then the other. "Jeanne, I will allow one thing and that is you can talk with your first Daughter Rebecca as she is rightfully her sister in blood. However, this is not normally done but I can feel your pain.'' This seemed to ease things somewhat for Jeanne. The children were in danger that was true and as a Mother, she must protect them at all costs from the danger to come.

Chapter 10

George Kernow had left London the day before and was now entering Cornwall. He had picked up the connecting coach from Exeter escorted by his trusted bodyguards, as usual, on his way to visit Rebecca and Joshua. He had been invited to their wedding but really needed to talk with them on other matters.

Six months ago, after rescuing Jeanne from the dungeons in France, he appeared content with the way things were and the personnel within his West Cornish team. However, in hindsight and a continual feeling of unease in his gut had made him change his mind. Jacques, Jeanne's partner, was on his mind but it was the nagging doubt towards Henry Hosking that would not go away.

Something had to be done and it was his job to do it, so change it will be. They may not like it but tough, his loyalty was to his Queen Anne and the safety of this Country.

He had thought long and hard about what to do for the best. His main thought was the exposure of the shores on the Lizard peninsular. Jeanne, he could trust completely but Jacques, being allowed to go free and live with Jeanne, due to his faithful promise of cooperation and end all alliances and communications with France, was another matter. Yes, Jacques has been true to his word, that was good, but George felt that the Sennen Farm, where Jacques lived with Jeanne, was just too a strategic place for his operations and really needed more reliable persons in its trust. Given more time to prove himself, George may think differently about this now non-combatant Frenchman. However, at this time Jacques was under house curfew at the Sennen Farm for three years and it was too early to take risks.

George was staying at the Red Lion in Helston and had sent messages to the other people he wanted to speak to and for them to meet him either there or at the Blue Anchor that night. He had also sent orders to Rebecca and Joshua that he will visit the cottage at Marazion the next morning and that Jeanne should be in attendance.

Henry Hosking, George Kernow's right hand man in Cornwall had confirmed his attendance and that he would meet him at the Blue Anchor. George needed to talk with him urgently above all others and it wouldn't be a pleasant discussion but he had to do it. Something wasn't adding up with this man's ways and means and, when that happens, George gets very concerned. Nothing was clear or obvious but it was little things adding up over the years and George would not and could not tolerate any further suspicions of people who worked for him. He decided that this night and tomorrow, he would completely sweep clean any cobwebs of doubt with all his new team members and implement his new planned intentions.

Rebecca, Joshua and Jeanne were now all at the cottage in Marazion. Joshua was outside preparing the gig for them all to ride into Penzance for the day. Joshua and Rebecca had indeed received word that George Kernow was visiting them tomorrow and thought a bit of fun beforehand would be good. Jeanne and Rebecca were inside talking quietly around the table. Jeanne wanted to clear the air and explain all that had happened. Little George and Christine were out playing on the beach with Queenie and Cecil, the little Jack Russells. The children's supper was already made for their return and once eaten had been told to go straight to bed, the both of them.

"Mother," Rebecca said," I had this feeling about them the first time I saw them. I couldn't say anything to anyone but I just knew from the first moment they were introduced to me by Henry Hosking. Does Henry know they are yours and Jacque's children?" "No, he does not my darling, and what's more he must never know, he loves me for himself, he has told me many times, even on operations he wouldn't give up on me. I have told him over and over that I love another but it's as though he doesn't or won't accept it and that scares me. No one knows except, except I can't tell you her name." Rebecca then quickly said, "You mean except Zelahnor?" "That is right my dear, only she, but don't say it so loud." "Mother I am not afraid to say her name to you, she knows everything and I believe it."

Rebecca carried on, "O Mother, please stop crying, we will get through this and all will be well". Rebecca was like her Father, very pragmatic and it was a trait that Joshua adored in her. He would often get a little muddled over a decision on what to do for the best, where as Rebecca would accept things for what they are and deal with it. Jeanne, however, couldn't help the tears from flowing. She couldn't quite think straight and her Motherly instinct of emotional love was confusing her thoughts. She felt fully responsible that she herself had put her young ones in danger.

"Mother, when did you meet Jacques, was it when Father was alive?" "No my Darling, it was not, I loved your Father dearly and when he passed away I wept continually. It was at this time when Joshua's Father and

George Kernow came on the scene, offering me to take over your Fathers work in the game you and Joshua are now in. Dangerous as it was I took it and was able to keep the cottage here at Marazion. It was quite a while later, feeling alone and unloved that I met Jacques in a Monastery in France whilst on an assignment."

"But Mother, we took these children from Henry Hosking. He is their guardian, I remember him saying to Joshua and me that they were on the streets and he felt sad for them so took them in himself, he must know, surely." "No my dear, that's not how it was. My very best friend in Helston took them in, bless her. When she caught the smallpox, she sent word asking me what to do about them. It was then that I suggested Henry Hosking as he was living very well in Truro with servants and so she organised everything and portrayed the children as being hers of her late husband.

On seeing the children of good nature and knowledge he agreed subject to five hundred pounds paid in advance. So, I gave her all the money I had, and she paid the rest. God bless her. That's how it was." "That lying bastard, he told us that he was the Good Samaritan and, we bloody believed him." "My dear, he comes across as butter wouldn't melt in his mouth but there is something about him, but as to what, I don't know."

"And what about Jacques, does he know," Rebecca asked. "I have told him nothing on what Zelahnor has told me. He adores them as I do but realises that it would not be any good if people knew their Father was a Frenchman." Both Rebecca and Jeanne went silent as though a little time of quiet was needed between them.

"When does Zelahnor want to start this?" "It is to start on the Saturday after your Wedding at Church Cove. She will send us a message then." Rebecca got up and went around the table to cuddle her Mother and said, "Well let's enjoy their time with us now. Zelahnor is the trusted one of Love in this county of Cornwall and we must always do as she asks." Rebecca then said in reassurance, "it's not that we won't see them again Mother and if they are in danger, then it is right for us to get them away to protect them."

"Thank you for being so understanding my lovely darling daughter and loving big sister to the little ones." They both leaned forward together and hugged each other tight and as they did so Joshua opened the front door and said in a jolly tone, "Ready when you are ladies."

Chapter 11

''Good to see Bull, how is the wife and St Just, still attached to Cornwall?'' Bull chuckled saying, ''Yes Mr Kernow, both are well and still attached.'' Bull was a brute of a man and didn't do the covert working stuff but, he and his team did do the back up whenever and where ever it was required. Kernow had the utmost respect for him, hence his decision to meet him in the Red Lion an hour before going over to the Blue Anchor, for the more formal discussions with the likes of Henry Hosking.

''Bull, thank you for coming at so short notice I appreciate it.'' ''No problem Mr Kernow, what will you have of me. ''I need to change things around here for the benefit of safety to others.

I cannot go into detail right now but I would like you and your wife to live in the Farm at Sennen and protect the side coast off from Penzance and Mousehole.'' ''But I thought you had given that to Jeanne and that Frenchman.'' ''You mean Jacques.'' ''I mean the Frenchman.'' ''Bull, I do understand your thoughts on this man but, without him, we would never have foiled the French operation or, got Jeanne back.'' He continued, ''Bull, it is important to me that you understand this and maybe give a little. Our kind of work is sometimes not easy and sometimes we have to look at the bigger picture.'' Bull felt that the man in front of him was asking for his help and so should really relax a little more towards Jacques. Then in a calmer response Bull replied, ''Alright, 'I understand, and yes putting it like that, maybe I have been a little too harsh on him.'' ''Thank you Bull, I ask nothing more but it is important that you take over and live on the Farm.'' ''The Farm and its land holding are very large, how would we manage its up keep."

"Bull, I want to bring you closer into the circle but need you still to maintain your support team as you do now. The Farm is not far from you at St Just as you know and your present monthly allowance will increase from ten pounds to twenty-five pounds per month plus an initial purse of one hundred pounds to get you started. You can use the Farm as your own and work it as you see fit. Should you and your wife stay there for five years and wish to continue and we are happy also, then we will hand over the full rights until your passing."

Bull went quiet, thinking about what George Kernow had said, "It sounds good Mr Kernow and thank you, when would you like this to happen?" "This Monday morning coming?" Bull knew this was a good offer for him and his missus but, also knew the dangers and the short notice. Kernow waited for a reply but decided to continue the conversation.

"Also Bull, as from this evening you do not take any further orders from Henry Hosking but from Joshua Pendragon." 'Why, what's happening with Henry may I ask?' "He is retiring from our service this very night." Bull again went quiet. He had worked with Hosking's for many years and got on quite well. As for Pendragon, he didn't know him that well but had worked with his Father whom he trusted and liked. Bull was no spring chicken as he was well into his fortieth years and so decided that the offer of the Sennen Farm versus his present lowly lodgings at St Just and any on coming danger was to say yes. He also knew his wife would love the Farming life. "Very well Mr Kernow, the answer is yes we will take over the Farm." "Excellent Bull, that's good news I will tell Joshua of your decision. Now let's have a Brandy together and then I must be off."

"By the way Mr Kernow are you going to his wedding this Saturday." "I got an invite but no, I will not be going, why do you ask." "I heard that Henry will be there." "Good for Henry I am sure he will enjoy himself, but I have to be back in London."

They both drank the brandy in one as a toast to Bull's new position and once completed they shook hands and Bull headed back to St Just. He needed to talk to the missus and get things sorted as the move was only a few days away.

As the Blue Anchor was just down the road in Coinnagehall Street, Kernow decided rather than ride would walk with his guards following. Time was moving on and Hosking's would probably be there by now.

As predicted Henry was waiting at a table by the fire. As Kernow entered he got up and went to him. They shook hands warmly and then walked back to the table. A bottle of Brandy was already opened with two glasses. "Shall I pour George?" "Please, and thank you Henry, we can then get on and talk."

Once both were settled, Henry took the lead and went first, "So George what's on your mind, you needing to come all this way to lovely Helston." George thought about putting his words gently and buttering Henry up but, time wasn't on his side and also, he had to be definite in his speech.

"Henry, you have done good service to our Lovely Queen Anne and her people and we are thankful for your dutiful service. However, things have changed now and time has moved on so have decided to offer you early retirement."

"What are you talking about George, I am still full of life with much to give and I don't think I want to retire. George knew things could go either way on what he said and from Henry's response so far, it wasn't going to go the way he intended. "Henry, I am sorry but there is no discussion with this, I have been ordered to implement this change." "By whom?" he quickly retorted. Henry Hosking wasn't ready for this, he normally had time to prepare questions and answers and put on a veil of deceit but, he didn't see this one coming.

"I cannot tell you that Henry, you know the rules." Kernow was remaining mature and calm and his speech balanced but Hosking became very agitated and started raising his voice. "You are telling me, with no prior notice and with all the work and danger I have put myself into protecting this bloody County for our Bloody Queen Anne, that I am done with like some kind of bloody unwanted puppy dog who is no longer needed." "Henry, please lower your voice and calm down." Kernow had never seen this side of Hosking before. He always knew him to be level headed. The two body guards standing at the bar looked over.

Hosking then realised what he had said and more to point how he had said it. Realising his mistake, he immediately changed tact to minimise his outburst of rage and limit any damage. In an instant, he became calm and controlling.

With a lower sweeter tone of voice, Henry said, "Of course George, I apologise, I was a little surprised and taken aback, that's all, when would you like me to retire." "As from immediate effect Henry, as from tonight, you are a free man to do whatever you wish." "I understand, thank you George, and what may I ask of my house in Truro." This was tricky as normally these grace and favour houses are assigned till one dies and then looked at to see if it can be transferred to another member of the family for mutual and beneficial use. However, due to handing over the Farm at Sennen to Bull and the other cottages he had on his books, he couldn't afford for Henry to stay there. George Kernow had presented his superiors with his forecast and budget plans and, for them to sign it off, they requested the town house in Truro to be sold, to balance the books. When George tried to argue the case they simply responded by saying, "You look after the South West region, we look after the whole Country, money is tight and doesn't grow on trees."

"I'm sorry Henry, it has to go." "And what of my monthly stipend of fifty pounds George?" George was the boss here and so started to get a little irritated with Henry's attitude of arrogance. However, he did have a plan. "Henry, as you know when a person retires, he retires. However, I have taken into consideration your dedication and loyal service and it has been agreed that if you downsize to some other property we will take thirty five per cent of the Truro house sale and give it to you as a thank you for your good work. Your stipend will of course be reduced in line with your retirement and will be fifteen pounds per month." Kernow waited for a reply and could not quite believe what Henry said and more importantly the way he said it. "Thank you George," Henry said nice and calmly, "That's very kind and reasonable and I accept your fair offer with much gratitude. Please may I also say George, it was really good working with you and all the others, and may God save our Queen."

"Well Henry, we would like to thank you, so why don't we fill our glasses and raise them to your good future ahead." They both drank in unison but George felt uneasy. Henry played his game well by then once again saying in a warm sincere and meaningful manner, "Thank you ever so much George." Henry then stood up and offered his hand in a farewell handshake, as men do.

When Hosking had left the Blue Anchor it gave George time to think and gather his thoughts. Well, that is another piece of the new puzzle completed, so far so good. He sat where he was, poured himself another drink and relaxed a little. Then with a nod to his guards, he got up and together they walked out heading for the Red Lion just up the road and a bed for the night after a few more tipples. Tomorrow is another day he thought, and that day started with a trip to sunny Marazion.

What George and his guards didn't see when they exited the Blue Anchor was Hosking waiting in the dark shadows watching them with venom and foaming at the mouth. He would not let this go at being treated like some sort of stray dog on a street corner being kicked about for others to gain. He would not let that Frenchman go for taking his beautiful Jeanne away from him either. He would not let this go, he would show them all, that he, and he alone, should be the boss and, Jeanne's lover too.

Chapter 12

As arranged, Kernow arrived at the cottage at Marazion in time for lunch. He and his guards had ridden gently from the Red Lion Inn at Helston and taking a little over an hour.

"Good afternoon George, please come in," Joshua said. The guards knew instinctively what to do and that was to wait outside and keep check all around the building and protect. Once George had entered he took off his hat and said with a fondness, "Thank you Joshua, it's been a while."

All were in the main room of the house with the fire gently alight for cooking purposes. George said his greetings to all present, being Rebecca and Joshua, Jeanne and the children. Once the initial niceties were over Rebecca asked, "Would you like tea George or something stronger?" "Something stronger please Rebecca and thank you."

Jeanne looked at the children and suggested they go with the dogs to the beach or the village for an hour or so as we grown ups have to talk.'

George Kernow felt completely at ease with these people. He had worked with them for a long time which included Jeanne's husband and Joshua's Father. It was most unlike last night in the Blue Anchor when he felt very uneasy and nervous talking with Hosking.

Rebecca poured George a tankard of cider and suggested that the stew is simmering nicely and will be around twenty minutes.' "Thank you Rebecca, I haven't had a homemade stew for a long time. Now, are we all sitting comfortably as what I say concerns you all and I need to hear your answers together."

"First of all, Rebecca, how are you now that your wound is healing?" "I am fine George, thank you." "And you Jeanne, how are you fairing?" "I am very happy George although in truth I think I am struggling mentally in coming to terms with my dungeon imprisonment for so long at Morlaix, but Jacques has helped me and been very supportive." "O yes, Jacques, and how is he?" "He struggled a little at first but is in good spirit and content with the decision he made to you to retire." "That's quite understandable Jeanne, thank you for your honesty, I too am glad that he kept his promises."

"And Joshua, how are you my good man?" "Couldn't be better George thank you especially as in a few days I will be married to the woman I love." "O yes, congratulations to you both and thank you for the invite but as you know I cannot attend." "We thought that would be the case George and we completely understand."

"Now let us now get down to business. There have been some changes above my level of authority which affect the future way we operate on the ground and in the field." He lied, it had nothing to do with anyone else, these were his changes and his alone due to the unease he felt about some people's loyalty and talent under his control.

"Firstly, Rebecca and Joshua, as you are both being of one unit on Saturday, we would like you both to live in Joshua's cottage at Gunwalloe, what say you both?"Joshua looked at Rebecca and after a few seconds of silence Rebecca asked, ''When would you like this to happen?'' ''Immediately, time is not on our side.'' ''But George, we have nothing ready.'' ''I had thought about that and have lined up some people with carriages to help with the move. They are on standby as we talk waiting for my message to act.'' ''What about the children,'' she asked. ''I will come to them in a little while, but first I must have an answer.'' Rebecca and Joshua were at eyes and then, with calm assurance, both nodded to each other. Joshua then took over the reins and said, ''We agree George.'' ''Thank you both,'' he replied gratefully.

''Now Jeanne, we would like you and Jacques to move back in here at Marazion and leave the Sennen Farm.'' All looked at Jeanne for her response as she looked at Rebecca for some kind of guidance. Previously Jeanne would have been more positive but the long time of being in the dungeons of Philip de Albret had taken its toll and her confidence was not at it used to be.

George was aware of this and gave her the time she needed. Rebecca felt for her Mother who had now gone silent trying to work out an answer to the question asked. She decided to help her by saying, ''I think that would be good for you Mother, after all this was your house before it was mine.'' Jeanne responded, ''But Jacques is under curfew at Sennen for another two years, what of that?'' ''We have talked over this very point Jeanne,'' George said, ''And have agreed he can move with you and support you, as he has so far done. His curfew address will be transferred from Sennen to here, but Jeanne, as you know there is here an underground pit in the scrub area which holds weapons and things, this can in no way be disclosed to him.'' Jeanne understood but felt a sense of guilt, as this is not the first secret she has kept from

Jacques. They had promised to be truthful with each other and be sole mates as well as in love. However, it seems she didn't have much choice. "Can we have the same assistance to help our move as you have with my daughter." "Yes of course." "Then I agree George." "That's good news Jeanne, thank you, please pass on my thanks to Jacques."

"Right Joshua, now the good news, I would like you to take over all our teams in Cornwall and report to me." Startled with what he had just heard, Joshua looked at George with a mystified look and said, "But Henry Hosking looks after Cornwall and we report directly to him." "You did report to him Joshua, Henry has decided to retire early, it took me by surprise also, but one must accept people's decisions."

Everyone looked at each other in amazement for some kind of logical reason as it didn't make sense why Henry would do this. George continued, "I apologise for putting this on you so quickly Joshua but I do feel that you are the right man for the job. Also, your stipend will be increased accordingly with the increase in responsibility. All I require at this moment is your approval that you will accept, I will send word for us to meet each other again at a later date so we can discuss things in finer detail."

Joshua looked at both Rebecca and Jeanne but they just kept quiet. Joshua looked up to the rafters and then out of the window as if somehow these actions would help guide him. He then looked at George and said. "I accept your offer George, subject to the finer details being agreeable when we next meet." "That's excellent Joshua, just excellent."

George continued, "By the way Joshua, I had a very strange message put on my desk last week. It said, 'the opportunity for 'Little George' to be an apprentice at Bristol Docks has been agreed, please liaise with Joshua Pendragon and arrive Monday week at eight o clock.'. Rebecca and Jeanne looked at each other in utter bewilderment at how she could have done this.

Chapter 13

The red hot ball of shot had left the muzzle at high velocity. It had no emotion only to go where its master had aimed and, he had aimed well. To help its straight trajectory the man's strength of grip had not faltered, even with the heavy recoil, he had held firm and true.

Zoe had just got down the outside steps of the cottage when Jon, the love of her life, ran out and caught her from behind. She tried to wiggle out of his grip but he kept her in his arms and both were laughing aloud like children. He then turned her around in his strong arms and as they faced each other he said, "I love you so much Zoe."

She looked into his eyes and said, "I love you too Jon, with all my heart." As he leaned forward to kiss her the deadly unemotional ball of shot came searing through the air from the small woods afar and hit him.

With a large splash of blood exiting his upper chest Jon fell to the ground motionless. Zoe, her face splattered with his warm blood, screamed his name with utter horror.

The man in the woods was still lying in the same position and musket still in the aimed position. He hadn't moved an inch and had watched through the musket's powerful scope, the complete flight. On its impact he simply and coldly said to himself, 'Target.' With operation complete, he withdrew to move to his next rendezvous point, south by south west. Picking his things up and making sure nothing was left, he crawled back into the small woods where his horse, already saddled, was waiting.

Once he was out of the woods and on the track, he whipped his horse into a gallop. It was good to feel movement again and the breeze of life, he had been laid down too long.

The three of them were waiting in the lounge area sipping their drinks and talking quietly. They had now been in the Inn by the harbour for two days. The sniper had said it may take anything from one to three days to do the job and, he would not be rushed. If they didn't want to accept his terms, then he suggested they find another.

The two men had now been joined by a middle aged lady of known intent in the circle of espionage. Through all the information they had gained they now knew the main part of the mission was going to be in Cornwall. Therefore, they will use their English aliases. The leader, being French, was Peter and the Spaniard, Alfred. The woman, who by birth was English and living in Plymouth, Devon, was Sarah. All three were nondescript and nothing stood out as they were all of average height and weight and all were average looking. Dressed in normal clothes of the day you wouldn't notice anything untoward if you passed them in the street. This is how Peter liked it. This is why he was successful and this is why Antoinette, the future Countess of Morlaix, had agreed to his fees because he would get the job done. ''I just had a thought,'' Alfred said, ''If you take our initials and add the A for Antoinette it makes ASAP, 'as soon as possible', just what she wants.''

Peter and Sarah both looked at him with a quizzical look of dry humour and just smiled at his offbeat train of thought. Peter then got serious and went over the mission again.

While they were chatting the front door of the Inn opened and in walked the sniper dressed in very casual gear as if just another person coming for a drink. He was also tidy, with a clean appearance. Peter had previously advised him that this was to be the case and, the sniper had listened. He had taken the time after his successful hit to clean himself up well. However, unlike the other three people sitting at the table, this particular man did stand out from the others. He was strong in appearance and athletic in build and, walked with a self confidence.

All three turned their heads and looked over his way but, as practised, he was to ignore them and go straight to the bar.

This he did, and as the barman came to him he ordered, in a little louder voice than usual, a large double of your finest cognac. The sniper then paid and picked up the glass. He drank the cognac down in one and with a sense of humour said to the barman, ''That hit the spot in just the right place, thank you my man.'' He then turned about and walked out the way he came in. The sniper knew his payment for the killing would be in the place as agreed and that is exactly where he was going. He also knew it would be there in full as he had worked with the Frenchman before.

The three of them had carefully observed what the sniper had ordered and heard everything that he had said. It was the code that all had gone well

''Well, it is on,'' Peter said quietly in English. ''The fuse has been lit and now that traitorous rabbit of a woman will lead us to our next destination.'' Peter then looked at Sarah and said, ''It is now your turn my dear.'' Sarah replied, "Are you sure she will come to Brest?" "With all the information we have are eighty per cent sure she will. Should she not come then we will activate contingency plans." With that, Sarah got up, said her farewells and headed off to the port of Brest. They had gone over their plans many times and Sarah knew exactly what had to be done.

The so-called Peter and Alfred clicked their glasses and sat back. They knew they too would be crossing the channel sometime soon, but until they received word, they drank heartily to the successful start of the mission.

Chapter 14

"And do you Rebecca take Joshua Cuthbert Pendragon, to be your lawful wedded Husband?" "I do." "Then I now have the great pleasure in pronouncing you both Husband and Wife and, may God bless you both in a long and happy life." Rebecca and Joshua leaned forward and kissed.

Little George was in the front pew and bored finding it all so embarrassing. Christine was watching their every move and found it all very romantic and loving.

Jeanne was sitting with the children and had tears of joy for her daughter, Rebecca. She was also crying for Christine and Little George as in a short while she would have to let them both go. Little George knew that in a couple of hours a coach will pick him up and take him to Bristol. He was already packed and raring to go and couldn't wait. George Kernow would escort him from Helston to Bristol where his ship building apprenticeship will start.

Jeanne and Rebecca had discussed telling him before he left for Bristol that he was in fact Jeanne's son from her lover Jacques and, Rebecca was his big sister. However, after a long time chatting over this issue, they eventually agreed that absolutely no good could come of it telling him at this moment in time. It would probably have the reverse effect in trying to make a better life for himself. Maybe when he was a little older and things were quieter. Yes, that makes more loving sense. They would tell him later in life and let him enjoy the freedom he deserves without burden.

Jacques wasn't present at the service as his curfew from the Sennen Farm wouldn't allow but, this didn't bother him as he was busy moving the last of his and Jeanne's belongings to the cottage at Marazion. Rebecca had already moved out and now living in Joshua's cottage high above the beach at Gunwalloe and only a short brisk walk from the Church where they are now.

With the service over, the small congregation made their way outside and head to the Halzephron Inn. Drink and food were to be served with joyful dancing taking place a little later to celebrate the lovely day.

Rebecca and Joshua got in the gig first and drove off to the Inn to get things ready and greet the guests as they arrived. There were about twenty people including Henry Hosking and Bull from St Just. Being in the game they were in, it wasn't prudent to invite people outside of their circle. George Kernow wouldn't be there, as he was heading back to London, but he had relented and gave Jacques a free pass for the evening only so could celebrate with Jeanne.

With most of the guests now there, Rebecca and Joshua sat at the head of the table laughing and full of happiness.

Not everyone had turned up yet but the atmosphere was one of pure joy for the bride and bridegroom. As time started to move into early evening, Jeanne took Rebecca to one side. ''Rebecca my darling, are you ready I think it's time to take the children?'' ''Yes, Mother I am ready, I will go and tell Joshua and make my excuses.''

Then gathering both Christine and Little George the four of them set off for the short trip to Joshua's and Rebecca's cottage above the cliff.

Little George was excited as in just over an hour or so the carriage will pick him up. Christine however, just wanted to get back to the joy and dancing at the Inn. "Why do I have to leave the party now Rebecca?" she asked. "Because you will want to wave your brother goodbye and we would like to talk with you afterwards, that's why." "Why do you want to talk with me?" she replied swiftly. "you will know afterwards." "Have I done wrong?" "No, Christine, you have done nothing wrong, you are beautiful and lovely and it's nothing like that." "So, what is it about then." "You will know when we talk with you and that is all I can say at this moment, so please no more questions."

Once they had arrived at the cottage Little George, helped by Rebecca, set about finishing off his last minute packing. It wasn't long after that they heard the sound of a carriage. As they all went outside, Rebecca and Jeanne hugged Little George with tenderness, as Mothers and sisters do. Little George tried to hug them back but as he was a young man now he was getting embarrassed. Joshua had previously shaken his hand like a man and wished him all the best as men do. The coach driver helped load his luggage and once all were on board and Little George was safely sitting next to the driver on top, they started waving him their goodbyes. "Next stop, Helston," shouted the coachman.

Walking back to the cottage and with tears in Jeanne's eyes, Rebecca suggested they talk with Christine now as time is running out. So as the three of them went in they went over and sat around the cosy table. As Rebecca started to talk, Jeanne held her breath and Christine, was quiet as a mouse. This had to be handled delicately as Christine was so young being only twelve years. Jeanne and Rebecca had decided to tell the truth as best they could with that youth in mind. ''Christine, your brother Little George is now all grown up and entering the life of a young man, are you happy for him.'' ''Yes, I am, we talked about nothing else since he was told a few days ago. He is so happy and I for him but I will miss him.''

Rebecca had to get to the crux of the matter soon but she was struggling with this roundabout way of getting there. Rebecca went quiet and looked over at Jeanne as Christine looked at both of them. There was really no way around this and so decided just to come clean and out with it.

''Christine, what do you know of your past?'' ''What do you mean Rebecca.'' ''I mean; do you know who your parents are.'' ''No I do not, both my Mother and Father died when I was born and Mr Hosking is our guardian. That's all I know.''

''Well, as Little George has become a young man, you are soon to become a young lady. As you know we are not a normal working type family, you know this, yes?'' ''Yes, I do Rebecca, but I am to keep this to myself.'' ''That's right Christine, never to be told outside of us. Firstly, the time has come to tell you that this lady here is your real Mother and that makes me, your big sister.'' Silence came across them all.

Jeanne got up and went around to her little daughter and got down on her knees. Then in a loving voice, Jeanne said, ''O my lovely beautiful little girl, at last we can tell you the truth." "Are you really my Mummy?" "Yes Christine, I am but we couldn't tell you until now, I am so sorry."

Christine didn't say anything but naturally bent forward and hugged Jeanne tightly around the neck. Rebecca started to cry with love and so also got up and went around the table to cuddle them both. Christine looked up at Rebecca without letting go of Jeanne and said, "Are you really my big sister." "Yes, I am Christine and I love you very much." They all stayed wrapped together with tears flowing with love and happiness.

After gently explaining all what went on before and why this and that had happened, with many stops and questions from Christine, the subject of the looming danger arose.

"So where am I going?" "You are going to a beautiful lady and her family whom we trust completely and will protect you." "What is her name?" "Christine, for a little sister, you ask an awful lot of questions," Rebecca said. And then both of them giggled.

Whilst Rebecca and Christine were chatting, Jeanne was getting a few things packed for her little daughter. Jeanne then came back and spoke, "Christine my child, you will be safe and loved but we must get you away from any danger that is coming. Please kiss your big sister goodbye as we must be on our way to meet her soon and, we cannot be late. Rebecca also kissed her Mother and then went outside to get her horse and ride back to the Halzephron Inn.

Christine was very excited and just couldn't stop talking. Jeanne inwardly adored her incessant questions and tried to answer all as best she could. They were to head back down to Gunwalloe Beach where she had arranged to be as the sun was coming down.

Christine took her shoes off and toyed with her feet in the sand filled with the new love for her mum and sister bulging in her heart. As the red shine of the fading sun shimmered over the gentle sea, Christine noticed a moth, no, it was a butterfly and there's another one. These beautiful blue and crimson butterflies flew closer and joyfully danced around Christine. "Jeanne, sorry, Mummy, look." Jeanne turned around and smiled with delight as she saw these beautiful creatures flying around her young daughter.

Then one came so close to Christine's face she could have kissed it and then immediately flew back to its friend.
Then both of them came in close and flew away again. Christine couldn't take her eyes off these lovely creatures and said, "We must follow, they want us to follow as the old poem says."

One in the air
Nothing to show
Two in the front
Follow ye go

Jeanne smiled as she too knew the tale well as did all the Cornish so took hold of Christine's hand and followed the beautiful creatures of colour. The two butterflies were now floating nearer and nearer to a dark cave's entrance which lay at the far end of the beach. It was getting darker but the butterflies seemed to shed a warm light like some sort of path making Jeanne and Christine feel safe and comforting.

Getting to the rocks close to the cave the butterflies then changed direction and headed out towards the sea but still hugging the rock line. Then out of the blue, a small red squirrel jumped down off a rock and ran to Christine's feet and then rubbed her ankle with its small neck. It then went ahead to follow the butterfly's pathway, stopping every six or seven jumps and then looking back encouraging Christine and Jeanne to follow.

Christine looked at Jeanne and both followed as gently and boldly as asked by the little red squirrel. Christine wanted to pick it up and give him or her a big kiss. It was just so sweet and cuddly she thought.

The butterflies and the squirrel passed the smaller caves on the left and were heading, it seemed, to the furthest darkest one. Slowly they moved forward and as thought the last cave it was. The butterflies then dashed in followed by the squirrel. Jeanne took hold of Christine's hand as they edged to the mouth of the cave. "Are you afraid Mother," Christine asked. "No, I am not afraid, are you." "No, I find it really exciting." Jeanne nearly laughed at her youthful confidence but said nothing.

While still holding hands they entered the cave but saw nothing. Then a shiny blue haze of light started to shimmer at the back of the cave. They both stood still and looked as the light gently edged itself forward towards them.

Jeanne squeezed Christine's hand a little tighter as they both slowly walked a little further into the cave. About twenty steps in they both stopped and stood still, as did the lovely blue light. They could both see it was Zelahnor, well, Jeanne knew, but Christine was just amazed at whoever or whatever this was.

Zelahnor looked at them both as the butterflies continued to buzz all around her and with glowing warmth turned her eyes to Christine. ''Hello Christine, you are so beautiful, I have waited twelve years to see you thank you for coming. I hope Ruby didn't scare you.'' Christine couldn't take her eyes off Zelahnor and just felt love and inner joy towards her. ''Who's Ruby?'' Christine asked. ''The little squirrel you saw.'' Christine smiled and giggled. ''No, she was very gentle and sweet.'' ''That's good, I'm glad, so Ruby, you can come out now.'' With that, the little squirrel poked its head out of the side slit of Zelahnor's black see through shawl.

''Christine, has your Mother and big sister explained to you why you are here?'' ''Yes, they have, I am to go with you for my protection as there is danger coming.'' ''That is quite true and how do feel about this?'' Christine turned her head to look up at her Mother. Jeanne smiled and squeezed her hand in reassurance.

''At first, I didn't want to go but they said it was for the best and I could see them both later when it is safe.'' Zelahnor looked at Jeanne as that was not what had been agreed between them. Only Jeanne could see Christine if it was fine to do so, not Rebecca. However, under the circumstances and in the name of love, Zelahnor said, ''That is also correct.'' Jeanne knew the lady of the Moor had just softened her agreement and smiled with gratitude.

"By the way Christine, do you know who I am?" "You are the Butterfly witch of Bodmin Moor." Zelahnor laughed inwardly with love at Christine's bold honest reply. "And do I have a name" "Yes you do, but I am not allowed to say it, everyone knows that." "Well, on this occasion, you can say it if you wish." "Your called Zelahnor." Jeanne knew what Zelahnor was doing and appreciated the softness, allowing Christine to want to go on her own acceptance.

"I have also brought someone with me who you may like to be friends with." Then a little girl appeared and walked up to Christine. Jeanne knew this to be the little girl whom she met when she travelled to the Bolventor Inn. The little girl now facing Christine said, "Hello Christine, my name is Deborah; I do hope we can be friends." Christine smiled as they both opened their arms and hugged each other. Jeanne looked at Zelahnor and without speaking mimed a slow loving 'Thank you.' Zelahnor smiled and accepted Jeanne's gratitude with warmth.

"Now, there is just one thing more to do then we must be off," said Zelahnor. With that, a massive but beautiful black panther came slowly out of the shadows. Jeanne stepped back in total fear but Christine and Deborah, now holding each other's hands, looked at him in total wonderment.

The beast went direct to Zelahnor and then lay down by her feet. "He is called 'Zoar' and he and his family live for our protection on the moor." Zelahnor then gently spoke to him saying, "Zoar, this is Christine; she will be with us now to complete my family and live with us from this moment, please go and say hello. "Zoar raised his powerful body and moved forward. Zelahnor felt the fear in Jeanne's body and said, ''Jeanne, don't be frightened, he will not harm anyone here.''

When Zoar reached Christine he lowered his massive bulk and gently rubbed his paw on Christine's side and purred. ''I think he would like a kiss Christine, Zoar loves kisses.'' Christine had to look up as Zoar's head was as big as her body, he was massive. Zoar, with his beautiful golden eyes and crisp black irises, bent his huge neck down and looked into Christine's eyes. Without fear or hesitation, she kissed him straight on his cold nose. ''Well done Christine, now he knows who you are.''

''Jeanne it is time.'' Jeanne nodded her understanding and with tears in her eyes went over and knelt by her youngest daughter's side. She then kissed and squeezed her tight for one last time whispering, ''Are you ready my little darling.'' ''Yes, I am ready Mother, don't worry.''

''Come my child,'' Zelahnor said, ''We have lots to do and learn and I will show you your new world." "May I ask how you know my Mother." "You will understand all when it's time my little cherub but now we need to go, we need to leave this cave and reach our rest place.'' With Deborah by her side, Christine followed Zelahnor to the back of the cave where the secret door lay hidden into the tunnels. Zoar stayed close and never left their sides.

Chapter 15

Jon was dead but Zoë still held him in her arms. His eyes were open but he was lifeless. Zoe, with blood all over her face, was in tears and shock and held him tight as though somehow this may awaken him. She just couldn't believe that the love of her life had been taken away.

She should run and she knew it for her own safety. But she didn't care, she just didn't care. While cradling his neck in her lap she bent forward and lovingly kissed each of Jon's open eyes and closed them with her lips. In doing so she said aloud, "I love you Jon." Her floods of tears were all over his dead face as she continued to sob uncontrollably.

It was then realisation kicked in. Yes, she was a traitor, she knew this, but it wasn't like that. Philip de Albret and his side kick Bouchier had recruited her at an early age to do their dirty work. She hated them, especially Bouchier, who was all over her like a rash and seemed to think he owned her. This must be some sort of revenge she thought. Did they mean to kill her or did they in fact want to kill Jon. Whatever their motives she had to get away fast. She had to run for her life, but where?

Whilst trying to wipe away her tears she managed to take the ring off Jon's finger and said, "I love you Jon and I will treasure this, our love, forever." A sense of hatred started entering her mind. This she knew was wrong as she had to be smart, she had to be logical. 'Think,' she said to herself. One second she wanted to stay here with Jon forever. The next second she wanted to run away. 'They are coming she thought, she must tell Jacques, they are coming. She laid Jon's head down slowly on the ground and took off her cloak and ever so gently covered him over. 'Survive,' she said to herself, 'if not for you then for Jon's sake, that's what he would have said, survive my love, no matter what.'

She left his body where he lay. She would tell someone of this and get him buried with her love but she had to go and go she must, this moment.

Zoe ran into their house and took every penny she could find. She had been paid well by the English for her loyalty in helping Jacques bring back his love from the dungeons of Philip de Albret. She knew the risks, but she had no other alternative. The English had captured her and Jacques too and then both had made a deal to work with them and live. Once the mission was completed, both were free to go and live quiet lives with their long lost loves.

Thoughts were racing through her head. She needed time to think, she needed safety. They would be watching her parents' house that's for sure. She stripped and washed away all the blood, redressed and loaded all she could onto the buggy which was standing at the back of the house. Once completed and she had taken one last look about, she whipped the horse away heading to the market town.

It took twenty long minutes to get to her destination and her mind was in turmoil. She was heading for the vicarage outside the town where the local parish priest lived. All the while driving she couldn't stop crying but once the buggy was still at the front path to the vicarage she got a hold of herself and wiped all signs away. Then after taking some deep slow breaths she put her shoulders back and got down and walked to the heavy wooden front and knocked.

While looking to her back and to the sides with nervousness the door opened. It was the priest himself who answered. Looking at her and seeing she was in distress he calmly said, "Yes, my lady how can I be of help." "Please Father; there has been a tragic accident up upon our farm. My loving partner Jon had an accidental discharge of his pistol and is lying dead. I don't know what to do, please help me." "O my dear Lady, yes of course, I will just get my things and you can lead me to him. Have you called on the constable yet?"

"No, I haven't yet; I am in such distress, I really don't know what to do or what I am doing." She was lying; she knew it but she just couldn't leave Jon lying there alone on the open ground. "I understand, now calm yourself my lady, all will be well, just wait there I won't be a moment."

"Father, I can't go back there, it is too distressing for a weak woman like me to see again." She started crying again but this time with louder sobs. Zoe fumbled into her purse, "Here, I have five Guineas, please, if you could just see to his burial in the true faith of our dear Lord." The priest looked at her with quiet disbelief then kindness took over him but with an inner feeling that something was not quite right. "Very well my child. Where is it you exactly live and where would you like us to take his body?"

Zoe explained the whereabouts of her small Farm and the location of her dead Jon. She also mentioned that she really needed to get to his parents and inform them of the tragedy and wouldn't be back for some time. "I understand, and these five Guinea's are for his funeral expenses I presume." "Yes they are, is that enough." "Well not really my dear, not if you want a headstone and my services to include all the paperwork thereof." "I apologise Father; how much is it you require." "Fifteen Guinea's will cover everything I am sure." She looked at him with tearful eyes and dipped her hand back into her purse while thinking, what a bloody thief.

Once the priest was happy with the names and places he went to explain what would happen. When he had finished, Zoe again said her thank you's then went to the buggy and took off. However, she vowed there and then that one day she would come back to Jon's resting place and be with him.

Zoe, not knowing at all where to go decided to head north inland. She was going to go south, south west to the port of Brest but something inside said 'No', not yet. She would double back South sometime and catch a ship but not now. She knew she had to somehow get to Jacque in Cornwall. It was whilst working together she had picked up some of his tactics in that when unsure or sure of the path to go you must always go in the opposite direction first, wait and then double back. She always thought he was over reacting but realisation now dawned on her that she was now the prey and it made good sense. She would ride all through the night and head to an unknown town where she would find some digs and lay low and wait a while.

The constable of the town was having a quiet lunch when the front door banged. Cursing aloud at being disturbed of his lovely lamb stew he got up only to find it was the local priest. "Yes, Father what can I do for you." The priest went on to explain the visit he had from Zoe earlier that morning and thought it best to inform him before he did anything. "Thank you Father, we will look into it. By the way, have you been paid?" "Yes, she paid me five Guinea's." "That's fine, so the council don't have to subsidise you anything." "No, she has paid me in full, thank the Lord." "Good, then please follow me up to the Farm this afternoon and we can take things from there." The priest went away with orders to back in two hours and bring along a coffin with carriage and some extra men.

On closing the door, the Constable immediately went to his desk and with feather scribe in hand shouted for his young errand boy. The Constable had been quietly informed some time ago by his superior that if anything happened like this, with a woman named Zoe, don't make a fuss. He was to send a letter to Morlaix and would be paid two Guinea's for doing so. Once the note was written he ordered the boy to ride fast without stop to the house of Morlaix and give it to the Countess Antoinette.

The body of Jon was still lying in the same position as Zoe had explained to the priest that morning. The Constable went over everything including the inspection of the body, then the house and outbuildings. He concluded that although there were no close powder burns it could have been an accident. But he knew through the experience of war, the size of the entry hole against the much larger size of the exit hole, that it was not a short range thing. However, this was not his problem. The man was dead and he had an eye witness stating it was accidental and the priest had been paid in full. No one else was involved so let's just get this man out of the way and buried. His verdict would stand up in court, he knew, and he also had other more pressing things to deal with. So with a decisive conclusion that the body be immediately buried the priest and his men took over.

Antoinette received the Constable's letter late in the evening and once she had read it, resealed it with her stamp and passed it to her courier to take it directly to the Morlaix Inn.

The Frenchman and Spaniard were using the Inn as a base for retrieval of notes and information. Their spies and touts were on alert all around the Country and information was coming in as planned. However, this one caught their eye.

It read: -

To whom it be concerned,
On orders of information it has become known that a man is dead from an accidental gunshot wound and that a lady involved is called Zoe.
Constable

The courier waited for a reply but there was none and was asked to leave. ''So, my Spanish friend the traitorous bitch has left the coup.'' ''When do you want to leave Peter,'' he replied. ''Thank you Alfred, I say we leave in the morning for further investigation on whom she talked with after the deed had been done and go from there, agreed?'' ''Agreed.''

Chapter 16

The gin laden prostitute had done her job very well. Henry Hosking was once again frequenting and abusing the local whore houses. It had become part of his life. Drink, whore, drink and sleep. How far had he come in life but now just didn't give a hoot. He thought about all the hours he had given, all the bloody hours and days of his life he had given them, and for what? Then bloody George Kernow, bloody pumped up little squeak Kernow tells him, you're finished.

Getting off the bed he walked across the room and delved into his trouser pockets which are lying neatly on the chair. Finding some loose pennies he throws them at the young girl still in the bed. He wants another drink and drink he shall get. He was Henry Hosking for Christ's sake, once the proud owner of a three story town house in Truro and, servants too. He was also once the top man in Cornwall for its inner defence reporting only to that bloody Kernow in London. Bloody Kernow, he thought, bloody Kernow.

He then thought back to how George Kernow had politely said, 'Henry, unfortunately you will have to move out of your town house and move away, we will help you of course.' Bloody prig. Henry was only forty-five years old and now out of work like a rag doll.

Henry was now living in a small cottage on his own at the bottom of the town in the cheaper part of Truro. He rides into town every day and drinks. No one calls anymore, he is not required, as he is not needed. He leaves the room and walks down to the bar and orders a cider then sits down by the window in the Red Lion in Lemon Street.

Henry likes it there, no one bothers him and the whores don't ask any questions.

It has been nearly a month now since he got the boot from Kernow whilst in the Blue Anchor in Helston. He couldn't believe it and wouldn't accept it either. All those bloody years of strife for the defence of this County of Cornwall and he gets thrown out like an unwanted crab. Bastards he thought. And look at how well they treat that French traitor Jacques; they give him a bloody farm. This is just not right.

It was three weeks ago he last saw the love of his life, his beautiful Jeanne, when he had been invited to Rebecca and Joshua's wedding reception at the Halzephron. She was there, his beautiful, gorgeous Jeanne. For some reason she had turned up late and then only once said, 'Hello Henry.' Other than that, she stayed away from him and had her arm in the Frenchman's arm all bloody night. Henry had worked with her many times in the past when she and Joshua's Father were all one undercover team. He had hoped every day then that she would be his but it was not to be. Like everything in his life, he lost her to of all people, that bloody traitor Jacques. That French bastard who one minute wanted to kill us all with a lethal chemical, mixed into our drinking wells and the next he wanted to help us. Since the wedding reception, Henry had travelled three times incognito across to Sennen in the vain hope of seeing her. It was then that his thoughts started to change from dreaming to possible reality. If Jacques was somehow gotten rid of, Henry had a chance and started to think about how this could be achieved. He knew a lot of people in England and abroad that's for sure. He had the contacts, money and brains. His once seemingly faultless allegiance to Cornwall and the Queen however was finished. It was his turn, why the hell should he suffer the way he is for the rest of his life. He then said to himself, 'I love you Jeanne, I am coming to get you my love and we can be together forever. He smiled to himself and ordered another.

Drinking faster he sat brooding on more reasons why he had been thrown away like a bag of rubbish. Even the children didn't visit anymore. Little George and Christine, all that he had done for them and they couldn't give a damn. Yes, it was true he took money for their charge but they didn't know that. He gave them a roof over their heads and what do they do, stay away with Rebecca, Jeanne's daughter. Jeanne, he thought, O Jeanne my beautiful love.

He then, with glass in hand, looked out of the window through the early dark night. On seeing the big white moon he raised his glass, smiled and started laughing aloud as though some sort of deal had been agreed between them. Am I going mad, he thought, but then easily justified it to himself that, whether he was or was not, life was simply not worth living without her. People in the bar heard his weird laughter and looked across at him but then quickly turned them back again and left him to it.

Jeanne and Jacques had now vacated the Sennen Farm and moved into her old cottage in Marazion which was once the marital home she shared with her late husband. Rebecca had moved out as planned and was now living with Joshua at his cottage in Gunwalloe.

When Jeanne entered back into her old cottage at Marazion as the new owner she had feelings of Déjà vu.

However, the move went smoothly and on time. Kernow wanted it all sorted by the latest Monday after the wedding. Jacques was not very happy about moving into another man's, Jeanne's former husband's household, but had no say in the matter. He was under a strict curfew and an oath of compliance. His honour and love for Jeanne were his means of acceptance to it. Jeanne knew him well and loved him dearly and made every effort to comfort his wounded pride. Without him, she would be still in that dungeon and probably dead. However, she knew now that as every day passed she was getting stronger, not just physically but mentally too. Also, Jacques was the Father of the two children and Jeanne had not been at all surprised that he had not once asked where they were, as she knew he trusted her fully. She also knew that if they needed help in any way shape or form he would be there for them. He was a good man she thought and in a very difficult position however, this would change as his time on curfew passed. Jeanne took the lead and organised the cottage the way she liked it and Jacques obliged her like a loving partner would in every detail. The weeks had now turned into over a month and although it wasn't nearly as big as the farm they were settling in nicely.

Rebecca, like her Mother, had also done the same at her new home in Gunwalloe. She and Joshua didn't have time for a honeymoon but she accepted this as part of the game of danger in which they played. She was in love and that is all that mattered. Joshua, like Jacques, had given Rebecca free reign to do what she wanted in his Gunwalloe home. But unlike her cottage at Marazion, this home had been a single man's place with no warmth or living comforts.

Over the weeks though, Rebecca had transformed it into a lovely and comfortable home for them both. Joshua had not been there a lot of the time to help her as his newly promoted role, previously held by Henry Hosking, was taking a lot of his time. He had yet to meet George Kernow on a formal basis to explain the full terms and conditions of his new role but, he had been giving initial orders to organise things as he saw fit and had written authority from Kernow to do so.

One of Joshua's first meetings was with the County Sheriff of Cornwall to be held in Launceston. The meeting went well and papers were passed back and forth giving Joshua authority to protect Queen Anne's Cornish land in anyway Joshua saw fit. An artist was brought in to draw Joshua's facial profile which was to be copied and shared around the area to people in authority acknowledging that this man was Joshua Pendragon. The Sheriff thanked Joshua for his loyalty to the Crown and his known bravery and suggested that if he needed anything he only need ask and it would be agreed. With that, they set up a message system which only they knew and, once that was sorted, had dinner together in the Sheriff's house and discussed matters of interest. Joshua had another two teams in Cornwall to manage and also to meet. One team was in Bedruthan, North Coast, and one in Mevagissey, South Coast. His facial sketches would also be sent to these teams with notes to communicate and to await his visit.

Joshua knew time was moving on and things were hanging in the air. One of the first things he wanted to do was secure his own South West cell. Now that Joshua had been promoted he was spending less time there and knew it was now weak on the ground. He would discuss this issue with Kernow when they next meet which he presumed would be sooner rather than later. As for now though, he wanted to see Bull which he had arranged for tomorrow. Mevagissey and Bedruthan would have to wait.

Joshua was glad to see Bull open the door and said, "Good morning Bull, how are you?" "We are very well thank you Joshua, please come in and have some tea." Bull's missus was boiling the water over the fire place but went to meet Joshua and took his coat and hat. They all settled around the table before Bull took the lead. "So, what brings you to this neck of the woods?" Joshua liked Bull and had worked with him in some difficult times and knew his character. "O just thought I would pop over and see how you are settling in." Bull knew Joshua was now head of Cornwall operations and also knew he needed to know things were fine.

"Well to be of truth Joshua it's a large farm and me and the missus have our work cut out if we are to make a success of it." Joshua looked at Bull's missus who smiled in a gracious and grateful type way. They both come from the St Just area and knew that this move was an opportunity for them to do well. However, it does have its risks.

After a little more chatting Bulls missus knew that the two men needed to talk more in private so suggested she should be getting on with her chores.

"Right Bull, now the missus isn't here how you are truly feeling. I won't be hurt but I really do need to know your honest thoughts because as you know, we are a little thin on the ground, and this farm on the shoreline is a strategic part of our operation.". "Mr Pendragon, we are good I can assure you. When George Kernow offered me and the missus this place we knew it to be an opportunity for us both so yes we are good.". "That's good Bull, did you receive the armour and ammunition and have you started the pit and tunnel as suggested?" "Yes, all is in hand, the armoury pit is finished, I will show you. The armour plated vests are unusual but we wear them every day as ordered. The missus is a simple woman and couldn't understand the need to wear them but accepted my wishes. The tunnel you mentioned has been started but will take many months to complete, maybe even a year, as the rock face we have to dig to is not close, but it will be done." "Bull, we both know the dangers of our work, have you made escape plans?" "Yes, we have." "Good, and what about your team in St Just are they all still good with things." "Yes, all are good." "I'm sorry for these questions Bull but I do need to know what our defences are at this moment." "Completely understand Joshua and may I ask how you and Rebecca are, it was a good reception what I remember." "We are fine Bull and thank you for asking."

Joshua's questions had been answered with pure clarity as he thought they would be; he just needed that reassurance.

Now though, he wanted to get back to Rebecca as quickly as possible. He hadn't seen her in a while and had missed her and the loving cuddles she gives him. Getting up, Bull took Joshua to the armoury pit he had dug in the scullery room and also to the entrance he had started on the tunnel. Joshua was pleased with what Bull had done and so shook hands firmly in appreciation and acknowledgement of their allegiance to one another. Joshua thanked Bull's missus for the lovely tea and left for Gunwalloe.

Riding back along the Helston Road on his loyal stallion, Joshua thought, that of all the people to have in a strategic place such as the Sennen Farm, Bull was a very good and trusted choice.

Chapter 17

The two men were hidden in the Sennen Farm tree line and watching the man ride out from the cottage. They noticed the stallion was of good breed and the man too looked of good appearance and dress. So they reasoned that the man must be of some importance. They previously caught sight of him riding into the farm an hour ago so decided to wait and watch and not to act until he had left. When he was out of sight away from the farm they waited a further ten minutes. With all now quiet, they made their move.

They would be quick, clinical and ruthless and when the job was done gallop fast away. There is no hanging about and no stealing just killing, then pay day. Henry had promised one hundred pounds each for just one man's death and, a French one at that. These men were from Bodmin, a rough neck town and also where the County jail lays. Henry was going to hire men more local in the Truro, Helston area, but that would be too close for comfort hence the reason he thought of Bodmin and two men in particular he had heard of a while ago. These men had also been quietly suggested by a local thug who Henry had been drinking with over the last weeks.

The two men got on their horses and rode down to the farm. One was armed with a loaded pistol while the other had a foot long razor sharp blade. They had done this before and their method was simple but very effective; surprise, shoot and stab and then quick exit. People paid good money for their work and they were good.

Riding up very close to the front door of the cottage they dismounted. Standing side by side with weapons at the ready they knocked on the door loudly and braced for action.

Bull was sitting at the table with his missus talking about Joshua's visit. On hearing the knocking, Bull's missus said, "That will be Joshua again, I wonder what he wants now, he must have forgotten something." Bull got up and said, ''I'll go.'' So casually he walked to the front door and opened it wide, not really looking.

"Bonjour Jacques," and squeezed the trigger. The flint cap went down but the strike was poor and produced nothing but a drab fizz. The other man standing by his side wasn't fazed at all with the pistols misfire, as these things happen, so struck forward with his blade straight at Bull's heart. It hit the target but didn't pierce the body as he expected only glancing off due to the armour under vest.

Bull was in complete shock and tried to slam the door shut but changed his mind and ran back inside to fetch his own pistol to fight back, his life depended on it.

The two men knew things had gone wrong but this didn't stop them from their method of attack and withdraw. They knew that going inside the Farm house was too risky and so with cold resolution turned and jumped on their horses and galloped away. They wouldn't get paid but they would live to fight another day.

Riding away from the farm for over an hour without stop they slowed down to a halt. Whilst still on their horses they took drinks from their hip flasks. Without a word said they knew they had been lucky to get away. On the other hand, the target himself had been lucky too. They had to get back to Bodmin to meet Henry Hosking, so with at least another two hours ride ahead of them, they galloped off.

Hosking was waiting for them in some grotty Inn at the top of town. All he wanted was the good news of Jacque's death and to pay the men off so he could then make plans to invade Jeanne's life. No matter how long it took, he would get her for his own, it's what he deserved. He was feeling a little anxious, as this day would be the start point in his new life ahead, so ordered another large one.

Bull was all the over the place as he couldn't believe how stupid he had been. All the years he had fought for Queen and the Cornish, how could he have been so bloody stupid? If it wasn't for those stupid mailed armoured under vests, in which he had sworn not to wear to his missus as they are being for girls, he would be dead. That's not exactly what he told Joshua, but his missus was insistent that he wear it for her sake and lucky for him he did as told. His missus was sat opposite him in confusion on why Bull was raging within himself. She had heard nothing, no shouts and no guns going off. "What is it Bull, what has happened?" "I tell you what has happened my love; I have just nearly been killed. It happened so fast and I was totally unaware of any risk. Like you I thought it was Joshua coming back." "Well who was it, if it wasn't Joshua." Bull suggested she please ask no more questions and fetch the brandy.

While she went to fetch his drink Bull stoked two pistols ready for firing and looked through the window surveying the front yard. The two men had ridden off as fast as they could and whoever they were, knew their job well. Bull reckoned that with the way they acted as they did they had done this before. Bull remembered the man with the foot long blade and how clinical he was in acting the way he did with absolute no emotion but to kill. Ice cool, even though his partner's pistol failed he acted very well. Bull could see things from the other side, and not the prey side, as he had been in their position many times. When she brought the brandy in Bull drank the whole glass in one and then kindly asked for another. She did as was asked and Bull thought how naturally kind she was to him and he loved her for it. Bull was acting rather calm in the circumstances but inside his adrenalin was running high. He kept thinking on how it could have been so different. But whatever it was, luck or something else, he was indeed still alive. He needed to get his missus to safety that he knew. He also needed to get to Joshua. He felt calm and calculated as he somehow knew they wouldn't come back.

Bull decided to get out and take him and his missus back to St Just but, as their old house was now being rented out, he would have to go to her mum's house. Once his missus was safe he would go and find his support team and ask they meet him in the Star Inn this very night. Tomorrow he would head off to Gunwalloe and speak with Joshua. The Farm would have to be left unattended for now as it was too dangerous to stay in. Bull explained the situation to his love and asked her to get things ready for the short journey. "How long we will be gone, she asked." "I don't know is the answer to that, but I must get you safely away as I need time to get this problem sorted." Without further a due she did as Bull asked. She knew he was doing this for her and she loved his manly actions of protection.

The two men arrived at the grotty Bodmin ale house a little early, but they needed a drink. The place smelt foul and the noise was loud. Henry was sitting over at the far side by the window. He may not think it but he stood out like a sore thumb. Henry was wearing good cloth clothing, clean and shiny leather boots and a hat. Most other men in the bar were miners or stall merchants and all dressed in scraggy filthy clothes. The ladies were of the night and didn't have much on at all and most were trying their luck with Henry, like bees around honey, as they knew he had money.

The two men walked up to his table carrying their drinks and before sitting down, told the two ladies hovering over Henry like a rash, to leave them alone. The two ladies were going to argue the case but just gruffed and walked off as they knew these men were trouble.

"Well my two friends, I have your money here, was there much blood?" "Save your money Mr Hosking, or whoever you are, we didn't kill him he survived." "What do mean you didn't kill him, tell me and tell me now what exactly didn't you hear of my direct orders to do so." Henry started to become louder after hearing the two men's failure to kill. It seemed his listening skills had vanished being replaced with some form of mental anxiety that if he raised his voice it would somehow get what he wants. Whatever it was it had no effect on the two men. These guys do not get spoken to this way. One of the men calmly pulled his pistol out, cocked it and pointed it a few inches away from Henry's face. The people in the Inn saw and heard what was going on and all went silent. You just didn't mess with these men or their families.

"Listen to us you pompous arse, we don't explain anything, to anybody you understand. We told you he had survived and for your information you weird twit he was wearing some form of protective under vest, get it. Now pick your pretty hat and purse up and get out of this Inn and Bodmin now. Do you understand those orders?''

These guys were in no mood for anything. Henry looked at them and then turned his head to the bar area. All of them were looking at him in deadly silence. It didn't take long for Henry to realise, especially with a loaded pistol sticking in his face, that he was in deep water and so without further word, got up and did as told.

Chapter 18

Zoe didn't know what to do, it had been many weeks since Jon's shooting and she still couldn't understand why. Did they make a mistake or did they want to kill her, she could not stop thinking about which. O my beautiful Jon, she thought, then cried again.

She had travelled from place to place, from Inn to Inn. She had to keep moving. What was she to do? She had money which was good and she was alive but only just. Whoever had done this killing had done it for a reason but what reason she couldn't work out. She knew in the end that she would have to go and find Jacques. No, she would not, she thought, yes she would, she thought next. Yes, she must do it and do it soon, but how?

If it were the English who had done this then Jacques would also be dead. If it were the French who had done it, then he would be next too. No, no she thought that can't be. She was getting confused again, but why would they do this?

Zoe was in another Inn somewhere miles from the little farm she had shared with Jon. She had started smoking and drinking again but she didn't care. She had many times thought about going back to her parents, but this, without knowing why or what is what would put them in danger

She could just accept Jon's death and simply leave things at that and get on with her life, if indeed, Jon was the intended target. If that was the case then she would be left alone but that didn't ring true. Jon was a law abiding man who never caused trouble and who she had known from a young age.

Jon was just a young farm hand on her parent's small estate when their love started to blossom. That was until that bastard Philip Albret came along and convinced her parents to take her away on promises he did not meet.

She couldn't carry on the way she was that was for sure. She had to do something. On pouring another brandy and reaching for the pipe she made up her mind that there was only one option and that was to somehow get to Jacques. If she was killed in doing so then so be it she would then be with Jon. Her eyes started to water again. At least Jacques, if still alive, would know what to do. Her mind was set.

Moving from place to place over these last weeks had affected her appearance and her clothes smelt. She needed to get new clothing and start looking after herself better. This she would do in the morning and then slowly move to the coast towards Brest and get a ship across the channel. She felt better that a plan had been made but also knew that she would need to keep a low profile, that's what Jacques would do. In her mind, she knew that Mousehole was her destination.

So, with steady moves and lying low it took over a week to get there but, the port of Brest she had made. The town she found was bustling and the ships were many. However, first things first she thought was to get some lodgings. Zoe knew she was an attractive woman and the number of men trying it on was becoming irritable. As nice and flattering as this was she wanted little attention but she just had to get on with it. She was going to go in disguise, which would be good, but what is the point. She was Zoe, and wouldn't be intimidated to be someone else by people she detested and who had taken the love of her life. She would be strong and be herself, hold her head high, and do this for Jon.

After getting some digs and settling in she then waited for the early evening before venturing out to the port. On walking to the harbour she started to feel nervous in that everyone seemed to be looking at her. Get a grip she said to herself, you are becoming paranoid. You are just a simple woman trying to get a ship to Cornwall, that's it, so don't make any more of it than that. Keep it simple and act with ease.

Being asked many times by sailors to come on board for a drink she eventually found someone with some sense. He then pointed to a little cabin on the dock. Entering the said hut a man seemed very busy but looked up and said, "Yes, Mademoiselle, what I can I do for you?" "I am trying to get to Cornwall to see my family and friends and was told that your ship can help." "That is correct; we sail for Falmouth in five days once everything is loaded and customs passed. We are awaiting a few more supplies which will then make my voyage worthwhile." Zoe's really wanted Mousehole but thought Falmouth was close enough and maybe even better than going straight there anyway. She could get a horse and ride over in a more cautious way. "Have you room for me?" "Yes, we do mademoiselle, if you have the money?" Once costs were agreed upon and the deposit handed over she was told the boarding schedule.

Sarah had been in the port Inn overlooking the docks for a month. Nothing would deviate her from her task and her task was to watch. This is why she was in the team. Every day and every night she would sit and watch through the window and scan the docks back and forth looking for Zoe. Twice she thought she had seen her and twice she had acted to get her, but both were false alarms. She would eat, drink and sleep at the window and just watch the town and dock area. She had waited for news from Peter, her team leader, but nothing had come so she had to keep to the basics.

Then she caught sight of her walking back and forth from ship to ship, asking questions, and looking a little lost and out of place with the others around. This she knew was it, her prey. Her woman's looks, gait and posture fitted Zoe's description perfectly. Sarah smiled and started to prepare herself. No rush she thought, steady and professional. So Sarah stayed where she was out of sight and kept watch on the traitorous bitch.

Sarah quickly thought that if Zoe didn't want to disguise herself that was up to her but she definitely would.

Sarah was forty five years of age and quick. However, her persona was to change from that to being an oldie woman with no aspirations and drably dressed. A woman who had been wronged and hadn't the energy to fight back.

When she saw Zoe go into a Hut on the quayside was when Sarah quickly got up and went out. She stayed close to the houses and Inns well away from the quay but kept an eye on where Zoë would go next.

Zoe came out of the cabin and decided to go straight back to her accommodation, have a large drink, smoke and lay low. She would also push away any bloody Sailors who came on to her.

Sarah saw everything as her eyes were completely focused on Zoe, the target. She then moved further away outward from the quay so she could see Zoe's movements on a wider scale. She watched her walk quickly to the left of the port and then saw her enter a small Inn called 'Les Tara.' Sarah moved closer to the Inn, sat down and unassumingly waited. An hour passed and Zoe still hadn't come out. The time was eight in the evening with a clear sky above.

Unlike Zoe, Sarah didn't drink or smoke. Zoe didn't give a hoot and the brandy and pipe she enjoyed. Waiting another hour and still no sign of Zoe, Sarah went back to her own accommodation and coldly planned the next move.

Late next morning Sarah started her act. Looking sad and gloomy she set out in a down and about way. She ambled over to the quayside and asked a couple of workmen about where that ship was sailing. Both times she pointed to a ship that was opposite the small cabin on the quay where she had seen Zoe enter and on both occasions she was advised it was indeed going to Falmouth.

Entering the same cabin on the quay as Zoe had done the day before Sarah asked for passage across to Falmouth.
The man gave his usual answer and so Sarah thanked him and paid her deposit. She then went back to her digs, fetched a heavily laden bag and made her way to the Les Tara Inn.

When Sarah went into the Les Tara she saw an empty seat over by the window. So making her bag seem heavier than it was for an oldie type lady to carry, struggled her way to it. A young waitress noticed her come in and saw how she limped slowly with the heavy bag. Once Sarah was seated the waitress walked over and asked if she was alright and did she want to order anything. Sarah acted out her role well and so with a softer, slower and higher pitch tone of a heartbroken woman, asked only for a small drink and if it would be alright if she could have a little croissant too.

The waitress looked at her and immediately felt pity for this lovely old lady with such gentle manner. Sarah saw her reaction and so started to whimper a little as her shoulder was sore carrying such a heavy bag. ''Would you like me to come to the bar with you and help you carry them back my dear?'' The young waitress felt real sorrow for this woman like she was her own Mother and replied, ''Thank you, but please this is what I do, you just sit here and rest yourself and I will be back in only a few minutes.'' Thank you my little flower, you are so very sweet and kind, thank you.''

With the first act over, the waitress went to the back of the bar and told everyone what a lovely woman there was over by the window. All the time while the waitress was away Sarah never looked up from the table and maintained the rubbing of her shoulder in such a delicate childish way.

On hearing the waitress coming back with the croissant and drink, Sarah looked up and smiled the sweetest of smiles. ''There you go Mademoiselle, enjoy.'' ''Thank you my dear, how much will that be?'' The waitress knew the real cost but said a little less just to help this lovely customer. Sarah started to fumble in search of her purse and once found slowly counted each small coin in turn for exact payment. While feebly handing the money over to the waitress, Sarah spoke with near tears in her eyes, "Thank you ever so much my child you are so kind." "That's really alright my lady." Then feeling guilty on just going back to the bar and leaving such a lonely lady on her own the waitress leaned closer and asked, "May I ask what you are doing in Brest?" "My husband doesn't want me anymore and so I am going back to my little empty cottage in Falmouth which my Mother left to me when she passed to the good Lord three years ago. That's when I met Anton and he promised he would look after me but now says I have become old and useless and that I have to leave." Sarah then started sniffling and fetched her hanky to dry her eyes and blow her nose.

"Men," they don't know the half of it, you are much better off without him. How dare he just kick you out, have you the passage and fare?" said the waitress. Sarah waited a few seconds to answer and let the sadness of the situation melt in further. "Yes, thank you my dear, I have a few days to wait for sail but thank you for your caring thoughts." "Well, if I can be of any help please do ask for me, they call me Petal." Thank you Petal, thank you so much, but I will be alright.

Sarah watched the young waitress walk away and thought 'stupid bitch.' However, she was sure the waitress will now spread the word and tell everyone in the Inn about the little old lady's sad situation including that traitorous bitch Zoe.' The bait had been laid now all she need do is get up and shuffle away with her head down, carrying her heavy laden bag, and wait. On reaching her digs she went for the quill.

Peter,
The Rabbit is here make ready the cottage at Falmouth.
Sarah.

Chapter 19

Christine and Deborah were playing with the cubs inside the shack which lay out of sight in a large crevice deep into the vast wilderness of the moor.

Zoar was away escorting Zelahnor to a meeting with others of her ilk from Scotland, Wales and England. Christine and Deborah didn't know what a Country was but Zelahnor said she would teach them all these things and to be patient. Zelahnor was excited about the meeting and it all sounded really important.

The cub's Mother was beautiful and calm but the cubs were boisterous and looking for fun. They wouldn't leave either of the girls alone for a minute. Zoar was their Father but as he was away with Zelahnor, his Brother Zareb, who was as big and as lethal, lay close.

The two girls had indeed bonded as Zelahnor wished. As they were about the same tender age their naivety and lack of maturity made them trust each other without doubt.

Christine loved her new life with Zelahnor and Deborah. She knew she was different and had been chosen, as with Deborah, to lead a life of love and protection. Zelahnor was their teacher and loved both of them dearly.

The shack was always warm and cosy and the butterflies flew around all the time as if discussing things with each other. It was their home too and there were thousands of them of all different shades and sizes. The fire was glowing and the air was one of life and love. Laughter and love were it, there was nothing else. Love and kindness would see all things through. This is what Zelahnor taught them every day.

Zelahnor had shown them the beauty of the elements such as the moon, the sun and the rain. Yes, even the rain had its beauty. It was nature's gift to feed the plants and all who were thirsty. Today was no different than yesterday. It was to enjoy the life they had been given. Love everything and be joyous in kindness. Feed everything you can and let nature love you.

There were always the daily chores to do like cleaning and washing but again, they were shown you must always do these with love. Christine and Deborah were amazed at all the animals coming across the moor to the shack just to see them. Even the butterflies inside the shack somehow knew when to sleep and play or when to keep silent. Singing and humming were all part of the day and the girls loved it.

Zelahnor loved them all and they her. Zoar with his whole family was no exception to this loving. However, they and they alone had the authority to go above this means of love if it meant the only way to protect.

The meeting between the four princesses of the lands had been arranged and agreed upon last year when they last met. The secret meeting of the 'Ladies of the Land' had been held for centuries and never missed, ever. It was always held in a different place every year depending on the situation as it was and, always at the end of autumn.

This year it would be held in Wales and the Welsh lady of the Valleys would organise all. Last year it was held in Scotland with the Lady of the Glens and the year before was England by the Lady of the Forest. Zelahnor knew that next year's meeting would probably be held in Cornwall.

Although all these meetings were held in secret, sometimes when Country is in need, such as an increase in civil unrest and tension, a special visitor of high importance would be invited to consult. However, on this occasion a person had asked for their help, knowing they could never mention meeting these ladies of the Lands. If they did they would, through pain of losing everything, live a lonely life in this world and their eternal spirit thereafter. Therefore all that had visited before had kept that oath.

It had been well known over the long years past that some people of the Cornish had, through either drunkenness or debauchery, mocked their 'Lady of The Moor' and in doing so had much raised people's anger. In their revenge they had them killed or forced out of their homes. The sheriffs and justices all knew when this occurred and always gave no charges. They would never dare go against the people and their true beliefs. They too simply loved the Princess of the Moors as their true spiritual living legend.

Due to the new union of the four joined lands the people's anxiety had increased and assaults from inside and out had risen. People were living in fear of the unknown and things needed to settle down. That's why this visitor had asked to attend the meeting in the Welsh Valleys as a matter of urgency. That one visitor, as in the hundred years past, was the head of all, The Queen.

Zelahnor lay quietly with Zoar gently stroking his back in an underground chamber deep in the valleys. It had taken five nights riding on her beautiful Cornish moor pony to get there as they only travelled at night and lay low when the sun rose. When they could use a trail or track they would but mostly it was cross country, it was safer too. When they did lie low all three would sleep together but in reality, Zoar would never sleep as he was always on alert. He also knew Zelahnor felt more secure when he was laid by her side. She had left the children with Zoar's brother for their protection. Zelahnor loved them dearly and would be their surrogate mother for many a year to come.

The meeting of the coven was to start at midnight tonight and to be held in the perilous marshes of the lower stream. These meetings went on through the entire night and, there were to be three meetings this year. The first was with only the four Ladies. The second night was to include the special visitor and the third was again them four only. The route to the marsh area was tricky and dangerous and, although not far in distance, would take an hour to get there. Cuddling closer to Zoar, she closed her eyes and slept.

Awakening refreshed, Zelahnor got her things together and with Zoar in front securing the lead and the pony behind, they slowly walked out of the chamber into the beautiful clear dark night. Zelahnor stood silent for a while looking up at the crystal stars above and thought how wonderful and marvellous the universe is. She then got on the back of her pony as Zoar moved off to guide their pathway forward to the marsh.

Getting close to their destination Zelahnor could see the glow of the fireflies ahead. Reaching the first of them she knew that her own animals could go no further, it was the rule. Now only Zelahnor could go forward so dismounting, she gently kissed both her animals on their cold noses and told them to be good. They understood and would wait unseen and silent until her return.

As Zelahnor walked forward, passing the guiding firefly's, she lovingly thanked them all for their help. Then going deeper into the wet marshy area the firefly's were replaced with many butterflies and moths who swooned all around her. She smiled and said, "Hello to you all." Getting to the small riverbank Zelahnor stood still and waited. The night was ghostly silent and only the rushing of the stream could be heard. She looked up at the dark sky as the full moon shined its massive thoughts of the unknown.

Then she heard the rustling in the dense undergrowth. It was coming from just to her right and it was getting closer. Standing very still she saw a massive black Welsh hound appear and head straight at her. The large animal didn't rush but slowly and without fear moved ever closer to her. Once by her side the beast bent down and rubbed its head gently on her bare feet. Zelahnor knew this was a greeting of love and once over it slowly turned about and moved off in a different direction. Zelahnor followed.

Chapter 20

Joshua paced up and down the main room while puffing on his pipe. "So, let's go over this again Bull, but let's take each bit at a time." Bull knew Joshua needed to get the picture right in his head before he could decipher whatever he was deciphering.

It had now been four days since the attack on Bull outside the front door at the Sennen Farm. Joshua had been away in Bedruthan meeting the team he now managed. It had been Rebecca who had got word to him that he needed to get back home urgently.

Since the attack, Bull had not been able to speak with Joshua so had got on with things without him, as best he could. His missus was now safely out of harm's way, living with her Mother in St Just. He had also met with his team and discussed things.

That team meeting in the Star Inn had achieved its results and activated his men into a covert action to find these two attempted murderers or at least find something they could work on. The clinical method the two men used to attack indicated to Bull an experience of killing and this, with their ruthlessness, proved to Bull they were no amateurs and had done this before. So Bull weighed these facts up and came to the assumption that they were most probably hired as a proven team to get a job done. He again emphasised to his men to concentrate on the simple double method in which the two men use to kill. His team were then sent in pairs to scour the Inns and haunts of Falmouth, Truro and Bodmin. Their job was to quietly get any information on which these men may be known and get this information back to Bull as quickly as they could.

After a somewhat quiet three days, the Team and Bull met again late on the third night in the Star Inn. The Falmouth and Truro pairs had come up with nothing of real interest but the Bodmin pair had something.

It would appear from the information gained that two men were quietly known in the area of Bodmin Town for 'Shoot and Stab' techniques and no one messed with them. These men were regarded by the locals as brutes and they always drink at the top of the town. That was their ward and they ruled. When locals heard that 'Shoot and Stab' were on the way round people got out of the area and went elsewhere. The Shoot and Stab information wasn't a lot to go on but it was something and it got Bull's attention and Joshua's too.

"So, let me get this right Bull." Joshua was still pacing around the fireplace but now talking aloud. "The men came to the Farm door just ten minutes after I had left you and your missus?" 'That is correct Joshua." "So, they must have watched me leave before they made their move." "That is correct again." "Very interesting," Joshua murmured back.

"So when you opened the door thinking it was me coming back again as I had forgotten something, the man with the pistol calmly said, 'Bonjour Jacques,' before firing." "That's exactly what he said."

Joshua started thinking who, in the close knit world of his work, would know that the turncoat Frenchman was living at the Farm or was it simply coincidence. But Joshua knew that coincidences don't happen in his world but again, don't over complicate things. He needed facts and had to look at the bigger picture as his responsibilities were now all of Cornwall, not just him and Rebecca, as it once was. Bull sat quietly sipping his cider waiting for Joshua's decision on what to do next.

''Alright Bull, you and your team have done well. I say that before we do anything we go to Bodmin and question these two men. We can then act as we see fit on their answers, what you say?''Joshua was wise enough to know that to directly order Bull around to do things he wanted was the wrong way. Like himself, he liked to be asked to do things rather than be bossed. It didn't cut well both ways to be a dictator especially to an experienced man and so suggestion with guidance got the best out of both of them. ''I say your right Joshua, when do we go?'' ''We go this very night, get your men ready.''

Rebecca ensured that Joshua was fed and watered for the night ahead and also checked his armoured vest. Rebecca knew the game she and Joshua were in and knew Joshua liked her care for his well being. He wanted to discuss with Rebecca what had happened with Bull and the pistol man and on their words spoken, 'Bonjour Jacques. 'However, he thought it better not to as she would then worry about the safety of her Mother, Jeanne.

Joshua knew he had to get answers quickly and quell any further attacks on his men, so hopefully tonight, he would get them. Bull and his team arrived around four thirty. It would take three hours to get to Bodmin so having checked all men and gear were ready, they galloped away.

At eight o clock, they arrived on the outskirts of Bodmin but before they went into the town itself they pulled off the highway and rested a while. Bull then gave a last minute briefing session. They were to go in pairs to scout the town and bars with all to be back within the hour, no later. He and Joshua would wait here for their return and then act on the information gained if any.

On their return, two teams found nothing but the pair who had gone to the top of town had found two men fitting the description drinking in the 'White Hart Inn. Based on this news everyone then got ready and prepared. The two men they were after were ruthless and known to be hard as nails so they had to be very careful. Also, only one man out of their whole Team could identify the two men wanted. As that was Bull he knew that he had to go into the Lion's Den. Joshua knew this too and so asked if he had his plated vest on. Bull nodded and said, "Thank you Joshua, yes I have." They both smiled knowing the seriousness of the situation. Once again Bull went over on what was to happen.

Two of his men were to secure the two exits of the Inn and two were to enter with Bull and Joshua. One man was to stand guard over the horses for a quick escape and the last man of the six was ordered to go to the Bodmin jail and find the Chief Constable of the town. He was to explain what is happening and that Joshua Pendragon with the authority of the Sheriff of Cornwall was conducting this arrest. Once everyone acknowledged their roles they rode into town.

The two men alias 'Shoot and Stab' were indeed in the White Hart Inn. They didn't need to be in there as they had already been tipped off two days ago that some strangers had been asking questions, or more specific, about two men using Shoot and Stabbing techniques.

They could have just stayed out of the town and let things calm down a little but that would have meant pussyfooting around and running away. That would have seriously dented their bad reputation and that just wouldn't do. They had clout in the town and people feared them. They would show these big outsiders who was boss around here. They owned Bodmin.

The man detached from Bulls team arrived at the jail asking for the Chief and on being received quickly informed him of the situation. On hearing this news the Chief shouted, ''O my God, have they left for the Inn yet?'' ''Yes, they have, they should be there in the next few minutes.'' ''Wait here, while I fetch my guards as they will need help. These men are notorious in Bodmin town and they will have got wind something is happening, they will be prepared.''

Bull's team and Joshua arrived at the White Hart Inn after just a short fifteen minute ride. Once dismounted they all went to their positions and with pistols hidden but checked and loaded for immediate use, four entered as planned.

The place was loosely packed with people drinking at the bar or chatting at the sides and ends. The first to enter was the two support men, followed by Bull and then Joshua but no sooner had the four walked in when the first shot was fired hitting the team's front man in the shoulder who then fell to the floor like a sack of potatoes. On seeing their lead man go down the second man could have simply withdrawn or rush back out of the Inn. But he was a brave old boy and remained where he stood and dived down taking cover and Bull and Joshua did the same. Just as they did this move more shots were fired but all had aimed high and missed. The injured front man was still laid on the floor in the open so the second man reached out his hands and grabbed his feet dragging him back in behind their cover. He was alive but bleeding heavily. All four were now stuck on the floor behind the low level wood panels but it now gave the three of them time to draw their pistols. Bull, lying on his chest, snaked forward to see if he could see anything but soon realised he would only see something if he lifted his head above the wooden rail that was protecting them. If he did this he knew his head would be shot off so stayed down and looked back at Joshua.

People who had come into the Inn for a cosy drink and not connected with the 'Shoot and Stab' men, started to scream and run around scared out of their wits. Glasses were being smashed all around as they fled from the shooting.

The two men known as Shoot and Stab had two of their mates with them and all four were reloading ready for the next movement of attack. However, once their pistols were ready, they started to laugh aloud and mock the intruders. The man known as 'stabs' shouted, ''Come on then girls, come and get us you cowardly gerbils.'' With that, they all raised their glasses of brandy and laughed louder.'' They knew this was a serious and possibly fatal situation but they simply accepted their fate as it would happen. The brandy consumption certainly didn't help matters but this was the way they lived.

Joshua tapped Bull's legs and jerked his head back towards the doorway. Bull understood and tapped the man in front and then all three keeping tight to the ground crawled back out the way they had come in, dragging their injured friend with them.

Once back outside in the relative calm Bull said, "Well that went well Joshua, now what do we do?" Joshua, trying to compose himself replied, "I'm not sure Bull, but we need to regroup and find a way to get this sorted one way or the other." Joshua's main thought was to get these men alive so to question them as he knew they must have been hired by someone and he wanted to know who.

It was then that the Chief Constable and his men arrived in force. The Constable was an experienced man and could see immediately what had happened and so ordered his men to surround the building.

Once the order was given he walked over to where Joshua and Bull were standing. Holding out his hand Joshua said, "Constable I am Joshua Pendragon, thank you for coming, I believe we just may need your help." The Constable shook Joshua's hand and whilst doing so answered, "That's why I am here Mr Pendragon; as soon as I heard what you were intending I knew there would be trouble. The men you are after don't care about anything or anyone and would kill their own Mother if the money was right."

Joshua then introduced Bull and asked if there were any medical people about as one of his men was injured. The Constable gave orders to fetch the local physician.

Things outside were now more calm but time was moving on and nothing was happening. All men were in position waiting. "Joshua," the Constable said, "We can't allow this stand off to continue much longer we need to sort it out." "The two men I want are inside with pistols loaded and, I need to question them." "I understand that but I have a job to do and that it is to protect the people of Bodmin. If these men get away with this tonight and, with what they have done in the past, their status of villainy will be sky high and mine will be nothing."

"So what are you saying?" "I'm saying, to keep any future law and order in this town we need to get in there and force them out now and if they don't come, we kill them."

Joshua understood the Constable's position and suggested a compromise. "What say I try and talk with them first and if they are persistent in their fiery defence then you take over and do what you must." "That sounds fine with me but be careful Joshua, they will shoot you without a thought." Bull then commented, "Joshua, the Constable is right, please do not go in there, if you must talk with these men then shout your wants by the doorway."

Joshua weighed things up. If he couldn't get them to talk he wouldn't get the information he needed. If he bravely went in against the advice he had been given he could be killed and then he would achieve nothing. If all went sour he would have to find another source.

After careful thought, Joshua agreed with the advice given and so all three men devised a plan to talk and attack.
It was Bull's turn to say to Joshua, have you your vest on?"

One main compromise was the Constable's request that it was Joshua Pendragons orders they were following, not his. If word got out that he or his men had killed these villains at their discretion there would be local reprisals from their so called followers and touts. Most locals would be joyful that these thugs are gone but he had to be careful, he and his men lived and drank in Bodmin.

Shoot and Stab and their two mates were still at their table drinking and laughing inside the Inn and had allowed the other people inside to hide out of harm's way as with the Landlord too. The Inn now appeared to be empty except for the four men. One of the men asked 'Shoot,' ''what are we to do?'' ''We do nothing, you coward; we stay where we are and fight so fill your glass and drink. If they take us alive we will hang anyway. If we fight and win we have a chance of getting out and besides we already got one of them.''

As those last words were spoken by the man 'Shoot' they then heard Joshua's voice from outside. ''You men in there, you know whom we talk, lay down your weapons and come out. You won't be harmed we just need to talk, that is all.'' Joshua's foot was holding the door ajar but his body was outside with pistol held down in his hand. He looked back at the Constable and Bull as they all waited for a reply.

Then it came, ''And who are you,'' shouted Shoot. ''I am a member of the Cornish Agency under the protection of our good Queen Anne and I order you all, under the good laws of this land, to come out unarmed. The four men quietly looked at each and said nothing but filled their glasses and drank them back in one. Banging the empty glasses down on the table 'Shoot' replied on behalf of them all.

"Well, Mr Cornish Bloody Agency, you can tell that so called Fat Wench Anne to run back home to London where she belongs and, while you're at it, you can also tell her Bitch, The Witch of Bodmin Moor, to go suck a duck." That last comment about the Witch of Bodmin got the other three laughing aloud. "Come and get us, he shouted loudly" and then fired his pistol through the window at the attackers outside.

Hearing those last words of defiance and the pistol shot going through the window gave the final clear message of their stance to fight. Therefore there was only one way to deal with it. So with nods to each other, the Constable and Joshua's men with full speed and aggression attacked from every angle.

The siege took just fifteen minutes and was total carnage of fire and blade. The four men lay dead around the table they had so violently defended while shouting abuse and firing their pistols at all who came at them. The Constable and Joshua's men took casualties but none were life threatening, bar one.

"Well Joshua, it is over," the Constable said. "Yes, and I thank you and your men's bravery, I am only sorry it had come to this." "Unfortunately Joshua these men lived by the sword and died by it, they would never ever had seen reason. What will you do know Joshua?" "Well, we will go home, lick our wounds and regroup and find other means to get the information we wanted."

Joshua went on to discuss that their visit to Bodmin should be kept quiet and to use vagueness to squash any gossip.

"By the way," Joshua said, "What was that they said about the Bitch of Bodmin?" "Don't ask Joshua, in these parts of Cornwall nobody messes with our beautiful Lady of the Moor, nobody." "Yes, I have heard this old witch's tale, her name is Zelahnor or something." "Shhhhh Joshua, you are not allowed to say things like that, be careful.

With that, both men shook hands and said their farewells. Joshua then went over to Bull and his men and asked if they were ready for the off. It was a long ride back to Gunwalloe for Joshua but even longer to St Just for Bull and the others.

Just before they left, Joshua asked Bull if he could be at his Gunwalloe Cottage in two days. The farm at Sennen was now lying empty as Bull and his Missus were now living at St Just and he needed to get this sorted out quickly due to the security issue of that particular coastline.

Chapter 21

Henry Hosking was again acting strange. He was forty five years of age and forced against his will into early retirement with nothing to do except drink and whore. He needed to get a life but what. All he ever kept thinking about, apart from Jeanne, was those bastards, all that effort and work he gave and for what, thrown to the wolves, those bastards.

How is it he thought, you can turn traitor against your very own Country and that other Country gives you everything you want. How can that be right?

Henry was standing in a corner of his bedroom facing and talking to the wall as if this was a normal thing to do. He was wearing only his pants and socks. He turned around and went back to his bed but he couldn't sleep, he needed a drink. Getting back off the bed and with the lighted candle in hand he went downstairs.

Pouring a large one he went and sat on the floor and looked into the red embers of the dying fire. He had not bothered to dress any further than what he had on and so that there in just his socks and pants. A silence then took over him as his eyes burrowed deeper into the heated coals as if they were somehow giving him advice on what to do? It seemed so unfair that he should find himself in this situation, all alone and lonely.

The small house was just about affordable if he was frugal. Only a few months ago he had it all, prestige and clout and now he had nothing, but that Jacques that bloody French traitor had it all and he also had Jeanne. They were living together and have everything while he has nothing. This can't be right so he poured another large one. He drifted back into a sort of dream like state, remembering bit by bit on how he had suffered for his Country and his fellow Cornishmen. He started laughing aloud.

He visualised, when he was so very much younger and had joined the service of his Queen and Country and how he was so full of life and energy. Fun, kissing and danger were the order of the day. He didn't shy from anything. In fact it was this energy and not being afraid that got him noticed. For anything that required courage, Henry would not shy.

He started laughing again at a particular time in his life when he was abroad in active service. He was on patrol in a foreign land when he and his mates were patrolling the back streets of a city. A young woman was sweeping her front door step, as they did in England and on walking by her she turned and asked them if they wanted servicing. Henry was a virgin, he had never done it before and didn't really know where things went. O the naivety he thought. It was only after his mates had agreed to her costs that Henry also agreed. When it was his turn he remembered trying to tenderly kiss her as he thought that's what you do, but she responded by saying 'no kissy, no kissy, you pay, you pay'. Henry looked at her in a quiet bemused way and realised this was real life and she was probably a very nice lady doing things she wouldn't normally do, but for the sad situation she found herself. Henry then threw some logs on the fire and poured more of the hard stuff.

His mind was switching from his active service memories to his outside so called normal life. It was confusing him.

In the marines, he had to be tough but in normal life he had to be wise, both ends of life's spectrum. Was it normal to defend a position while being attacked and your mate next to you had forgot his bolt for his gun? He remembered that night well with everyone laughing at the absurd situation. Henry smiled and giggled.

Many times he had been scared but never allowed to show it. He saw hands being cut off at a sweep and friends killed due to a simple mistake. O my dear he thought, what a waste.

His mind then went to the time when he was chosen to find a hidden ignition point where a large cache of gun powder could be denoted. He knew that other men had died doing this but when the officer had asked if he would do it, he did it, without hesitation.

He could feel himself tense up at the mere thought of this action. He also thought of the other men's relief that he and not they were doing this act. Once again his mind found itself in a deep tense. He tried hard to arrange his mind to clearer thoughts of love and happiness but for some reason found it hard to concentrate on these kinder things of life. In the marines there was no show of emotion which seems now to have affected his loving side, in that to do so, would be weak. Why couldn't he do what seems to be quite easy and normal for other people. It was this particular lack of emotional thought that hurt him more than anything.

He then went over the time when he found himself outside the main defence in a forward observation post. It was the dead of night when he heard the enemy stealthily advance towards his covert position. He immediately sent a runner to inform the officer that an attack was imminent and that he wanted to withdraw back into their main defence.

The runner came back and told Henry that the information would be acted on accordingly and, that he must stay in the undercover position he was in and let the enemy come through. Henry understood the order but once again found he was in a life and death situation that he could nothing about.

Henry couldn't help but think, even to this day, that if they had been found he would have been tortured and killed most inhumanly. He thought of his life as worthless and tortured himself thinking how other people saw him as a waste of space, but he had so much to give. It wasn't long after his continuous bravery that he caught the attention of people in authority and after a few more years of service he was transferred out and put into the secret world of internal defence in the Cornish region.

He had enjoyed his time with the Cornish teams especially when he worked with John Pendragon and Jeanne. Though saying that, in his last mission with them a few years ago, he was not as brave as he once was. His brain was telling him not to be brave. He felt then that something was not quite right in his mind and tried to work it out. What was wrong with him? He was tired.

Getting up from the floor he stumbled, with bottle in hand, back up the stairs and lay down on his bed. He felt nothing in the physical sense but mentally he just couldn't stop the thinking, analysing and trying to find solutions. He felt he was going mad but why would he say such a thing and then analysed why he had even mentioned it in his mind. After closing his eyes he started to cry. He needed help. He thought of beautiful Jeanne and the loss it gives him. Then after a few more slugs of the brandy, sleep found him.

She then appeared like real life as if he could touch her. She was shouting at him but he couldn't understand what. The little boat, they were all in then touched the galleon and he scaled up the rope first. He wanted to help Jeanne up and saw Joshua's Father quickly put the paddles away and for some reason, he smiled. Then the explosion from a French cannon ball and the little boat went flying with both Jeanne and Joshua's Father still in it. He screamed and shouted. He was in a daze shouting and crying when he heard a loud banging noise going on and on in his head which woke him up back into the world of reality. Somebody was knocking on his front door. He was sweating profusely

Henry shouted out at whoever it was at the door to shut up and wait. Henry got his feet on the floor and grabbed the brandy for a quick swig. Only a few months ago his maid would have done this for him.

Getting to the standing position Henry fumbled his way down the stairs. The banging was now getting louder and so eventually with shaking hands he unlocked the bolt and opened the door.

The first thing Joshua saw was a man who looked bloody terrible, skinny and smelt of drink. ''Henry, you look bloody awful.'' Seeing Joshua took Henry by surprise and didn't know what to say, he wasn't expecting this. What was up, he thought. ''Joshua, what brings you here.'' ''If you let me in Henry I will tell you.''

Henry did as was asked and allowed Joshua in. It was only a simple house with two rooms downstairs and two rooms up above. Joshua walked through the door and stayed in the main room looking at all the mess. He didn't want to go any further, especially into the filthy washroom come work room, it was disgusting.

''Henry, what on earth is going on here, this place is a pig sty.'' Henry had to wise up and think quickly. ''O, I went out last night and did not get back to very late this morning, you know how it is.'' Joshua wasn't convinced as he could see this place had not been cleaned in ages. He looked Henry up and down and saw he wasn't wearing any clothes apart from his socks and pants.

''Henry, you have no clothes on?'' Henry started to wake up as he had to be on his toes with Joshua. ''Apologies Joshua, I think I am still hung over, I thought the banging was probably some rag woman selling something or other if you know what I mean.'' ''Yes, I do know what you mean Henry but please get some clothes on as we need to talk.'' Joshua sat in a dirty chair and waited for Henry to come back down hopefully with some more clothes on this time.

Henry was frantic. He was putting some clothes on as advised but couldn't stop his brain from thinking. What does he want he thought, what does he want? Calm down, he said to himself and act naturally as if you know nothing, and take it all by surprise.

After five minutes Henry entered back down to the main room. Joshua had cleaned the hearth and was relighting the fire. ''Have you any tea Henry?'' ''No, I haven't, I really do need to get some groceries in, would you like a brandy?" "Henry, it is only nine in the morning and no I do not want a brandy, thank you." Henry stayed silent as the two sat down in their seats, albeit filthy ones.

"Henry, I have come here on two counts, one is to see how you are and the other is to ask you a couple of questions, that is all." However, Joshua could see this man in front of him was not at all well. He was gaunt and unshaven and had lost an awful lot of weight. Joshua also noticed he had cut marks all over him.

"I am fine Joshua, thank you for asking." Henry knew he had to be careful here. He needed to play the game as he always plays it, tell them nothing but tell them everything. Joshua didn't answer and just looked at him in silence. "Well Henry you do not look well and what are all those cut marks on your body about, how did you get them?" "O I went berry picking last Sunday. It was such a lovely day but guess what, I decided to take my clothes off and then would you believe it fell into a bush of prickly thorns. I was so embarrassed Joshua." Henry then started to laugh aloud at the answer he had just given. Joshua looked at him in bewilderment and knew something was seriously wrong.

Joshua felt sad for Henry's state but he needed answers and carried on. "Henry, what do you know of some men who are called, Shoot and Stab?" Henry's heart nearly fell into his mouth as he started to think about what has gone on. What do they know? Say nothing. Then in a controlled manner, Henry replied, "Sorry Joshua, I have never heard of them." "Hmmm," Joshua mumbled.

A few seconds of quiet went by and Henry asked. "Why do ask Joshua has something happened." "Yes, something has happened Henry." Joshua weighed things upon whether he should tell him or not. Henry was not on the payroll now and retired out of service, but something in Joshua decided to push it a little. Henry remained quiet.

"Someone tried to kill Bull at his farm in Sennen." "But I thought Jeanne and that turn coat Frenchman lived there." "That's right Henry, that's exactly my point. It seems that when Bull opened the door to these men, only ten minutes after I had left, the gunman's opening words were, 'Bonjour Jacques,' before squeezing the trigger. Luckily for Bull, the pistol misfired. So it is our conclusion that the assassins meant to kill Jacques and not Bull." "But how do you know this to be Joshua?" "We don't know it for sure Henry but after going over it again with Bull we both agreed that this was the most likely case." "Bull could have been mistaken in what the man said." "That is correct Henry but we go on what we think to believe is true."

"Also Henry, immediately on the pistol misfiring the other man stabbed Bull with full thrust. The under armour vest which I had ordered Bull to wear deflected the blade and both then ran off. The way in which these men did their work made Bull aware that they were not amateurs and had probably done this move many times before."

"So let me ask you again Henry, what do you know of these men known as Shoot and Stab." "As I said Joshua, I do not know them." "Well, that's funny Henry, as Bull seemed to remember that it was you who had mentioned it to him a few years ago." Henry remained silent and started to sweat. "I'm sorry Joshua, but I cannot recall ever mentioning these people, Bull must be mistaken. I have also been under a lot of pressure lately. Have you these men in custody?" Joshua could see Henry was shaking nervously and felt something was wrong but decided to quickly finish what he had to say and not let this man in front of him, who once was a loyal colleague, fret any more on his behalf. "No, we do not, we had a standoff in Bodmin a few days ago and they were both killed along with two other men." "Did you get to talk with them, did they say anything?" "No we did not get to talk with them and their last words were actually shouts of rebuke at our Queen and our Cornish Lady of the Moors. It was when they mentioned the Moors Lady that the local constabulary lost complete patience and went for the attack. They were killed instantly through our pistol fire from all directions."

Henry seemed to relax on hearing that these men were dead and replied by uttering a single word, "Zelahnor." He then went icy cold at the thought of mentioning her name aloud. "One day Joshua, you will come to understand that name. To the Cornish, she lives and breathes for their very souls of life". Joshua looked at Henry in a surprising way as he was now talking calm and factual. Henry then said, "What do you know of this woman Joshua?" "I know that she lives Henry that is all, why, do you believe in this fairy tale." "This is no fairy tale Joshua, how do you think we came to know of the Frenchie's planned attack on Mousehole last year." "What are you saying Henry she can hear and gain information from sitting on the Moors?" "I am not saying that Joshua. What I am saying is this lady, whoever she is, has the ears and hearts of the people. I was in your position for ten years until only four months ago and people of much higher rank than I fully respect her position as the one who knows. It has been heard that she even has secret meetings with them but nobody can say this as it is not allowed. No one will have a bad word said against her. She is meant to be beautiful and full of love.'' Henry could not stop himself from talking about her. ''Joshua, you have been away at sea and abroad for a long time but you know the old tales and you know the truth and yes, I do believe.''

Joshua thought a while about this Zelahnor. It was true that when he was a little boy growing up in Cornwall he had heard the tales. Joshua smiled to himself as he remembered the 'Butterfly.' But how did she know about the planned French attack and more importantly, how does she know the right people to inform to stop the attack.

Joshua considered all that had been said but brought the subject back to the present. He knew Bull had not lied on remembering that it was Henry who told him of these men. Then again, it is also quite possible that he could have been mistaken but whatever the truth he couldn't do much about it now. What he did know was that the man in front of him is in a very bad way and needs help. Henry had fought for Queen and Country for a long time but all Joshua could see now was a dishevelled drunkard of just skin and bone.

Henry looked at Joshua waiting for him to say something of Bull remembering, as it was indeed himself, who had told him of this killing team known as Shoot and Stab. Henry knew that Bull was telling the truth so waited for Joshua's authoritative response.

Joshua knew his questions were not being answered to his satisfaction and was now in silence weighing things up as to the right balance of reply. What would he gain in taking things any further with this broken man? Joshua then made up his mind and spoke, "Henry, whatever has happened has happened we will leave things at that, but Henry my friend, you need help, you know that yes?" Henry looked down at his feet and started to cry.

Chapter 22

Zoar lay silent in the rushes protecting the south side of the meeting when his ears pricked at the soft beautiful singing that had started. Zelahnor had now been gone for over two hours and all had been quiet. Zoar was doing his job well.

The night was fresh and dark with a crystal sky showing the large full moon and only a very light breeze was about. The four ladies of the people sat tightly together on the flattened reeds holding each other's hands and all facing each other in a circle. Their eyes were closed and they were singing an old Cornish chant and when they had finished they started humming a Welsh song. Afterwards, it would be Scottish and then an English ode. They didn't rush their tunes and were in perfect harmony with themselves and the rustic wild nature that surrounds them. It was as if they were thanking the moon and night sky with their love and gratitude. Thousands of butterflies, moths and all other small creatures fluttered around dancing in full joy.

When they had first met they all kissed each other tenderly and thanked the earth and spirits for keeping them and all who they protect safe. This included everything that moves and breathes including the trees and flowers. These ladies knew that all that was on this earth had been given freely with no charge and were bound in faith, love and loyalty to protect these gifts of life.

Before they had started to sing, information and rites had been quietly shared throughout all the four lands. The new Union of the Lands had caused raised anxieties and unrest among all the people. Other nations such as the French and Spanish felt threatened by this new combined strength that the four United Nations gave. The Ladies knew this would happen, they felt it years ago when talk of the union started and it was part of their journey to calm, where they could calm, through love and affection to each and all of the people. Information flowed between them without hinder or judgement as they listened and learnt from each other about what was happening in their Lands. Knowledge and love were all, this was their strength.

Now that their smooth and melodic chanting and singing had stopped they started to get even closer together. When almost touching each other's noses they lowered their heads and huddled together as one. With voices now lowered to a deep whisper, the butterflies and other animals moved away as if knowing that secrets were now to be passed.

After nearly an hour of whispering had passed they hugged each other with warm loving tenderness as if they were one body. Still holding hands they then kissed and stood up and danced slowly round and round while all facing up to the moon. Once this last ritual dance was completed they separated as the meeting was ended. They all needed to get back safely to their respective caves whilst the dark of the morning night still gave protection. The meeting with their visitor tonight had been arranged and all knew what to do but for now, they needed rest and daylight was in a couple of hours.

The carriage had arrived at the old isolated Inn on the main drag in the Welsh domain with a small lady sitting inside with four armed men. Outside the Inn on their arrival were ten horses with riders waiting for orders from one of the four armed men.

Once the carriage was stationary one man stepped out and ordered the ten riders to immediately surround and secure the Inn. They had no idea who was in the carriage and only knew to do as told. The ride from London had taken two days.

Once all men were in place and the armed man was happy he went back to the carriage to escort the lady down.
Once she was out he held her hand and hurried them both into the Inn. It was the end of the afternoon and in a couple of hours, she would be informed on what to do.

Sitting in her room contemplating what the evening would bring she took a large nip of gin swirled with fresh orange. She was dressed as a pauper with a large scraggy hat pulled over her head. As the minutes ticked by slowly a little light knock on the door was heard. The pauper looking lady looked up at the door and spoke in a posh orderly voice, "Enter." The little girl entered and in perfect English with a beautiful Welsh lilt said, "Good evening my lady, my name is Aerona, your pony is ready." The pauper lady knew this to be true as 'Aerona' was the code word that had been sent to her by undercover sources only three days ago. "Thank you my dear, I will be there in five minutes." With that, the young girl nodded and went back out.

A few minutes later the armed man knocked and went into the lady's room asking seriously if she was prepared to do this alone. He too didn't know why, where or what this lady was up to and it was his job to protect this woman at all times. If he slipped up in any way from his guarding her then his head would be simply sliced off. He had also been forbidden to say exactly where they were going when they left the Palace in London. It was put about that she was going hunting in Scotland and all people closely linked with her accepted this as true as they knew she liked this game of sport. If they knew that she was in fact in Wales to meet unknown people in an unknown location deep in the Valley marshes, they would have called physicians for help and guards for her restraint.

The time had come for her to go and again the man offered to go with her as protection but she would have none of it. "I cannot tell you where I am going or who I am seeing but, I do this for my people. If I am not back by daylight I suggest you leave this place henceforth and go directly to my Cousin George at the House of Hanover." Although she said this with gusto and pride she was, very nervous.

The man who was indeed in the order of her guard knew when to back off, as he did now, with a bowed reluctance. Then she spoke again, "Please do not fret for my safety my trusted guardsman, you have done everything you could to protect me. I have left a written memoir in my safe at Windsor that you tried in vain to stop me and that your head will not roll because of my actions"

Taking a last drink of gin for courage, the disguised Queen of England and the new Crown of the Union left her room. The main commander followed her out and then sat down in his seat outside her bedroom door. She carried on alone pulling the scraggy hat further down over her face went out the back way of the Inn, as advised, towards the stables where the beautiful pony was waiting for her. Anne was a good rider and confidently jumped on its bare back. She had to say no words of command as the pony knew what to do and where to go. For the first time since she could remember Anne felt the thrill of excitement once again. She felt free and rebellious as when she was a young girl and miles from the thought of being the Queen of England.

The dark of the night had now fallen and the moon was getting ever closer to its prime position to rule the earth. Anne was holding firmly onto the pony's mane which allowed him to gallop with freedom. Maybe it was the gin or maybe the thought of meeting her devoted princesses of the people that she ruled over, that she felt young and alive.

As the moon moved slowly watching her a good hour must have passed but Anne didn't care. For the past five years, she had been manipulated, told what to do, how to dress, and what to eat by many people out for their own gain. She had always steadied the ship through the give and take process of politics and she was tired, she needed advice herself from her people who cared.

Anne had heard from top sources that these ladies exist but never took it further than hearsay and gossip. While her reign continued into the years all sorts of problems had come and gone. Her advisors should give her council but over time things had become vague and disjointed. She felt they were not advising as they should, something was wrong. It was then that she quietly probed to find out more about these princesses or witches as some people call them. After using full discretion and only her very private ways of gaining knowledge that word had come back to her. If she would swear upon the oaths of loyalty and faith to the people and never disclose names and knowledge a secret meeting would be forthcoming.

Gently looking around at the vast dark open moor all she could hear was the pony's hooves and his heavy breathing. At the top of a rise the pony slowed itself down and while looking ahead down into the valley below saw a wonderful sight of tree tops shining in the moonlit night. The pony then slowed to a stop by a small copse and, as the Queen sat silent and waited, then heard some rustling noise and saw a small person emerge out of the clump of thick bushes. It was Aerona.

''Good evening my lady, I have some clothes for you to put on but they must only touch your natural skin. I will care for the clothes you are wearing until you are finished.'' The Queen jumped down and took the bundle. ''Thank you my dear.'' Anne then walked into the bushes to change.

Untying the bundle the Queen found only a see through shawl of pure white lace and nothing more save a butterfly hair pin. She tried to make sense of what she was doing but sense didn't seem to come to her.

Anne, with some reluctance, started to take off her clothes but as she got to her underwear she stopped. What was she doing, she was the Queen of bloody England and people took their clothes off for her, not her for them. She looked up and was just about to have a tantrum when the large moon caught her sight as if waiting for her outburst.

For some reason, seeing the big white moon comforted her. Then rather than cry and scream like a child, that she would not do this, she smiled and accepted her fate with inner happiness, calm and humbleness. When Anne stood naked she looked up once again and with mild humour asked the moon, 'there, are you happy now?'She then put the shawl over her head and slid it down over her body like smooth oil. She then pinned her hair up with the glittering silver butterfly and when all done, took a deep breath, bundled up her rotten clothes and went back out to Aerona.

Aerona was talking to the pony when she heard the Queen come back out. Anne gave her the bundle to look after and waited. Aerona looked her up and down and said, ''You look lovely my Lady but I am sorry your shoes too please.'' Without saying a word, Anne did as told but noted that she was now being corrected from a young eight year old child

''Thank you my Lady the firefly's are now coming to escort you down into the crooked wood.'' Anne looked down into the valley and saw a swarm of light heading her way. What she had failed to see was Zoar, who had been lying quietly in the copse where she had just changed.

The swarm of firefly's got to Anne and after a short period of flying around her, flew slowly back down from whence they had come as Anne followed on her now bare feet. The firefly's took their time as if knowing this lady would be slow. As she went further down into the valley the trees in the oncoming wood seemed to be getting taller and taller. She found that quite weird.

The firefly's then entered the crooked wood of tall trees and Anne followed but once in, she couldn't believe what she was seeing. The trees were twisted and warped and had never seen trees like it. It was as though they had had an argument with someone, and lost. She was used to woods of the highest standard with splendid straight oak trees to fit that of royalty. This was the complete opposite. She was just dumbstruck with the oddity of the whole situation and just stared at the trees and their weird altered state of being. It seemed as though they wanted to talk with her and then shook her head in disbelief at just the thought of what she had just thought. The firefly's were hovering around close waiting for her to move as they needed to move on deeper into the crooked dense wood.

Anne had to get a grip of her thoughts so she rubbed her face roughly with her hands as if this would clear her mind somewhat. Looking up, she again shook her head in a kind of reluctant acceptance of disbelief. Now though, she must move on in between these crooked, twisted beasts to get to the meeting place. With a deep breath and finding some inner courage, she started to gently walk forward following the light of the flies. The crooked trees looked on as she felt again the inner sense that they were indeed talking about her. With bare feet and only a silk see through shawl over her naked body Anne felt vulnerable.

The walk was continuing on a downwards slope when all of a sudden Anne noticed that the firefly's had vanished. One minute they were in front of her, now they were gone. She stood still and looked around but couldn't see anything as all was dark. She then heard quiet singing coming from just off her front right and so went forward towards it. Coming to the end of the crooked tree line she saw them, all four of them, and they were beautiful.

They all looked at her with smiles of radiant love so Anne smiled back like a young child and without dread or fear walked towards them. The Ladies were all huddled together holding hands. They were in a small pond with steam coming out of it. "Come Anne, we have been waiting for you," the Welsh one said.

Anne went forward and stopped at the edge of the water looking on in amazement. "Come, come further please, the water is lovely." Anne tiptoed into the water realising by surprise that it was hot, not cold as she had thought. Once up to her waist, the Ladies separated, allowing Anne to join their circle. When Anne had steadied herself they started to sing an old ballad which she knew and so sang with them.

While they were singing this lovely ode Anne couldn't take her eyes off them. She also couldn't quite believe that, with all the hearsay and folk tales she had heard over all years, these Ladies actually did exist.

The moon was now full and its radiance reflected on the water all around them. The stars too were many and all glittering in the dark moon lit night. Anne, for the first time in many, many years felt eased and non-combatant. It was as if she was with friends who wanted nothing from her. In fact, she felt it was the complete reverse, in that they only want to protect her and for her to accept their love.

When the calm and beautiful singing stopped all the ladies looked at Anne and then one by one they kissed her very tenderly on her forehead. As each one did this they walked away out of the water until Anne was on her own in the water looking at them all on the dry bank. "Come Anne, it is time for us to talk."

With that, all five of them went into the crooked wood and once again the firefly's came to light their way. Once they got to a clearing the Welsh lady sat down and they in turn followed suit making a circle with all touching one another. The time was now nearing the midnight hour. Once all were comfortable they introduced themselves to Anne and explained to her their duty to love and protect the people of these good lands. Remaining silent throughout, Anne was starting to wake up to the fact that these Ladies were indeed what and who they say they are.

As this meeting was in Wales, the beautiful Lady of the Welsh took the lead. "Anne, our Dear Queen of our new combined Kingdom, please say you swear never ever to tell of this meeting." "I swear to you all this day that this will indeed be the case." "Thank you Anne, we love and trust you as we have your descendants for thousands of years." Anne wasn't surprised in the least at this information for she had heard rumours of the tale from when she was a child.

"Anne, you asked for this meeting through channels and people we secretly know, please ask what you will and be not afraid." Anne did indeed put the word about and ask for this meeting of the people's Ladies but wasn't expecting it to be like this. She thought it might be around a table in some warm Inn somewhere with her servants in attendance and all her courtiers about. Not in a crooked wood, unbeknown to anyone, in the middle of the Welsh marshes, on her own, half naked and alone.

Anne smiled; she could see all of them and their beautiful loving shining eyes looking at her. ''Thank you, did you say you have met all the Kings and Queens of this country?'' ''I did not say that Anne I said, we have met descendants of yours for well over a thousand years.'' ''What about Oliver Cromwell,'' she asked quickly. ''All four Ladies started to giggle with tenderness at this somewhat upstart question. ''That was over fifty years ago Anne and no we did not, we felt it was not the right thing. Our loyalties and love are to the crown bloodlines of this Kingdom and the people and creatures within. We live, love and protect only for them''

Anne calmed herself and so started asking more relevant questions as was advised. She had rehearsed these over and over so as not to forget and was astonished at the clear unequivocal answers coming back. It was then that full discussion took place and went on for many hours. All subjects were broached including the most important, being the new alliance of Great Britain and the consequences and defences thereof.

When all were finished and hugs and kisses given, Anne made her back with the help of the firefly's. Aerona was waiting for her as promised as Anne quickly changed back into her scraggy clothes. Anne thanked the little girl for her help and once she was ready jumped on the pony's back and galloped off back to the Inn. One hour more and the sun would be rising.

On entering the Inn via the back way she went straight up to her room. On reaching the corridor she saw the guard sitting outside her room. The guard heard the footsteps but once he saw who it was looked at her in astonishment. ''My lady, you have returned, thank the

Lord." As she got closer he continued to say, "Are you alright, you look different." With a warm smile she replied in a sweet voice, "Yes, I am very well thank you and thank you for asking my dear good man. Having heard the way she had just replied to his question he again looked at her with a confused face. Anne noted his confusion then realised how she had just spoken to him as a tender loving sister would, and not as the Queen of Great Britain would, talking to a guard.

Getting to her bed chamber and closing the door behind her she quickly took off her old clothes and put on the silk lace shawl which she had been allowed to keep. She then went to the full length mirror and couldn't believe how young she looked. All her wrinkles had gone and the anxiety and pressure she had felt all these years had also gone. She then looked at the beautiful butterfly pin held in her hand and closed her fingers around it and as she did so felt the most loving warmth go through her whole body. Going over to her bed she pulled back the covers and gently got in then fell into the most peaceful, beautiful loving sleep.

Chapter 23

Zoe was ready but nervous as rushing around her native France was one thing but trying to keep safe and travel across the open sea to Cornwall was something else. She had very few friends now if any, and so sat on the side of her bed with her feet on the floor looking at the empty wall. She felt so alone.

Only a few weeks ago she was so happy and in love with her partner Jon. O Jon, I love you so much, I am so sorry, she said to herself. Then with the vivid last moments of Jon entering her mind with the silly childish love he gave, she burst out crying.

Through her sobs, she reached into her pocket and pulled out her pipe. She had given up smoking when she got back with her true love as he didn't like it. He said it wasn't lady like and then she laughed at the simple thought of it.

She wiped her tears with her sleeve and reached into her other pocket and pulled out a small brandy bottle. Taking a gulp of the cognac and then the flint to light her pipe, she eased herself into a more accepting view of the situation. She wasn't happy, she knew that, but an inner strength was coming through, she could feel it. Be strong she said.

She had been on the run now for what seemed like months and things were running a little low. She still had money but that wasn't going to last forever. Her clothes were also minimal. She looked around her room and saw the lonely case sitting in the corner which just confirmed her sorry state of affairs. Jacques would help her, she knew he would but she needed to be very careful. She had also sold her horse the day before.

She took one last big puff of the pipe, inhaled it all and then dubbed it out. Picking herself up from the bed she looked up and swore aloud, 'You Bastards, I will survive this, you watch me.' She went over and picked up her bag, looked around the bare room one last time and then headed for the door. The galleon was set to sail at high tide in a couple of hours but she was ready. She paid her bill at the Les Tara and on leaving the Inn through the front door walked across the quay towards the waiting galleon.

It was then that Sarah saw her leave the Les Tara. She had been waiting and watching quietly and had not moved from the window of her room. 'So, my little tramp, you think you can just leave France and do what you wish,' she thought to herself. Sarah had already packed her things ready for this moment and only needed to get her makeup on to make her look a little older and also heartbroken. Her clothes were just right as not too bright but not too peasant looking. The case too was just right being a little too heavy.

There was no rush but the timing had to be right. The ship wasn't set to sail until early evening and as she looked out through the window could see that it was still being loaded. Double checking everything and making sure all was in order, she went to look in the mirror one last time. She was pleased with her appearance and thought how her boss, Peter the Frenchman, would be proud of her. Ten years ago she had bedded him when they working on another job in Holland. He wasn't good at all but she played the game and said he was the best and then thought about the five hundred guineas he had promised her for this job. Clearing her brain from Peter and the money, she refocused on her target and headed for the door. The galleon was set to sail at six giving her just thirty minutes which was excellent and just right.

Sarah got to the gang plank fifteen minutes before sail and all was chaotic with everybody rushing around sorting last minute details. She showed her ticket to the young sailor man who quickly said, ''Please mademoiselle, please go on board quickly, you are late.''

With a soft voice she replied, ''Thank you, I do apologise for being late, I am so forgetful lately.'' With that she slowly and with hunched shoulders picked up her case, and with a deep sigh of its heavy weight began to shuffle up the plank.

The young sailor man, although busy with other tasks saw her struggle and feeling pity said aloud, ''Would you like a hand with your case mademoiselle?'' She stopped, turned around and said sweetly, ''No, thank you Monsieur, I can manage, please don't worry.'' With that, she turned back around and with heavy laden feet headed on up.

The man at the top helped her on board. ''Thank you Monsieur, you are very kind.'' ''Please, think nothing of it Mademoiselle, it is my pleasure.'' He then politely directed her to her quarters. Well, they were not exactly her quarters they were more a section of the ship, one deck below, for female passengers only. He also said that the top deck was available should she like some fresh air. ''Thank you,'' she said, ''What time we will reach Falmouth?'' ''Well we are heavy laden with wine and the wind may not be in our favour but I would say two days Mademoiselle. We aim to be in the dock, subject to good clearance from the port customs checks, by no later than midnight Monday."

Sarah's boss, the so called Peter the Frenchman, was in the Chateau Morlaix with the lady Antoinette, the soon to be known, Countess of Morlaix. "So, Monsieur, you have news?" "Yes my lady, we have identified one of the traitors and one my colleague is in pursuit as we talk." "Excuse me I am just not interested in the minor goings of your pursuit. What I want is the person responsible for the killings of my dearest people so I can personally eliminate them. Now tell me, have you found that person?"

"No we haven't but we are closing in and thought it would be good to update you." "Well I thank you for that courtesy but all I need to know is when?" "Would you be interested in where" "Yes, that would be of interest, obviously." Peter was used to dealing with these arrogant rich people. He didn't like them for they never seem to see the real world and the poverty in which real people live. But, they paid him well and so accepted their priggish behaviour as part of his working life.

"Cornwall, is where things are heading." "Did you say Cornwall," she replied. "Yes, Cornwall is where we think this may all end up." "Well, that's fine with me, I quite like Cornwall. I went there once, I think we went to Plymouth for the day when my Husband had some business to attend to over there." "Excuse me my Lady but that is Devon, not Cornwall." "Don't be silly, they're all the bloody same." He was going to argue the case that it may be the same to her but knew that the people of Devon and Cornwall do not see it that way.''

With the brief meeting over, Peter the Frenchman bowed his and withdrew from the drawing room and shook his head in disbelief at the pure arrogance of Antoinette. Yes, the money was important but the sheer ego of the woman and the status in which she thinks she lives is beyond him. However, he was shrewd enough to know that only one person can award her the title of 'Countess of Morlaix,' and that was the King or, maybe somehow, one of his devious and egotistical Sons. Dread the thought.

Peter rode back to the Inn at Morlaix to discuss the next moves with Alfred the Spaniard. Whilst riding, he thought to himself that yes things were a little slow but traction was starting. He had received the letter from Sarah and had made good the cottage at Falmouth. He now needed to get the Spaniard across the water or his silent assassin, or both.

Sarah saw the deep steps leading down to the deck below but had refused the help of the Officer even though her case was very heavy and that it would be dangerous. Step by step she very slowly and awkwardly scuffled down acting out the old lonely woman role with pride. However, as she went down further she was continuously scouring the deck without anyone's notice when she caught sight of her. Zoe was at the back corner, off to her right, sitting down with her knees up to her breasts. She also noticed that Zoe was watching her. Sarah carried on shuffling downwards and didn't move her drooped head once.

With four steps to go, Sarah fell forward with her heavy case in hand and both went crashing down onto the deck floor. It was a great move. She was sprawled out and blood was coming from a cut on her head but she didn't ask for any help and didn't make a fuss but she did make every effort for people to see that she was struggling. On her hands and knees, she drew her case close to her body and started to sob but not too loud, just enough. A little girl then rushed up to her asking if she needed help. Sarah, still on the floor looked up and smiled the sweetest of smiles saying, 'thank you my little child but please, I am alright, thank you so much.'' Eventually, Sarah got to her feet and while keeping her head down, shuffled along to find an ideal spot to work her devious plot. On finding the right position, Sarah sat down with open exhaustion. She was not close but again not too far away from where Zoe was sitting and observing.

Zoe realised that this must be the lady the waitress called Petal had talked about back at the Les Tara Inn where she had stayed these last few days. Poor thing she thought, what is the world is coming to, how sad. Zoe, although sympathetic to this lady's plight then thought of her own problems which she had to deal with. Sarah, through squinted eyes, saw the empathy coming from her target and smiled inwardly saying, 'I will get you, you traitorous little bitch. She brought her knees up to her chest and dropping her face into both hands started to cry.

Chapter 24

''Thank you driver,'' Sarah said and then got down onto the ground. Zoe stayed in the cart to hand down their luggage and then jumped down herself. Sarah paid the driver and with both of them now on the ground side by side, the driver flicked the reins and drove off. ''Well this is it Zoe, it's not much I know, but my sweet Mother left it to me, as I told you.''

It was a little two bedroom terrace cottage made of granite and slate. It had a small back yard and nice green fields beyond heading on an upwards slope. As the cottages were built on a steep slope, steps had been laid right up to its front door. There was another terrace which had been built on the opposite side of the track lower down and then, for some unknown reason, they were given even numbers and the upper row had been given odd numbers which just didn't make sense.

Dracaena Ridge is a couple of miles inland from the docks just out of the town heading out to the main routes of Truro and Helston. It was in quite a rural area and out of the way as Sarah described to Zoe while on board the ship. When Zoe heard this, her ears pricked up as its location was excellent and very attractive to her needs.

Over the last two days, these two women had really got on well. Zoe felt much pity for her but on the other hand, she needed somewhere to stay. She could have found a place further inland like an Inn or something but that would cost money. Here she could be housed for nothing, keep out of the way, and still go about her business as she pleased. Yes, Zoe was rather pleased with herself that she had met this lady.

Sarah went in first and showed Zoe about. Although rather small it had two bedrooms upstairs and downstairs was a small kitchen area with an eating area. The toilet and tap for washing were outside in the back yard.

"It is very dusty, I am sorry Zoe, but will get on to it now." Zoe, again felt empathy for this lovely woman in just trying to please. "That's alright Sarah, it's a lovely little place, your Mum has done you proud." "Thank you Zoe, you are so nice." "Tell you what," Zoe said, "You do the dusting and I will make good the fire and boil some water, do you have any tea?" "That would be lovely Zoe, yes the tea leaves and caddy should be in the larder over there." Zoe again felt a sense of warmth between them. When both had finished they sat down together in front of the warm fire. "I have made your bedroom up as best I could but I didn't touch any of your things as I didn't think it right." Zoe smiled and replied, "Thank you Sarah, that is very respectful."

Feeling very relaxed, Zoe asked if she could smoke. "You smoke?" "Yes, I do, I gave it up for a while as my Husband to be did not think it was lady like, but now he is gone I decided to take it up again." "Where has he gone Zoe" "I couldn't really tell you on the ship as I didn't like to but he was taken away from me a few months ago and I loved him dearly." "O, I am so sorry Zoe, yes please do smoke, I don't mind in the least."

Zoe made and lit the pipe and as habit had it, pulled the hip flask out of her pocket and took a shot of cognac. Sarah looked on in silent amazement at this woman doing these things in front of her without a care in the world. Zoe looked at Sarah's bemused face and then both burst out laughing. Zoe, extended her arm towards Sarah, offering the hip flask but Sarah said, "I'm sorry Zoe, I don't drink or smoke, my Mother would have had kittens." Again, they both laughed together at the very thought.

It was only midday but both were very tired and so Sarah suggested she bring in the metal bath tub for both of them to get cleaned off. Zoe got the pots on the fire to fill it with hot water.

They both agreed that rather than have an afternoon nap, they would walk down into the town and have tea in one of the new fashion teashops and then go to bed early for a good long sleep. Falmouth was a sailor and shipping port and the Inns and Taverns thrived off their drinking. However, a couple of new tea shops had indeed arisen like the ones in Truro but sited away from the dock area.

Over the next few days, Zoe and Sarah got on well and felt really comfortable with each other. Zoe liked her very much but did notice that Sarah never said too much or too little.

As the days passed Zoe was getting anxious to move things on and knew time wasn't on her side, so started thinking about her next move. She felt the cottage was a good bolt hole, in a great position and Sarah was a good friend. She also felt the need to inform her friend that she would be off soon to visit some places but will come back. Zoe only really knew of one place to start her search and that was the small port at Mousehole. Jacques had a contact at the docks there and remembered when she trailed him saw speaking with a man. She hoped he would still be there and that he would have the information she needed. Zoe also needed to buy a horse and stable it in Sarah's, her lovely friend's, small back yard. She would leave early tomorrow or the day after.

It was late that very night in the darkness of a half moon the sniper entered the rear of the cottage at number twenty four directly across the street from number twenty five, Sarah's terrace cottage.

He had tied his horse further back and walked in with his gear on his back. These two cottages were owned by Peter the Frenchman and were excellent for this type of work. All could watch, learn and act as they saw fit and communicate easily by signal or leave a message in a hole in the ground at the far end of the upper terrace under a tree, or if needed, they could meet there. Number twenty four was occupied by an old Cornish couple of French descent. They had long served the French way and their house was an undercover safe place. It had been provided for them for their loyalty and devotion to the Catholic cause and paid no rent. They were well liked in the community and had been there for five years.

The couple had been notified of the sniper's date of arrival and so was expecting him. The door was unlocked and he simply walked in with confidence and air. They were both sitting down comfortable but couldn't help but look at this powerful tall man in fear. He nodded his arrival to the old man who nodded back and pointed to the stairs. With all his equipment the sniper went up without saying a word and started to get his things sorted out. He would now be known as Charles, their Son, who had come home.

The old couple knew they must carry on with their day to day existence as normal as neighbours get very suspicious when things start to change. They had always played the game well and the sniper had been informed that they were excellent cover.

Normally, the old couple would sleep in the front bedroom directly over looking number twenty five but this was now given up for his work. So they had moved their things out into the smaller back bedroom overlooking the top of town out over the downward sloping fields between.

Late that same night Sarah was on her bed up in the front bedroom and when the time was right she got up and with lighted candle moved to the window. She half opened the curtains and put the lit candle on the right hand corner of the window sill and waited. Then, on the stroke of eleven, a lighted candle was seen glowing from the front bedroom window of number twenty four opposite.

Dousing the flame Sarah waited silently till midnight before acting. Quietly she tiptoed down the stairs and with a shawl over her shoulders headed out into the night through the back door. Getting to the little gated exit of the backyard she stood still and waited but heard nothing, no movement inside or outside the cottage. Good, she thought and then moved off towards the large oak tree in the field at the end of the terraces.

Getting to the tree she stopped and then cautiously stepped forward. She then saw the man leaning confidently against its trunk and when only a few yards away stopped again. "Come here," he said in a deep commanding voice. She did as told without murmur. She went up to him and stopped only when her body had touched his. He towered over her. The man then took his large hand and put it around her throat saying in a menacing deep whisper, "When I say come, you come at once." She didn't say a thing but only nodded. When he took his hand away from her neck she silently reacted by taking her shawl off over her head and stood there naked.

He again took her by the throat but this time forced her to the ground. Without a word, he took her violently and she let him do with her as he wanted and she loved him for it. She felt like a prostitute and totally free in some weird way and, he never kissed her once, it was the way he was. He was cold and severe but she didn't care at all, he was strong and unemotional and that's what she liked.

Once he had finished and was satisfied, only then did he talk. They exchanged information on the task at hand and what should happen next. Sarah told him everything.

At around one thirty Sarah was back in the cottage creeping up the stairs and into her bedroom. Once back in her bed and lying down under the bed sheets her hands went to her throat to feel the marks he had made on her. The thoughts of the sensuous night had pleased her very much and knew too that she had pleased him. 'Charles,' she thought, 'you know me well.'

"Good morning Sarah," I have made some tea, would you like some?" "Yes please Zoe, that would be nice, did you sleep well?" "Well, yes and no, I woke up around midnight for some unknown reason and tossed and turned a little but then drifted off back to sleep." Sarah didn't say anything but thought carefully.

While they were both sipping their tea Zoe said, '' Sarah, I may need to go away for a few days soon.'' ''What do mean Zoe, I thought you had nowhere to go.'' ''I don't, it's just that I need to meet someone.'' ''Who?'' ''I don't know that either.'' ''Zoe, you're not making sense, are you alright.''

Zoe had to be careful, she liked Sarah that is true but what she had to do, she had to do alone. ''I promise I will let you know when things have sorted themselves out but really I can't say more than that. Please Sarah, will you allow me to come back.'' ''You silly thing, of course I will, in fact, I will go into town this very day and get another key cut just for you, that's what my Mum would have done.'' ''You are such a good friend Sarah, thank you so much.'' With that, they got up and hugged each other.

''I tell you what Sarah, I will come into town with you as I need to buy a horse.'' ''A horse, you're a little dark horse yourself. Alright, but can I help you choose.'' ''Yes, that would be nice and can I stable it in your backyard?'' ''Of course you can Zoe, when do you think you will be going away, wherever you are going and how long will you be gone?'' ''I will start off early tomorrow and probably be back in a couple of days.'' ''Right, then I will be up as well and make you a cup of tea before you leave.'' Zoe smiled as one smiles at a good friend. Once they had got themselves ready both headed off into Falmouth town.

In the main bedroom, standing back in the shadows of the window at number twenty four, the sniper watched them leave.

Sarah handed the key to the locksmith but decided not to wait for the duplicate to be made as they both wanted to get to the blacksmiths and find the horse for Zoe. "What do want he said, a stallion or a mare and what do you want it for?" "Well, I prefer a mare but I may need a stallion as I will need to travel quite a lot." "When you mean a lot, do you mean like travel trips to London and back?" He started laughing at his own question. Zoe didn't see the funny side of his remark but understood what he meant while Sarah remained quiet and listened intently.

"No, I would not say London but places like Penzance or Truro or maybe Bristol at a push." "Then I would say either would be alright for that distance." He then asked them to follow him.

On the field, there were dozens of horses of all sorts of sizes and colours. "How much money do you want to spend my lady?" he asked. Sarah then interrupted by saying, "Let's see the horses you recommend first and then we will ask you a price." Zoe looked at Sarah in quiet surprise at how purposeful she had suddenly become. The blacksmith was not used to dealing with women but backed down and said, "Very well." He then ordered his apprentice to fetch three he felt would do the job and after catching and reining them in the young boy walked all three to where Zoe, Sarah and the Blacksmith were standing.

One horse stood out from them all being the black stallion with a white face and white tail. "How much for the stallion" Zoe said. "Five guineas," he replied. Zoe looked at Sarah for her thoughts. Sarah couldn't have chosen a more stand out horse for being easily recognisable. "I think he is perfect for you." "The Blacksmith then said, "If you want, I will throw in a saddle and reins with the horse for six guineas." Zoe thought for a few seconds and said, "If you can get all things sorted and deliver him with all the gear to twenty five Dracaena Ridge this afternoon then yes I am in accord." "Done," the Blacksmith replied.

That evening Zoe and Sarah chatted by the fire but Zoe's mind was elsewhere and was feeling a little nervous about tomorrow and where all this will lead. Sarah sensed this and so suggested they bed early tonight ready for an early start and Zoe agreed.

As before, Sarah shone the candle at the window. Within five minutes the reply came so Sarah put on her shawl as the sniper liked and sneaked out of the cottage as quiet as a mouse. Zoe's Stallion saw her but didn't move or make a sound. She then waited silently inside the backyard by the gate just in case Zoe had heard her movements. Hearing nothing she moved on to the oak tree.

At six the next morning Zoe came down the stairs. "Good morning Zoe, I have made us tea as promised." "Thank you Sarah, you have been very good to me." They chatted once again and Sarah helped Zoe as best she could but Zoe was on a mission and the efficiency to do things herself kicked in. When Zoe had packed her things and got the stallion ready, Sarah asked, "What have you called him," "Called who?" "Your horse, silly." "I never thought, why don't you name him for me." Sarah thought a while and said, "Why not call him Arthur after the king, he looks strong and regal." Zoe laughed and said, "Why not, Arthur it is." With that, they hugged each other, and Sarah said, "Please keep safe Zoe, I will miss you." Zoe got on Arthur, blew Sarah a kiss and rode quickly rode off. It was six thirty in the morning and the sun was not even up yet, but nearly.

The sniper had to make a decision in which way she would turn. He had been up since four that morning to get into position. As there was only one main road out of Falmouth before hitting a fork, Zoe would then have to head for either Truro or Helston. Therefore, he had to get to that main fork three miles out of town before she did. He had done well and was well camouflaged. He knew from Sarah that she would be leaving the cottage around six thirty to seven, so that means she should pass his position about fifteen to twenty minutes thereafter.

Slowly chewing on some old salted meat he laid low and waited. He heard the hoof sounds first before he saw the horse and rider, as described by Sarah the night before. He smiled a grimace smile. The jet black stallion with its white face and tail was indeed well chosen. 'Well done Sarah,' he thought, the horse stands out like a sore thumb.

Without moving a muscle and still chewing on the grizzled meat, he watched her with cold intent. Zoe got to the fork and reined Arthur into a stop and the horse did as asked without any fuss or ado. The signs read Helston to the left and Truro to the right. Gathering her breath and thoughts she chose the left and galloped off.

The sniper let her go but then quickly got up and ran to his powerful waiting horse. If it was Helston she was going then fine, he would find her and stalk her there. If it was further on that would also be fine. Either way, he must get to the main Helston fork for the Lizard or Penzance before her, to find out.

Spitting the final juices of the now worn meat out of his mouth he rode off like the wind heading cross country for Helston. He knew where he was going as he had checked the maps and scoured the countryside prior. He had also checked the back route to Truro just in case she took that fork. Preparation and planning were his forte.

Chapter 25

''Joshua, I think I may be pregnant.'' It was very early in the morning and both he and Rebecca were sitting down in the cottage overlooking Gunwalloe cove. Joshua had now been away for quite a while and had forgotten what it was like to just sit down and relax.

Rebecca wanted to tell him yesterday when he had returned home but she let him have a good night's rest first.

He looked at her with loving and warmth and said, ''Sorry Rebecca, you are what?'' ''I am pregnant you silly oaf.'' He couldn't quite believe what she had just said. He was thirty seven years old and had lost his first daughter and wife a long time ago in Bristol. He thought he would never feel that love again but when he married Rebecca three months ago he had been hoping and praying.

With his mouth still agape, he got up and went over to her. He kissed her tenderly on the lips and said, ''I love you Rebecca, would you like me to run you a bath or make you a cup of tea or something.'' Rebecca started giggling with the love at his silly heart filled questions. ''No, Joshua, I do not want a bath but thank you for asking but I do think we, especially you, need some time away from the pressure of work. Can you ask George for a few days off?''

''I will send word this very afternoon Rebecca, we could go away to Truro, you like Truro, are you sure you don't want a cup of tea?'' He was like a big excited child. ''Alright Joshua, yes, a cup of tea would be nice, thank you.'' As he went out to boil the water, Rebecca smiled and thought, 'men.' and then giggled again.

Joshua got himself tidied up and couldn't stop the spring in his step. 'Pregnant' he thought, Rebecca is with child, his child.' He remembered back to when they first met on that cold wintry morning at the gate of his bungalow where they now lived. How things turn out when you least expect, he thought.

He then smiled at the thought of when they first slept in the same room when they had acted as husband and wife, on their first assignment together. She had put a big wooden bed divider between them as a warning sign that she did not mess around. He started to giggle at the thought when he heard Rebecca shout, ''Are you alright in there Joshua,'' ''Yes, am fine thank you, will be out in a minute.''

''Joshua, I have been thinking about Mum and Jacques and how it would be nice if they could get away and come with us also. I haven't told Mum yet and we could all have a merry time together.

Joshua thought about this question. Jeanne, Rebecca's Mother was not a problem but, Jacques would be. He was on curfew at the house in Marazion and would need to get special clearance from above for Jacques to go to Truro with them. Then he thought, well, as he was now in charge of Cornwall, he had the authority himself, but then thought again. A Frenchman, albeit a turned informer, being seen drinking and laughing in Truro just didn't bode well at all, he had better get that permission or at least mention the fact to George Kernow, just in case.

"I tell you what Rebecca, that would be a really lovely thing for them, especially your Mother but Jacques is in curfew so maybe best I mention it in my dispatch. George is away presently at Bristol so a reply should be with us by no later than Thursday, are you alright with that." "Thank you Joshua, I understand the position you are in and will wait the reply before I ask them, or not as the case maybe." "So, Rebecca, hopefully it is Truro we come." "Yes Joshua, I was thinking, if we get the reply on Thursday and all is well, we could leave first thing Friday and go for a long weekend and stay in a hotel or something." "That's fine with me, I will ask for this weekend coming as holiday."

Joshua continued, "I will get the message sorted and send it by our courier friends directly. However, before I do this I need to attend and clean the armoury plus the cliff tunnel is due for inspection too." "Tell you what Joshua, you do the tunnel and I will sort the armoury." "Thank you Rebecca but are you alright opening the hatch and climbing down the steps?" "Joshua, I am pregnant not an invalid, now go do your chores and the message before I throw something at you." Joshua smiled with love and sincerity at his wife's attempt to be hard with him.

As Joshua walked to the door, for some reason he knew not, thoughts of Christine and Little George came into his mind. Trying to ignore these strange thoughts he carried on to the door but couldn't help but to stop and turn around to ask, "By the way Rebecca, have you heard from Little George or Christine?" Rebecca's face went from smiling to immediate tension of dread. She was taken completely aback by this straight awkward question. "Sorry, are you alright Rebecca, you look a little shocked?"

"No, I haven't heard anything but understand that they are doing well, why do you ask?" "Nothing really, it just came into my head to ask you, I don't know why." Joshua then went on to say, "I know Little George is in Bristol, but I have never really asked where Little Christine is or how is she doing."

"I believe Christine is in Plymouth, safe and staying with some friends of Jeanne. I have also heard that Christine is being well educated and that she is happy. She is becoming a young lady, from what I can gather from Mother." Joshua shrugged his shoulders and replied casually, "Just thought I would ask that was all, I will see you in a little while my lovely."

As Joshua closed the door, Rebecca sat back and sighed with a sense of relief. Why had he asked that question she thought? Again, she had lied to Joshua, her husband, but she had to. She had made an oath to her Mother that she would never speak of Christine's true whereabouts, ever, as Zelahnor would know if she did, she listens. Rebecca must talk to her Mother soon.

Joshua did as he was told and enjoyed the new found skip in his pace and heart. He would go and do the tunnel now and get it out the way and also George liked to see reports when things had been completed. Yes, he would do it now and then organise the message. He had plenty of time as it was still very early in the morning and the Sun hadn't appeared yet.

Walking around the back of the cottage into the area of the garden with heavy undergrowth, Joshua got to the entrance of the tunnel. On opening the hatch he saw the candles and flint in the correct place and ready to light.

Joshua checked his pistol was loaded and ready as although he had travelled this tunnel many times it always gave him the fear of the unknown. Then striking the candle alight he went down and down into its darkness. As with the old Cornish tunnelling ways every hundred feet was placed something of note. It would be either a mark or a turn off or something. Joshua always thought this was excellent as even if you had no light you could somehow crawl your way out.

Down and down he went checking the walls, ground. Rats, bats and other animals had been here, he knew, and if he found any he had to kill them. The tunnel had to always be clear and clean, it was that simple. The tunnel itself carried on for two miles down to one of the caves on the left side of the beach. But that was just this direct one from his bungalow. This tunnel also had many off shoots going in different directions but he wouldn't do them today. He would check them next month.

Eventually, after nearly an hour of slow movement in near total darkness and with scary shadows coming from all angles from the flickering light he got to the bottom and stopped. He was now at the cave wall down on the beach. All he need do now was pull the stone door open towards him and take a good look inside then his tunnelling duties for the month would be completed.

The cave door from the tunnel side was always awkward to move as it was made to be pushed open from the other side allowing people to come in from the cave and not exit back into the cave. He put down his pistol and candle to get a good grip and with both hands pulled the entrance stone open. As the stone door was about half way open he caught a glimpse of something shining inside the cave. He quickly went to pick up his pistol but as he did so hundreds of butterflies from out of nowhere came swarming around his head. Trying to see and focus on what he had just seen while all these things were flying around made him panic.

He started to thrash his head from side to side while using one hand to keep the door open and the other to get the pistol. The candle had now also gone out which only added to his confusion. Now in total darkness and still fumbling for his pistol his sweeping hand touched it but also nudged it forward as it dropped into the cave. Still disorientated and while bending backwards and forwards he then lost his footing and fell back onto his bottom. When this happened the butterflies and moths then simply flew away back into the cave as if knowing their job was done.

Joshua sat there in the silence of the dark but still had one hand on the door. He calmed himself down and began to take stock and then shuffled forward to peer again into the cave at what had taken his attention before.

''Good morning Joshua,'' the beautiful little girl said in a sweet crystal clear voice, ''Why do you not believe Zelahnor exists?'' Joshua couldn't believe what he was seeing or had just heard. He was a grown hard man of the world.

The little girl was standing inside the cave looking directly at him with sheer confidence and showing no fear, but what really shook him, was the massive black cat standing by her side which she had her arm around in comfort. The cat was enormous and powerful with bright golden eyes and who also was looking directly at him.

Trying to make sense of what was in front of him and with all the darkness and flickering lights of the cave, Joshua let go of the door and rubbed his eyes hard with both hands as though this would clear his brain. It was then when he took his hands off the stone he had so painstakingly pulled open that it rolled back into the closed position. Joshua quickly went to grab it but he struggled with its force and so jerked his hands out of the way.

After taking a few deep breaths Joshua went through the procedure to open the door. Pulling the door back into the open position he decided to put a stone underneath to lock it. He then moved his body forward and looked back into the cave so he could simply make sense of what he had just seen and heard from the young maiden but now, she was not there. Not there, how can that be, he had just seen her. Joshua rubbed his eyes and looked again but saw nothing, she and the cat had vanished. What is going on here, he thought. What is going on?

Joshua slowly scanned his eyes all around the cave but again nothing but he did notice his pistol lying on the floor of the cave just below him. Without further thought, he jumped down, picked it up and quickly checked it over. He then pulled the flint lever back into full position ready for firing and then started to feel a little more confident. The cave wasn't that large so it was easy to see things but the little girl and her beast were simply not there. That's just bloody amazing Joshua thought and walked to the cave's entrance to look across the beach but saw nothing. He then looked down at the wet sand and noticed massive paw prints. So, he wasn't seeing things after all, which means whoever they are, were here. He then thought about what she had said. What was it now,

171

'you believe in Zelahnor?' No, that wasn't it he said to himself, she didn't say that. He thought hard to recall, then he had it. She had said, 'Good morning Joshua, why do you not believe Zelahnor exists?'So what was that supposed to mean, he thought.

Walking away further out of the cave and onto the sand he stopped and decided that before he left the area he would need to go back into the cave and take one last look. As before, he didn't see anything or anyone but did notice that the deep paw prints he had just seen had also now gone.

Joshua shook his head in disbelief and thought, as big and strong as he is, he would take the longer route back to the bungalow across the open beach and over the cliffs and not back through the tunnel. He laughed at himself at the fear of going back into the cave. The little girl he had seen was not the issue it was the massive beast that shivered him.

Something is not right here he thought and he meant to find out what it was and while walking the long way home tried in vain to work it out. He did need to sort the message and get it sent to Kernow but that can wait as he wanted to talk with Rebecca first.

As Joshua walked into the bungalow he caught sight of Rebecca coming out of the ground from the armoury hatch in the scrub area. ''Rebecca, I need to speak with you.'' ''Joshua, what are you doing back so soon, have you done the Tunnel duties and the messaging to Kernow already?'' ''Well, I have done the tunnel but the message to Kernow needs to wait.'' ''Why Joshua, what's happened?'' ''Rebecca, please could we sit down and talk." Joshua went over what had occurred in the cave and Rebecca listened in silence.

"So, let me get this right Joshua, you fell back on your backside while hundreds of butterflies were over your face.
Then, when you got your wits about, you looked back into the cave and the little girl and beast had vanished."
"That is correct Rebecca." "Joshua, you need a break, you are seeing things." "Rebecca, I know what I saw, and I did see them." "So, you saw them and then they disappeared and so you just casually left the area and strolled on home, does that make sense to you Joshua?" Joshua realised what he was saying did not make sense at all and Rebecca, not one for dilly dallying, did not hold back her pragmatism.

Both were silent until Joshua, now realising that there was no logic in any of what he was saying calmed himself and said, "Alright, it doesn't make any sense but just say, just say, what I am telling you actually happened, what would you say." Rebecca heard in his voice a feeling of sincerity and the need for her calm advice, so she played along.

"Alright Joshua, let's say it did, what exactly did the young girl say." "She said, Good morning Joshua, why do you not believe Zelahnor exists."

Rebecca fell silent and contemplated her reply. She knew of Zelahnor and the way she works and the way the Cornish adore her. She also knew that the little girl was Deborah as described by her Mother and the black beast was Zoar. Her little sister Christine was introduced to them both when her Mother Jeanne met Zelahnor a few months ago on the day of the wedding.

Rebecca was struggling with an answer to placate Joshua and could not say anything about what she knew as was under oath and promise. "Joshua, I have never asked this before, but do you really not believe in Zelahnor." Just the thought of saying the name Zelahnor out loud brought a shudder of fear through her body. "Of course I don't, it's all a load of poppycock and old Cornish wives tales."

"So Joshua, on one hand, you fully believe that you saw and heard these things this morning and then, on the other hand, you don't believe she exists. What is it Joshua?" With these last clear and direct words from Rebecca, Joshua shook his head in his hands with the senselessness of his argument.

Rebecca continued, "Joshua, no one was harmed from your so called encounter in the cave this morning. So, let's not dwell on things and concentrate on getting that message to Kernow for our little break in Truro, we need it and you are working too hard."

"Alright Rebecca, you win, I will go and saddle the horse and be off." Joshua bowed his head and walked away in a quiet shy way. Rebecca saw he was not sure of what was right or wrong and felt sad so she got up and went out after him. "Joshua," she said aloud. When he turned around she hugged him saying, "I love you Joshua, please be careful." "I love you too Rebecca." "Tell you what Joshua, let me make you a nice cup of tea before you set off." "Thank you Rebecca, I would like that very much."

Whilst the water was boiling Rebecca asked, "So, my dear Husband and Father to be, have you any ideas on names for our new child?" She noticed this question had done the trick as an inner warm smile instantly came over his face. "Well Rebecca, funny you should ask that.

Chapter 26

The surgeon held the skewer tight as he pushed it firmly down in a slow twisting motion. Henry Hosking's skull was clean shaved and this operation was needed to make him better.

Henry had been escorted by Bull and a couple of his men to the Asylum which had been sanctioned by George Kernow on the information sent by Joshua.

George could have washed his hands of the whole affair as Hosking's did not work for him anymore but Joshua had insisted that Henry was not well and feared for his safety and his sanity.

It was only a few days after Joshua had left Henry after his unexpected visit to his house in Truro that Bull had been ordered to fetch him away. No ifs or buts, take him away for his own good. Henry did try and fight them off but Bull had his orders and so gently but strongly overpowered him and tied him up. They then all rode to Exeter without delay with no stops just breather gaps when they or the horses needed.

On arrival, three Asylum men were there waiting for them as Henry again tried to fight them all off but he was gagged and restrained and taken in. Bull and his men with their job now done turned their horses and headed back to St Just. However, they were all very tired so stopped off halfway at an Inn near Launceston and got merrily drunk and slept the night like babies.

Henry had been at the Asylum now for two weeks under strict observation. He had been analysed, talked with, and subjected to treatments such as leeches and cold baths but he still had not changed his traits of seeing things that were not there or speaking with himself.

Henry knew he was not well but this type of treatment he didn't want. What he wanted were gentleness and love but most of all, he wanted Jeanne. He had lost a lot of weight too and so the asylum fed him every morning, noon and night which he accepted as he knew he had to get stronger. They may think him mad but that didn't bother Henry at all because when he was strong enough he would escape. His thoughts of getting his beloved Jeanne generated a manic hatred of Jacques, the man who had so twisted her mind. That bastard traitorous Frenchman will pay for taking the love of his life. He would save her. He would do what it takes to get his love back.

The doctors and alchemists had tried to talk with him many times but he was just not interested in talking back to these stupid so called doctors who thought they knew it all. Yes, they could all act posh and clever in front of others to show off their so called skills of intelligence, but could they fight the Spanish or French soldiers in close combat in the cold light of day. He laughed many times imagining these puny men he now found himself around doing what he had done in battle. What Henry didn't know was that he was being watched day and night and after many careful discussions between the alchemists and doctors, they all agreed that the only course of action to heal this sick man was trepanning the brain.

For safety reasons, Henry was strapped at all times to the bed which gave him no chance of escape. He had to get the straps off and get people away from him long enough so he could get away. Henry reasoned that if he did what they say and act the way they want he may convince them that all was getting well. They would then have no choice but to let him free or keep him in but under less supervision. Both options agreed with Henry's thought process of escape.

However, this reasoning was a little late as he was now in a strange quiet room strapped tight in a bed with lanterns brightly lit all around his head. He tried to make sense of what was going on but had been subjected to large doses of opium which made him very light headed and so chuckled thinking it all was rather funny.

It was then that he felt the searing pain of something trying to puncture his skull. He screamed in agony at the pain of it but couldn't move a muscle due to the heavy strapping. He then screamed again as the alchemist pushed the skewer ever deeper to make the hole and as he did so the pain was so intense Henry passed out. They checked his pulse and it was beating so carried on to complete the operation in the belief that this procedure would drain any excess pressure in the brain area that was causing his affliction. Once the cranium hole was pierced and the one inch skull fragment removed, they would then let the internal brain matter seep out and then bandage him up. The seeping may take up to an hour and then, keeping him strapped down, wheel him back to his room to recover. The hour passed and the fluid drained so in keeping with their agreed strategy, started to wheel him out. As the two porters did this, the surgeons shook hands and congratulated themselves on a successful operation and now only need wait for the patient to get better.

Chapter 27

The small two horse open top coach was waiting outside the cottage at Marazion. Joshua told the coach driver they would be ready in about ten minutes.

The message had come back from George Kernow that he himself didn't mind Jacques going with them to Truro but orders from his superiors had disagreed and said he should maintain his curfew in line with the agreed contract. What they actually said was, that an order of restraint wasn't a bloody pleasure cruise for the traitor's enjoyment, but Kernow thought it best just to say, they had reluctantly overruled him.

Jeanne and Rebecca were feeling gay going to Truro for the weekend. Jacques felt the complete opposite and although putting on a brave face could not help but think that his life was going backwards and the control of the authorities was tightening. His love for Jeanne was all, but for the first time he started to question what he has versus the adventurous free life he once knew.

"I'm sorry Jacques," Joshua said, "I thought they would have let you come with us" "Thank you Joshua, but I understand their apprehension, I am sure over time things will ease." "I am sure this will be the case," Joshua replied, in a somewhat unsure feeling.

"Come on Jacques," Jeanne said, "I'm only going away for a couple of days, don't look so glum, you said you needed to work around this place anyway. Let's have a big cuddle and before you know it I will be back pestering you again." All four were around the table feeling a little sorry for him but there was nothing they could do, orders were orders.

"Your right my Dear," Jacques replied in a more confident tone, "Now you three get off and have some fun." As they all stood up Rebecca, said, "Tell you what Jacques we will buy you a gay tunic for you to wear." "Thank you Rebecca, and if you could put a couple of bottles of fine cognac in the pockets, I would enjoy wearing it much more."

With that final piece of humour, they took their things and headed for the waiting coach. Once everyone was on board and their things packed down tight, they were ready for the off. Jacques had helped Jeanne with her things and gave her another kiss for her farewell. "Don't forget Jacques," Joshua said aloud, "Harry, my stallion will get very jealous of your stallion, Arc, if he starts moving in on Rebecca's mare, Lilly." With a grin on his face, Jacques, replied, "I will try and keep them apart Joshua for their own good as I am sure Rebecca's mare will play innocent to both." With smiles and hands waving the coachman whipped the horses away. "O what a gay day," Jeanne said, and then lent back looking all around at the open views and the sea shore.

As the carriage rode off Jacques turned around and with his head down, slowly walked back to the empty house. Was this all worth it, he thought? For three years he had to endure this confinement. Three years and even then there was no guarantee he would be free as it was subject to the powers that be. He loved Jeanne, but this was breaking him and thought back to a time when he had buccaneered all over France with the freedom to do what he wanted and the power to do what he wished. Now, he was reduced to feeding the pigs and fixing the fence. As he went back into the cottage and slamming the door behind him he went for the Cognac. On sitting in the chair and looking out of the window with the large glass refilled he couldn't help but notice a great many butterflies on the window ledge. They seemed to be just sitting there silently watching him. He laughed aloud at this stupid thought and slurped a big mouthful.

The singing and dancing over in Truro was about to start in an hour. Jeanne, Rebecca and Joshua were enjoying themselves going shopping, walking and having afternoon tea on the estuary. They all had a siesta and slept well and now it being the Saturday evening a good sing song was in order. They were in fine spirits.

While Joshua was still getting himself ready, Rebecca was fully dressed and raring to go but first, she wanted to talk with her Mother. Kissing Joshua on the cheek she went out and knocked on Jeanne's door. Now both sitting together and chatting away Joshua's cave experience came up. "Well Mother, that's what Joshua said he had seen." "And you said he must be seeing things or hallucinating." "Mother, Joshua, just doesn't believe, what are we do, shall we tell him what we know?" "No, that can never be and never from our lips; it must only come from her. Zelahnor works in mysterious ways and we must trust and love her always, she is the way of the Cornish."

"Mother, that is fine and I understand but that is the second time I have lied to him and I don't like doing it." "Rebecca, my lovely Daughter, I also have lied to Jacques and agree with you, it is not nice, but we simply have no choice." "What shall we do Mother?"

"Rebecca my sweet, there has been no harm done to either of these men. Zelahnor will do what she has to do and, don't forget, she is the guardian of our Little Christine. I say we live and enjoy our lives with love, silence and trust her as she trusted us. I am sure Zelahnor will come forward to these men when she feels the time is right." Rebecca was now standing behind her Mother combing her hair and looking into the mirror at her Mother's face saw the warmth of love radiate towards her. "Alright, Mother, you are right." "Now Rebecca, we both have had difficult times over these last years. You are now pregnant with my grandchild which delights me, so tonight I think we need to let our hair down and enjoy ourselves, all will be well my darling."

The singing and drinking were going well and as the night turned into Sunday morning the band took a little break to rest up a while.

During the interval, Rebecca asked to retire as she was very tired. "Would you like me to escort you back Rebecca, Joshua asked?" "Thank you Joshua, but I'm fine, you and Mother are enjoying yourselves, I will see you when you are finished, now relax and enjoy Joshua you need it but don't forget though, you promised to row us ladies on the river boat tomorrow." "Alright my Love, as you wish, I won't be long I promise." After kissing both her husband and her mother goodbye she went up to her room feeling exhausted.

When the bar lady had come over and filled their drinks, Jeanne asked, "So, Joshua, tell me, how are things on the work side?" "Things are good thank you Jeanne." Joshua had no issue at all in openly talking to Jeanne as he trusted her completely. Although she was officially

182

retired, she had worked very closely with his Father and that meant a lot to Joshua. It also felt good he could just talk with someone he trusted and off the record if needed. "And how are you finding running Cornwall and reporting to George.

"Well, the two other teams, as you know, in Bedruthan and Mevagissey are good and the people in them are solid as far as I can see. As for George Kernow, well you know George probably better than I but I must say everything he has promised to do, he has done, and I cannot ask for more than that. He also allows me much freedom to act as I see fit and supports me." "You mean he gives you enough rope to hang yourself." "You may well be right there Jeanne but at the moment things seem alright and are working well."

"And how is Henry Hosking, now that you have taken over his job?" Joshua hesitated at this question as he had a feeling that something had gone on between these two but never really found out what. He decided he would tell her the truth and said, 'Unfortunately, he is not doing well." With that brief and clinical answer, Jeanne leaned forward and said, "Tell me Joshua, what has happened to him."

"I visited him a few weeks back at his small little cottage in Truro. It was disgusting and he was in a most terrible and vulnerable way. I asked Kernow's advice and suggested he be sectioned in the new Asylum at Exeter to be assessed by professionals and he agreed." "O dear," Jeanne replied but inside felt a somewhat feeling of relief. Henry's attention to her over the years had always been worryingly obsessive. "Yes," Joshua replied, it is a sorry state of affairs." "Well Joshua, you can only do your best;

other than that it seems things are running quite well for you.'' With a sense of pride, Joshua replied, ''Yes Jeanne, things are running smoothly and in good control, thank you.'' Just as he finished his reply the band started playing again.

It was another hour before Joshua and Jeanne retired to their rooms. Creeping into the bed Joshua cuddled up close to his wife to feel the warmth of her body. He moved his hand slowly and tenderly over her shoulder when he heard, ''Joshua, go to sleep.'' ''I thought you were asleep,'' he said. ''Well, I am not now turn around and go to sleep.'' With a sigh, he did as was told like some naughty school boy who had been caught out. Rebecca smiled but kept her position.

In the early morning, Rebecca heard the loud banging and so got up out of the bed leaving Joshua to lie in a little. She opened the door to find a young boy with a sealed message for her husband. ''Thank you,'' she said and closed the door firmly. The young boy knocked again so Rebecca turned about and opened the door saying, ''Yes, what is it?'' ''I was told I to await a reply my lady.'' ''Alright young man, sit in that chair quietly, we won't be long.'' It was only six in the morning. Rebecca was going to open it herself but thought better of it. She then thought about waiting a few hours before giving it to him but again knew this would be wrong too. Going back into the bedroom and shaking Joshua for what seemed like an eternity, he woke up asking, ''What is it?'' ''A message Joshua.'' Taking the paper from Rebecca's hand he shuffled up into a sitting position and after rubbing his eyes and temples carefully opened the message.

The message read:-

Joshua,
Hosking's escaped from Asylum, two killed.
Await your instructions
Bull.

Chapter 28

He had ridden like the wind over the hills and valleys to get ahead of her and was now in position. She had already passed Helston and was on the Lands' End road. He took his hat off to her as one thing he admired in people and that was determination. Now, on the Mousehole/Penzance cross junction, he laid out of sight waiting for her jet black and white patched stallion to show.

It didn't take long for her to appear galloping up the road and heading straight towards him. 'So you stupid traitorous bitch, which road will you take now,' he thought to himself.

Without a stop, she took the Mousehole fork. 'So, Mousehole you go is it, so Mousehole I will go.' With her passing out of site he scrambled out of the lair to his awaiting steed. Now he needed to be careful. Although he was the best at his job which was killing people at long ranges he was not built for spying and watching on open streets. One thing about this man is that he was a realist. He was six foot four inches tall with a lithe and strong body and stood out amongst lesser mortals. He was unemotional and always weighed up the odds against risks and success.

He would gallop towards Mousehole but tie up his trusted steed before entering the town. He would find somewhere out of sight but not too far away as to react quickly should he need. He would then walk in quietly and unobtrusively as best he could and mingle.

Zoe didn't waste time riding from Falmouth to Mousehole as she had gone past caring and wanted to find the person who she knew would know about Jacques. But she had to be extra careful as Zoe had lived in the north of Mousehole before acting as a gentle woman in a safe house. However, that was a mask for her real role in being the front person with Jacques for that bastard Count Philip de Albret, in his failed attempt at the chemical plot.

She had limited knowledge of the man she wanted to speak with. She had only seen him once when Jacques needed to get back to France and, without his knowing, she followed. All she knew was that he was one of the officers on board a Brittany ship that regularly buys the local seafood on mass, especially pilchards. The only other fact she knew was that when the ship was in the harbour he drank in the Smugglers Inn.

Dismounting from Arthur, her new Stallion, she tied in him up in the town's open stabling area where most visitors tie their horses. Young boys are always about to take a penny to watch the animals while their masters go into the dock area. If for any reason the horse is gone when their masters return the boy is whipped on his bare back, no questions asked and in front of everyone. Some have not survived this horse whipping but that was just the way it was. They took the money and must accept responsibility and fate should things go wrong.

"Penny for the horse my Lady?" a young boy shouted. "Yes please, that is very kind of you young man," she said in her best quiet English voice. She then pulled the shawl up over her face and with a hunch of the shoulders walked towards the shipping area.

With head down but eyes alert and looking all around, she walked to the harbour area but nothing caught her eye so stopped and sat down to think. Yes, there were ships in but not the one she had seen with the man. Waiting ten more minutes she got back on her feet and walked around again but as before saw nothing of any real interest, so decided to head for the Smugglers.

Walking passed its front doors she saw the place was busy with men, whores and drunken sailors so didn't stop. She again sat down and watched. She needed the information it was her only chance. Zoe, you have to be brave, she said to herself. She then thought that rather than pursue this line of enquiry which puts her in danger why not ask the young boy at the open stables who was holding her horse. These boys know everyone around.

The young boy saw her coming and got up still holding Arthur's reins. ''Excuse young man, do you know of a ship from Brittany, it's the one that buys all the Pilchards?'' ''Yes I do, it's called the Moonshine and docks every other Friday morning early. I know this because it's always our busiest time and I have to bring my baby brother with me to hold three or four horses each.''

''Thank you my young man, you are very knowledgeable.'' ''What does that mean?'' ''It means you are very clever.'' ''O thank you, my mum teaches us.'' ''Well, she is doing a good job. Now here is another penny and thank you for your help.'' ''Will I see you again Ma'am?'' ''Yes, you will see me this Friday morning and I will pay you double for looking after Arthur.'' Zoe got up in the saddle but before she rode off she bent down and ruffled the young boy's hair in a loving and friendly way.

The sniper was struggling away from his normal type of work and felt exposed walking through and around people in the open. He hadn't got that far into town when he saw Zoe's stallion ride past him back out of Mousehole, the way he had just come in. Without thinking, only that to keep tail of his prey, he turned and ran quickly to his tethered horse but then soon slowed down to a walk when he realised the prey had escaped. There was nothing he could do. He had done well tracking the bitch to this place and if he started asking questions to strange people in a strange place may lose what he has gained. It wasn't much he had, that was true, but he couldn't see any advantage in snooping about anymore. His only hope was that the bitch was going back to Falmouth. He decided to let her go for now and would rest up a while as it was still daylight. When the dark of night fell he too would take up the reins and head back.

Zoe tried to open the back door of the house in Dracaena Ridge but it was locked. So leaving Arthur tied up in the backyard she went round the front and tried that door but that too was locked. Sarah was asleep in the front room and heard the attempts on the door so got up. Zoe heard the movement and waited. Before Sarah opened the door she quickly peered out of the front window to see who it was and seeing it was Zoe, smiled brightly and thought, 'so the bitch is back.' With a big smile on her face Sarah opened the door and said with joy, "Hi Zoe, I thought you said you would be gone for several days." "Hi Sarah, yes I did but things didn't work out, can I come in." "Of course, don't be silly, come in, it's so lovely to see you, I will put the water on for a nice cup of tea and you can tell me all.''

The next night at eleven as per usual Sarah looked out of her front bedroom window and waved the candle from side to side. When she needed to talk this was her signal code and vice versa if the other wanted. She waited a minute or so and then saw the lighted candle appear from the terrace window opposite. 'Good, she said and got herself ready.

The Sniper was waiting under the tree as usual. ''Well, is the bitch back?'' ''Yes, and she has told me much.'' ''Before you say anymore you whore, get on your knees.'' She was waiting for when he would say these words of command, and so did as told. She knew what he was doing and what was to happen and would enjoy every minute.

Creeping back into her bed she smiled with satisfaction that the bitch in the next bedroom was being cornered and her own passions of lust had again been fulfilled this night. She blew the candle out and closed her eyes.

Zoe slept well and was glad to be back with Sarah, her good friend. 'What a lovely woman,' she thought, 'so caring and thoughtful.' As she down the stairs she smelt bacon frying and saw Sarah holding a pan over the roaring fire. ''Good morning Zoe, I thought I would do us a nice breakfast and maybe after we could go into town.'' ''You are so good to me Sarah, how can I ever thank you.'' ''You just being here and being a friend is thanks enough, I get so lonely on my own sometimes since my good Mother passed, it is lovely just to have you here.'' Zoe went up to her and both had a big cuddle. "I think I better see to Arthur first, it won't take me long."

Very early Friday morning at three o' clock the sniper made haste. He wanted to be in position, fully ready and waiting for whoever Zoe was to meet in Mousehole. He needed to find the right place out of sight to observe. The information Sarah had supplied him the night before was excellent. A few hours later Zoe too headed off.

"Good morning my Lady, the Moonshine is in the dock, I have been watching for you." "Thank you, you are a very good young man, here are two pennies to look after Arthur and another two will be given to you on my return.

Zoe once again covered herself up and walked towards the docks. This time she noticed the hustle and bustle of men running all about with the loading and unloading of goods. Moving herself a little further back from the harbour she sat down and watched the Moonshine men at work and wasn't long before she caught sight of him. He was giving orders from the ship's deck to some men on the ground. Well, she said to herself, it is now or never. She felt a dread of fear in her heart but knew she had to overcome it. She had to talk with him and that was as simple as that but decided to wait just a little while longer in the hope he would come off the ship and onto the dock.

After an hour had passed he still hadn't got off the ship and Zoe was getting anxious. Luckily for her, the harbour was bustling with merchants and traders all going about their business so she really wasn't being noticed.

Still sitting and trying to act casual she saw him walk on the gangplank. Should she wait a little longer and look where he goes and then make contact or, should she do it straight away? There was no choice and knew she had to act now and not miss the opportunity.

With decision made, she got up and walked boldly towards the ship and stopped at the bottom of the boarding plank.
He was about half way down the plank but his head was turned towards the Moonshine giving last minute orders to the people on deck.

Zoe held firm in his direct line of approach and as he turned his head back to the dock area he saw her. He didn't think much about it but as he got closer she didn't move from his path. He walked on and when only a few feet from her he stopped and without a hint of hesitation she said, ''Good morning, my name is Zoe, I need to see Jacques urgently, do you know where he is?'' The man immediately grabbed her while quickly looking about with utter fright. ''I know who you are, I have seen you before, what the hell are you doing here, it is not safe, you could get me killed, go away.'' ''I am not going anywhere until you tell me where Jacques is.'' All the time he kept looking about feeling very nervous when he heard, ''You alright down there Johan, need some help with the lady?'' He looked back over his shoulder and saw his men leaning over the ship's side all laughing and joking. ''Go back to your work you bloody stupid idiots,'' he shouted back.

''Well, where is Jacques, tell me and tell me now.'' Zoe was not messing about anymore; she had lost too much and was at the end of her tether. ''We cannot talk here it is just too dangerous. Meet me at the back of the Smugglers at noon and I will then tell you what I know." With those last words, he pushed her aside and walked away.

Zoe had no choice and also walked away from the dock and wait till noon, but if he doubled crosses her, she would ruin him. She now knew his first name was Johan.

The sniper saw it all. He was canny and had already sited himself in a small room upstairs in a quiet Inn which had a window looking at right angles across the whole harbour. His telescope had a true and superb zoom lens which he had optimised on both. With crystal clear facial precision he saw their body language, their agitation but much more important he could see and read their mouth movements. He would then mimic to himself their speech in real time as it was spoken. Sometimes it's pure gobbledegook but once he got into sync with their rhythm it worked well. So it was the Smugglers at noon. Also, the name Jacques had been said many times by Zoe and so logged the name in the back of his mind. This is what he was good at, being silent, alone and watch. He was satisfied that he had now identified the person Zoë so urgently wanted to meet and so sat back and looked at his watch and thought about his next moves. One of the first things he needed to know was the time of sail of the said officer's ship called the Moonshine.

At twelve noon Johan had kept his promise and now both of them were sat at the back, out of the way from anyone, in the Smugglers Inn. Johan started to calm down after he had swigged two large brandies. Zoe also drank with him.

"So Zoe, what the hell is going on, why are you here."
Zoe had nothing to lose so spilled out all she knew,
emphasising that these people, whoever they are, would
be after Jacques and she had to inform him of the danger
he was in. This was not quite right, it was her who was in
danger and she wanted Jacques to help her but it sounded
very good and plausible. "By the way," she said, what is
your full name." He looked at her in quiet disbelief but
could not see any reason why not to tell her as she could
now find out quite easily if she wanted to. "My name is
Johan Prideaux and I am a sub lieutenant aboard the
Moonshine." "Johan, you helped Jacques before please
help him now, he is in real danger and I really do need to
talk with him urgently." "I understand that Mademoiselle
but I am thinking about how to do this." "Please Johan, I
beg you." "It is true, Jacques has kept me informed on
where he is." This piece of news put a skip in Zoe's heart.
"But Zoe, it is not as simple as you think, I cannot take
you just like that, I have duties to perform on board ship
and people would get suspicious. I have some leave on
the morrow and the ship doesn't sail until full tide
tomorrow night which means I could take you first thing
in the morning." He in fact was on leave at this moment
until sail but wasn't prepared to lose his Friday night
drink and whore session for this woman's wants.
"Alright, she said, "What time and where shall we meet
tomorrow."

The sniper had clearly seen them both go in the
Smugglers at the agreed time and then watched Zoe leave
on her own. He put the scope down, leaned back and
rubbed his facial stubble in deep thought. He could break
cover and face the man down to get the information they
both had discussed or break cover and chase after Zoe.
Both of these options had drawbacks so needed to think

things through, but time wasn't on his side. He needed to decide on what to do. His mission's objective is to find the person ultimately responsible for the killing of Philip Albret and report that information back to his masters in Morlaix. If he acts rashly without that overall aim in mind he could jeopardise all his work and get paid nothing. He then realised he had no option but to take the man and take him now. Carefully, as he took the scope apart, three butterflies out of seemingly nowhere flew around his head. He swished his hand about to shoo them off mumbling, 'bloody creatures.'

Chapter 29

Zelahnor looked at him with love and said, "I know Zoar, my beautiful defender, you are getting impatient. Christine my sweet could you take Zoar out into the open for a while I think he needs some play time."

The meeting of the Lady's in deepest Wales had gone very well and the special visitor had been delighted. That was a few weeks back and the next one will not be scheduled for another two years. However, the venue had been discussed and all decided it would be held in Cornwall.

Zelahnor was delighted with little Christine and Deborah's progress as love and happiness were embedding into their very souls. Also, the habitat and all the creatures were accepting their purity and love. This is why Zelahnor of the Cornish existed. The previous Lady of Cornwall had lived for two hundred years and Zelahnor, although looking very youthful was in fact one hundred and ten years of age. She was beautiful in face, body and soul and looked only thirty.

Zoar was getting nervous over what he knew that Zelahnor knew on what was to come. The butterflies also talked with her about what they had seen and heard. Zoar had listened and understood all that was said. Zoar's wife was a sleek and beautiful black panther and very much like Zelahnor in her trust, love and kindness. She wanted to reassure Zoar herself but with the new cubs forever wanting found time difficult.

After taking in all the information gained about the danger to come, Zelahnor decided to wait a little longer before she acted. As the creatures waited for her answer on what was to happen, Zelahnor first wanted to talk with the stars and moon and then let her heart and soul dictate her decision. She thanked them all and went out on the moor alone. The creatures knew where she was going.

At around ten that night Zelahnor came back into the warm shack. Zoar and his family were waiting for her return as was Zoar's brother Zareb. Both brothers were equal in size and weighed four hundred pounds each, with large fangs and razor sharp claws.

"Now Zoar, I know your feelings and I too feel there is fine warrant in them to protect our good Cornish people." Zoar and Zareb were sat side by side on their haunches looking at Zelahnor's beautiful eyes and listened to all she said with quiet intent. Christine and Deborah were at the fire making the nettle soup and talking to the butterflies with love.

Then Zelahnor asked with simple ease, "Zoar, can you not stop this man without his death?" Zoar twisted his head in confusion. Zelahnor went on to express her thoughts why death, even on this evil man and what he is doing, must be avoided at all times when possible to do so. "What, I mean is, I know it may require more stealth and love on your part and put you at more risk but what I feel, I feel is the right way. "Therefore I ask you not to kill this evil being but to stop him and end his career in the killing of others for his own greed and self worth.

Zoar and Zareb turned to look at each other to understand and accept if they could achieve Zelahnor's wishes to injure rather than kill. After a few seconds in silence, Zoar turned back to Zelahnor and nodded his large head in agreement. Zelahnor smiled and hugged him saying. ''Thank you my darling, ''You are so brave.'' Even sitting on their haunches, both Zoar and Zareb were taller than Zelahnor when she stood up.

Christine and Deborah could hear all that was being said and were learning daily the way to communicate with each creature, no matter what. On over hearing Zelahnor's last words of guidance and love they both walked towards Zoar and kissed his massive cheek. They also kissed Zareb so as not to leave him out. Zareb purred his affection to them.

His job now was to take his brother's place in protective duties of all in the shack and on the moor until his brother returns. Zoar's wife with the young cubs went over to her husband and kissed him with much warmth. The love around was so radiant that the butterflies and moths fluttered their wings with joy. Even Ruby the little squirrel and her family joined in and, Zoar loved them all.

''Right Zoar,'' Zelahnor said, ''It is time for you to go. May the wind be with you and the angels of love protect you.''

Chapter 30

"You do realise the situation you are in?" the sniper said. Johan looked down at his feet and pitifully replied, "Yes, fully." "Good, then I will unchain you and you can carry on your life but don't forget that once have you pointed out the cottage to her, in full view of my sight, then and only then you are free to go." "I understand, but I am not a traitor as you may think." "I didn't say you were but if you do not do as asked you will be tracked down and hunted for the rest of your life until guillotined as one."

He found out the man who had talked with Zoe, and who he had just interrogated, would be in the Inn most of the night. He had waited and watched then took his chance to snatch him when the darkness fell as the man went to the filthy latrine out the back. The sniper attacked as the man was peeing and made it look easy with one hard smack of an iron bar to the back of the man's head. He then carried him out like a drunken sailor's friend would.

With Johan Prideaux now released to do his bit as agreed, it was time to check all the equipment, especially the cleaning of the long range musket and scopes. He would have a few hours rest then move out into position and wait. He was feeling really good and smiled quietly.

The next morning Johan was at the Penzance turnpike at the agreed time but, he was not feeling well. He was also very worried about his own life and was inwardly terrified of what the sniper would do to him on the information he had given out. But he had no choice he kept saying to himself, no choice at all.

After Zoe had left Johan at the pub she decided to lie low out of the way. Hanging around in Mousehole was just too risky as she may get seen by someone from her past which was the last thing she needed. She found some cheap digs near Penzance and slept the night badly.

At the allotted time she too got to the turnpike. Johan was there and greeted her with smiles in a somewhat over the top language of friendship.

The first thing she noticed was the bruises around his face and head. ''What's happened to you Johan,'' she said. ''O nothing, I got involved with some loud mouth sailor last night and he got the beat me all over the bastard.'' ''But you said you had to back for duty.'' ''That was right Zoe, then a messenger came just after you left and said, due to my good leadership I could take the weekend off.'' Zoe looked at him in disbelief but said nothing. However, she did very much notice that he was on edge and his hands were shaking. ''Are you sure you are alright, you look terrible and your shaking.'' ''Thank you Zoe, yes I am alright I just had way too much drink and feel bloody awful and I have a massive hangover.'' Zoe didn't answer this and hoped the fact that what he said had some truth. ''Well, shall we be off,'' Johan said. ''How far is it?'' Zoe replied. ''We should be there in about thirty minutes.''

The position of the shot would be straight and clear. The only thing that could possibly cause him a little trouble was the up rip of air coming over the cliff edge between him and the target. He had tweaked the special scope accordingly to counteract this possible thermal and had also estimated the range at seven hundred metres as the crow flies.

The cottage in which Prideaux had told the Sniper where the traitor Jacques lives was really very nice, he thought. It was a hundred metres back off the cliff, centre right looking from the Mount of St Michael. The Sniper could see the cottage also had a beautiful clear view over the large bay of Marazion and Penzance off to the right. So that's what you get for being a traitor, a beautiful home, he thought.

The sniper had embedded himself high above the cliffs just inside a small dense forest north west of Perranuthnoe. A most excellent position he thought. However, it had taken energy and time to find it in the time frame given. His horse had been fed, watered and now tied to a tree east of the copse for a quick getaway once the target was killed. The sniper was laid down and camouflaged ready for the shot. His mind drifted over his gun equipment and was pleased he was now using the new bipod as it steadied things better all round even in the kickback. The gun barrel had also been extended to improve accuracy aided by his expertise with site and bore. All was in order except his breathing but knew that was just a matter of him relaxing and waiting. The time was just touching eight thirty and the sun was up with good vision and very little breeze.

His objective was to take out the bitch Zoe with one shot to her upper chest as he did with her husband back in France. He smiled a big smile at that as it was a good job well done. She, the bitch, had now done her bit and had kindly led him to his next target and was now surplus to his requirements. Now he knew her contacts name and address, and in a very short while what he looks like, he would then, once Jacques flees from her dead body, trail him to see where things lead next. Excellent, he thought.

At just passed eight thirty he caught sight of them and was pleased that Prideaux was doing exactly what he had been told to do, good man. When they got to about a hundred metres from the cottage Prideaux reined his horse to a stop and started to point towards the cottage. The sniper started adjusting the zoom ever so slightly.

Then Johan said, ''This is as far as I go Mademoiselle, I must get back to the ship.'' ''Is he in?'' she asked. ''I do not know if he is or is not, he did say he was under curfew so I would say yes, but be careful.''

Zoe accepted his goodbyes but felt he was rushing to get away for some reason. She got down off her horse, tied him to a branch and walked towards the cottage. Getting closer she thought it wouldn't be good just to walk up through the front gate and knock on the door. So she circled the cottage and crept in near to a bush by the side wall and waited. The sniper adjusted the lens with her movements and muttered, 'you traitorous bitch.'

She waited out of sight for what seemed a long time but saw and heard nothing. While thinking on what to do she heard a banging of tin buckets or something towards the front of the building. So slowly, ever so slowly, she crept forward a little to try and get a glimpse.

''Jacques," she said as quiet as she could for only him to hear but he didn't respond. "Jacques," she said louder. This time he heard and turned toward the voice. "Zoe?'' "Yes Jacques, it's me." "What are doing here and come out of that bush, you look like a talking badger or something." She got up and ran to him like a terrified and totally spent woman and he hugged her tightly with love and affection. The last time they had seen each other was six months ago when the English had given them their freedom as promised on the oaths given on both sides. Zoe had gone back to France to be with Jon, but Jacques stayed to be with Jeanne.

"O Jacques it is so good to see you again." "Zoe, what are you doing here, you gave your oath that you would go back to France." "I did go back Jacques but something terrible has happened."

Jacques did not feel anxious at all at seeing Zoe as Jeanne was away in Truro and wouldn't be back till Monday. The cottage also was in the middle of nowhere. "Alright Zoe, now calm yourself there is no need to worry, you are with me now and I will sort things. Let us go on into the cottage and I will make us some tea." "I would prefer a cognac." "Alright, a cognac it is, now hold my hand and let us walk together.

The sniper watched as the two traitors cuddled each other. Keeping his eye on the target he pulled back the flintlock and resettled his aim. Steadying down his breathing he saw them both release and then hold hands. The cross hairs in the telescope were now on Zoe's breasts and so holding his breath one last time started to squeeze the trigger.

Just as he took the last pressure up on the trigger for bullet release he noticed two dark little figures move into his line of sight. As he took his eye away from the lens to look over the scope he saw two butterflies, and then without warning, heard the deepest roar behind his back. He immediately turned his body over and saw a massive beast in mid-air with paws, claws and fangs outstretched above him. He desperately tried to move the musket and fire but it was too late. Zoar, aided by the two butterflies for distraction, had successfully crept the final few feet without notice. Now his full weight was on top of the very bad sniper who was now pinned to the ground in the face up position and petrified. Zoar could have killed him there but that is not what Zelahnor wanted.

Zoar moved his head slowly forward looking deep into the man's eyes and saw only death. Keeping his eyes focused on his prey and with no movement of his head, Zoar swept his long tail around and moved the musket out of harm's way. The sniper was in total fear that in any second his head would be ripped off. Zoar, breathing with slow deep throttling breaths waited and did nothing but stare into the man's eyes. After three or four long minutes of utter stillness, Zoar moved his heavy right paw onto the man's throat and slowly pushed down thinking how best to stop this man from ever killing again. Then Zoar realised what he must do and how to do it. He opened his massive jaws to the man's right upper arm just below where it meets the shoulder joint. He then pushed his mouth a little further forward which allowed only his flat back molars to rest on the skin. When his teeth were in position Zoar squeezed his jaw closed and the man's bones and muscles cracked and crunched to dust under the power of Zoar's single bite. The man closed his eyes and screamed in the anticipated pain to come from this beast's massive jaws but, he felt nothing, no pain, just nothing. The sniper could not understand this, he must be dreaming, he must be mad. Zoar stayed in position with the sagging arm joint in his massive jaws and didn't move for ten minutes.

When Zoe and Jacques had turned to walk into the cottage they both heard what sounded like a man's deathly scream coming from away over on the cliffs. They looked about at where the wind had blown this eerie sound but shrugged their shoulders and carried on walking. They put it down to some screaming gulls or some other wild animal being killed which was none of their business.

Only when Zoar was content that the injury he had inflicted on this savage man could not be treated or repaired by any physician or alchemist on this earth, released his bite. There was hardly any blood as the constant pressure and Zoar's thick saliva had congealed the wound. The man, who had now simply fainted from total exhaustive fear, would live, albeit without the use of his most prized asset of ever being able to kill again. Zoar moved off the unconscious man and looked about at the weaponry lying all around. He picked up the rifle and threw it against the tree trunk then stamped on it until all was broken and in bits. He did the same to the scope and all the other tools connected with this man's means of death. Everything was destroyed never to be used again. Zoar then heard the man groan and knew that soon he would rouse from his fainting. He quickly turned and clamped his teeth on the man's coat collar and dragged him like a baby through the brush of the small forest towards his waiting horse. Zoar had no issue or complaints with the man's stallion and the horse seemed to know this so didn't move or try to get away. Zoar's job was now done and now had to get back to Zelahnor and the moors. He took one final sniff of the wound he had inflicted on the man and then looked at the two butterflies.

He then closed and opened his eyes twice in a slow movement as they had agreed when his job was done.

The butterflies nodded their understanding and with that Zoar turned swiftly about and ran like the wind. The butterflies would stay by the man, gently fluttering over his eyes and ears until he wakes, and, awake he would. When he was fully aroused, they would then fly away to a safer distance but would keep track of him no matter where he went. Their love for Zelahnor was all.

Chapter 31

Joshua waited for Bull to arrive at the hotel in Truro as there was no sense in him riding west to St Just when most likely he had to ride east to Exeter. The little courier boy waiting outside Joshua and Rebecca's bedroom had been told to relay the message to Bull and for him to get here as soon as possible. Bull was also asked that while he was on route to ride to Joshua's home at Marazion and pick up his stallion. Rebecca and Jeanne would stay with Joshua until Bull had arrived then take a buggy home to leave Joshua and Bull to sort. Rebecca was to ride to Marazion with her Mother then pick up her horse and ride back to her place at Gunwalloe

Bull arrived the next morning and after Joshua thanked him for his quick response asked, "What has happened, how did he escape?" "I have no idea Joshua only what was said to me as in my message I sent to you." "Well Bull I suggest we have some food and both get to Exeter as quickly as we can to find out."

The manager at the Asylum was trying his best to appease and act with a sense of professionalism. Joshua was having none of it and carried on asking direct questions but still got only vagueness in return. "Please Sir," the manager replied, "We too are trying to understand what exactly went on. If we could all calm down and go into my office we can talk better." Joshua was in no mood for this small talk as he had already discussed things with this very man before Henry was admitted and he gave Joshua full assurance of the tight security they give.

Joshua and Bull had ridden all the way from Truro but had stayed overnight at Okehampton and got up early to then push on to get to the Asylum. It had been a long ride and both were tired. They just needed the information so they could adapt. One thing Joshua did know is George Kernow will go mad once he knew of this escape.

When all were sat down the Manager began to explain. ''When Henry was admitted he was observed under tight security for quite a while and then assessed by physicians and alchemists who had all agreed that the best course of action would be to operate. It was only after this operation that he was moved to a less secure unit and the main reason for this was for communal love and respect.'' ''Communal love and respect, what the bloody hell does that mean, the man was sick.'' ''Yes Mr Pendragon, that is exactly right the man was sick but after the successful drilling into the skull to drain the excess fluid and decrease the brain's pressure the patient had shown a change in being calm and collective. The surgeons were very pleased with the outcome and our monitoring and support team were pleased also, hence the decision to move him to encourage mental recovery.'' Bull kept quiet and let Joshua do all the talking. ''Well, it didn't work, did it.'' ''That is not true Sir, we believe it did work, our only failure was the decision made in the security level category and the two people who had been killed.'' Joshua then realised that people had lost their lives and bowed his head in silence.

''Mr Pendragon, what I can do is take you and your friend to where the patient was bedded and go over all that we believe happened. But please note it is now full daylight on Tuesday which is a normal working day so will find things very busy with all staff on board. Therefore please keep in mind that Mr Hosking made his escape at our weakest time, being two in the morning on Sunday with a skeleton staff." Joshua, although not satisfied, started to appreciate more of the position this manager was in. What is done, is done, he thought. However it did not excuse the fact that there had been a security lapse, but again, this wasn't down to just one man's bad decision but had been made collectively. Once again Joshua had to see things from both sides of this and act professionally. "Mr Pendragon, I know it doesn't change the situation but we are sorry this man has escaped and we are working hard to make changes in our security staff and patient category levels."

As they left the Asylum all three men shook hands and said their goodbyes. The stable staff had already brought their horses round and once both were saddled they rode out at a gentle pace heading for the overnight stop at Okehampton.

On booking themselves into the Inn, Joshua was feeling the pressure and needed some well earned ale and Bull was in full agreement. As they sat at the table by the window Bull went quiet as something was on his mind and didn't know if he should say something or not. Joshua felt the silence and said, "Are you alright Bull, you look deep in thought, what's on your mind." "Well Joshua, I don't want to give any cause for concern but when I went to pick your horse up from Marazion, on my way to you in Truro, I noticed that Jacques wasn't there or at least I didn't see him, which I thought was odd." "So how did you get into the stables." "That's what I mean; I went through the front garden and knocked on the front door but there was no answer so I went around the back and again saw no one. I then went to the stables and found all was open and saw only two horses, your Harry and Rebecca's Lilly.'' ''That is strange, Jacques is on a strict curfew, he must be there somewhere.'' ''That's what I thought, it just doesn't make sense. After I got the horses out I thought about going into the cottage and check things out but thought I better get to you first.'' ''Thank you Bull, you did right.'' Joshua picked up his ale and looked into its golden brown liquid with deep thought.

Enjoying the beautiful bumpy ride the buggy then slowed to a halt outside Jeanne's cottage at Marazion. Mother and daughter jumped down while the gig man got their things untied. ''Thank you for a wonderful ride,'' Jeanne said and handed him a shilling. Picking up their things they walked to the cottage and as soon as they were in, Jeanne shouted, ''Jacques, were home.'' Putting their things down, Rebecca suggested she go and check on her horse Lilly in the stables. ''Jacques,'' she shouted again. Jeanne then went around the cottage to find him and started to get a little anxious. Where is he she thought?

Jeanne stopped the searching to put some hot water on for some tea but the fire wasn't alight which again she thought strange. She then knelt down to feel the embers finding all stone cold. Rebecca then came in and said, ''That's funny only Lilly is in the stables, all on her own.'' ''Jacques, is not here Rebecca.'' ''Mother, he has to be, he is on home curfew, maybe he's gone for a ride.'' ''Hmmm, maybe, but you say my horse is not there either.'' ''That's right, come and look.''

After an hour had lapsed and both sitting by the roaring fire drinking tea, Jeanne spoke up, ''I am worried Rebecca, this is way out of character.'' ''Mother, do not fret there has to be a simple answer.'' ''But he knew we were coming back today and if he did go riding he would have left me a note, that's what we agreed, that's what couples do. Rebecca, I have an awful feeling something has happened, I know it." Jeanne then started sobbing so Rebecca went over and cuddled her. "Mother, please don't cry." "I'm sorry my love but I always felt in the back of my mind that one day something like this would happen." "Tell you what Mother, I will make us some fresh tea and will add brandy in yours as a little pick me up." "But you have to get back to Gunwalloe, what about your little dogs, Queenie and Cecil." "Mother, I am staying here with you, Joshua will understand, and I am sure Mrs Stevens wouldn't mind having them for a little longer." Rebecca rationalised that when Joshua returns to their cottage at Gunwalloe and finds her not there he will put two and two together and ride to Marazion." While Rebecca got on with the fresh tea Jeanne got up and went into the bedroom but this time checked the wardrobe and, as she thought, his clothes had gone. Coming back into the main front room she said, " Well, where ever he has gone he has taken most of his clothes with him." Rebecca did not respond but handed her Mother the fresh tea and then both settled back into their seats, thinking on what to do.

Chapter 32

The sniper opened his eyes for just a few seconds but then closed them. The butterflies knew he was starting to awake so with their job done, they flew out of sight and waited.

He opened them again but this kept them open and saw the tree branches and foliage above him. He moved his head to the right and saw the underbelly of his stallion. His stallion had stayed with him but had got so close he was almost on top of him. Lying still, he started to think things through but it all seemed a blur. He then felt an aching pain in his upper right arm and moved his left arm to investigate but all he felt was loose clothing. He tried to feel his upper arm muscle but there was nothing just loose clothing and what felt like some dangly bones inside. He was confused as he had no pain. He got up into the sitting position and looked at his right shoulder and saw it was hunched over like an old man. He looked at the bottom of the sleeve and noticed his hand had turned blue and was extending further out of the cuff than normal, like some witch. He shut his eyes tight and then reopened them and what he saw was the same but how could this be. He tried to get up and stroke his horse but fell over so tried again with his left arm in support and succeeded. ''Steady boy, steady,'' he said. He went into the saddle bag to get some water but couldn't undo the strap so had to use both his teeth and left hand to get it. As he gulped the water his shrivelled right hand dangled further out of the cuff. He needed help. On resting his body against his horse he started to wake up more and take stock. After a few moments he then slowly, holding his shoulder, walked to the area where he was just about to pull the trigger and kill that bitch Zoe. But every time he moved he stumbled as his balance was way out of sync. Rather than walk straight he swayed from side to side with his right shoulder sagging down. Finding the site he saw it had been destroyed and the important tools of his trade were smashed into small pieces.

It started to sink in that he was either a very lucky man or someone knew what they were doing but how, how could this possibly be, he should be dead. Although his mind was very confused he wasn't one for moping about and crying like a girl, he was a man and the best sniper ever. He then thought of what he had just said about being the best sniper ever and realised with a grimace of never being able to ply his deathly trade again. He then dismissed the thought as rubbish, of course he could, couldn't he?

One thing he did know was that he needed treatment as a matter of urgency and also had to get back to Falmouth. However, it was now daylight and he would only normally move at night but decided he must take the risk and do it now as his very existence depended on it. So hunching over like an old man he got to his horse and somehow managed to heave himself up into the saddle. With his one working hand, he took the rein and whipped the stallion forward.

The old couple looked at him in total shock as he had scared them by literally falling through the back door. What they saw was not the gallant, strong and dashing man that had left two days ago but a dishevelled, aged old man looking weak and fragile. "Get a bloody doctor here quickly" he shouted at them. He then went upstairs to his bed and passed out. The old couple looked at each other in silence as their job was to keep a low profile safe house, not supply an on demand health clinic, that's why they were well paid by their French brothers. If they did get a doctor, suspicion would be brought onto the house and this would go against the value of why the house was so safe. It would also break their promise to always live quietly and alone with no visitors. They decided it would be best to talk with Sarah at number twenty five before they did anything. Yes, this is what they would do, Sarah is such a lovely lady, she would know. She would help them.

On hearing what had happened and the visual description of the terrible condition the sniper was in, Sarah suggested they do nothing for now as she would come over and nurse him later herself. The old man bent forward and kissed her cheek saying, ''Thank you Sarah, you are so kind.'' On the old man leaving, Sarah sat herself down and sighed heavily. Whatever has happened she thought, she needed to find out all that had gone on and then Peter, in France, would have to be informed. She got up and went about getting the bandages together and anything else she thought may help, including her cache of deadly night shade, Belladonna.

As night fell, Sarah, with bag in hand, exited the back door and walked quietly to the old couple's safe house. On waiting only a few seconds after knocking gently, the old lady came to the door and said, ''He is upstairs Sarah, thank you so much for coming over to help.'' ''That's alright my dear woman, now you and your good husband just sit tight in the warmth and leave everything to me.''

On sitting back down she said to her husband, ''She is such a lovely person, don't you think my dear?'' ''Yes, I think she is very lovely my dear, I don't know what we would have done without her, he is in very good hands."

Sarah opened the sniper's bedroom door and went in and noticed that a candle was already alight by the bedside but he was fast asleep. He looked like an old man of eighty but he was only in his forties, she thought. She took hold of the candle and moved it towards him and as she did he started to stir. "Snipe," wake up, it's me, Sarah. All these years she had known him she never got to know his real name as he was always known by his nickname, Snipe. Always the loner he never got close to anyone as he would do the job, get paid and leave. It was the same when they were passionate with each other, cold as ice and then leave.

"Sarah, is that you," he said in a quiet sleepy voice. "Yes it is, please don't move I am here to help you, tell me what has happened." The sniper opened his eyes fully and tried to focus. Again he tried to move his right arm but nothing as he had forgotten it wasn't there. Sarah put the palm of her hand on his head and felt it burning. He was in a fever she thought and needed to get that cooled down before anything that's for sure. "My arm," he mumbled, "A big black cat the size of a lion with huge fangs," then he passed out. He must be delirious she thought. However, she glanced over at the arm he had touched and noticed only a saggy outer sleeve with dried blood. Then she looked at the cuff and saw the horrible dishevelled hand hanging out from it. O my dear, she said quietly. Sarah took a step back to get an overall look at him and assess what had to be done. If he dies, she had no information to report back to Peter and that just could not happen. Therefore, she must get to work and strip him down, blanket him, and do whatever she could to heal the wounds.

She went downstairs and asked that plenty of hot and cold water be brought up. She also asked for blankets, sewing needles, some cotton and a sharp knife. ''Will he live?'' the old lady asked. ''He is in a very bad way but if all goes well, then yes. However, he needs urgent attention and may lose his right arm. Thinking of that, could you also be ready to bring up a red hot poker when I shout for it.'' ''Of course, we will put the poker over the fire now and we also pray for him.'' ''Yes, please do that.'' Sarah was really not happy at all with the work she had to perform. If she could have got the information from him now, even in the near death state he was in, she would have and then let him die. Now it was the complete reverse, she had to make him live and then get the information she required. She had to work fast.

Chapter 33

Joshua and Bull got to Henry's residence at Truro as it was their initial thought on where to find him. Banging on the front door several times and having no answer they went round the back to try. Again there was no answer so without any further fussing. Bull forced the door open and then both of them searched the house but found it completely empty.

"Bull, I don't like it, something is up and I don't mean just Henry's escape. Something is happening, I know not what but I can feel it. What I would like you to do is to get some of your men and secure the Farm at Sennen and when I am done I will meet you there as soon as I can." "I understand Joshua, I will get on it right away." Both men then shook hands firmly, walked to their horses and galloped off.

Joshua got to his cottage at Gunwalloe expecting his new wife Rebecca to meet him but he found the place empty and locked, exactly as he had left it before they went to Truro. He went to the stables and found Lilly wasn't there either. This was not the Rebecca he knew as she would inform him on everything and so he saddled back up and went over to Mrs Stevens at Cury. As always she was very pleasant but no, she had not seen Rebecca either. "Is everything alright Joshua, do you want to take your little dogs with you?" "Yes, all is fine Mrs Stevens, thank you, but would you be able to have for a little while longer?" "Yes of course, they are lovely little things and are no trouble." "Thank you Mrs Stevens, you are very kind." "Joshua, I do hope things are well with you both." "All is well Mrs Stevens, please do not worry yourself unduly, just a mix up on my part." Joshua lied as he was indeed getting worried and needed to get to Marazion, but something was niggling inside him and it did not feel good. Over the weekend away he had become a bit lax and hadn't worn his protective under vest so decided to go to his cottage at Gunwalloe first to armour up and then push over to Jeanne's place. He would also send messages to his other teams in Cornwall and, dread the thought, to George Kernow.

Joshua didn't get back to his cottage until very late in the evening and by the time he had organised his things, it was too late to get over to Marazion. He also needed some sleep and so decided he would move off first thing. Sitting down to write his messages he started to think that his promotion to manage all Cornwall wasn't easy especially when things out of the blue happen. Hosking use to do this with three teams but then Henry had always stood back and managed from a distance. Joshua had to do the same with only two teams and lead his own south west team too. He needed to talk to Kernow for more resources and, in the back of his mind; wanted his team rebuilt with Bull to lead it.

When the sun arose, Joshua was already nearing the cottage at Marazion. Careful, Joshua thought, careful does it. Some fifty yards from the front gate Joshua got down, tied Harry up and walked the rest of the way in. With pistol loaded and ready, he knocked on the door and stood aside. He heard some movement and then heard the bolt slide back and as the door opened saw his wife. ''Rebecca,'' he said. ''Joshua, where have you been, we have been waiting for you. Come here and give me a big kiss.'' Joshua put his pistol away and hugged Rebecca tightly and kissed her sweetly. ''What is going on,'' he said. ''Come in Joshua and I will tell you all but Mother is still in her bed so be quiet in your talk." "Where is Jacques?" "Come in and sit down Joshua and I will tell you."

Rebecca told Joshua all that she had heard and seen since she and Jeanne had returned from their weekend away at Truro. "Does he not realise what he has done," Joshua said." "Joshua, I am not sure of anything, only what I have told you." As they talked more and time went on, Jeanne appeared so Rebecca got up and said her good morning and made some more tea for them all. Jeanne then sat down and joined in the conversation and although she was deeply involved with Jacques and loved him dearly a certain hard inner resolve was in her tongue.

"So what do you think Joshua," Jeanne said. "I don't know Jeanne, what I do know is that Jacques has broken his oath and pledge and that he will now be classed as a traitor and could be killed on site." "That's exactly what I thought." "But Jeanne, he may not have gone on his own accord." "Joshua, I know him well and am sure if he didn't go of his own free will he would have somehow left a message. He also would not have taken all his belongings and my horse too." "He didn't take Lilly though did he," Rebecca said. Joshua listened to both women speak and then said, 'I think we may be speculating here, don't you think." "No, I don't think we are," Jeanne said, "But somehow I know and feel that something happened during our stay in Truro. In truth Joshua, I have felt for quite a while Jacques wasn't happy being stuck under lock and key." "You love him do you not Jeanne." "Yes I love him Joshua and he loves me, I am sure of it, but that is not the question here. This is not about love this is about life.'' Joshua knew exactly where Rebecca gets her resolve. The pragmatism was incredible.

''So what do you want to do Jeanne.'' ''I want out Joshua, completely. I have thought about it long and hard and wish to move away out of this and your way of life. I have been in it too long Joshua and my imprisonment in France took me to the edge as you know. Jacques and I were fine at first but deep down I knew that something like this may happen someday. Also, in my mind, this cottage is the marital home of my lovely deceased husband and of our beautiful daughter. I have saved my money and talked with Rebecca and wish to retire and move away with my memories intact into a little house or cottage in Helston, somewhere which is less remote and has life about. I would like to walk to an Inn for a gin when I wish or knit when I feel and care for Christine and Little George, should they ever need, and of course, my future grandchild.'' Joshua listened to Jeanne's heartfelt wishes with quiet and full respect.

When Jeanne had finished Rebecca got up and went over to her Mother and hugged her warmly. ''Mother are you sure this is what you want.'' ''Yes, I am sure my darling.'' They then both looked at Joshua for a reply but he was quietly thinking about his own Mother, if she was still alive, and stayed silent a little longer in her memory. Joshua, looked with more empathy at Jeanne's wishes and said, ''Tell you what Jeanne, how about if our baby is a boy we call him Richard in memory of your late husband and your father Rebecca?'' Rebecca smiled brightly with love at Joshua and Jeanne started to cry with heartache and joy at the tender sincerity of the people that now surround her. Joshua, then finished by saying, ''I will talk with George and get things sorted, Helston you say?''

"Yes Joshua, Helston would be ideal for me, I have always liked the town and the people in it and of course, I won't be too far from you both."

With all things discussed, Joshua asked to be excused for a while and went out into the fresh air to think. So Jacques, the French turncoat has flown the nest, what a bastard, he thought. He had to be caught, he knows too much as does that bloody Hosking who has also vanished into thin air. Joshua walked out through the front gate to head for the top of the cliffs. He wanted the sea breeze to run through him. He needed to stand up and take action.

He sat down on the soft turf as close he could to the very edge of the cliff. He put his arms around his bent up legs and let the sea and wind take its toll. He thought of how he was managing things and said to himself, like a twot, that is what, you have been given the task to protect the very good people of this County and your acting like some wet behind the ear politician, pussy footing around like a prat. Make decisions and act with confidence. No more gently, gently and pleases and thank you's. Joshua relished the power of the sea spray smashing against the rocks, 'be brave my son, be bold, be yourself and do it right.' He closed his eyes to let the Cornish sea air refresh and come into his very soul.

Chapter 34

Jacques had listened to Zoe's tale of woe and hurt and knew he would help as they have helped each other in the past. They had worked together for a long time and slept with each other too, both in France and England. Although Zoe talked and talked about her lover's killing, his mind was drifting on what and who sanctioned it. He also thought of his Jeanne and what she would be thinking. He knew that once he left the cottage at Marazion all oaths given would be broken. If he stayed, Zoe would be on her own and vulnerable. He started looking at his life in Cornwall and how he couldn't move, speak, or do bloody anything unless agreed in writing by Kernow. He wasn't used to anything like this and although his living and love for Jeanne was agreeable it came at a cost, his cost as a man. In some funny way, he knew that Jeanne would understand him. Maybe helping the English defeat Albret was wrong and now it is time for him to pay the price. But what he did then was for the love of Jeanne. Zoe, bless her, had accepted to go along with his plans to turn coat but there was simply no choice, the Cornish had uncovered the plot anyway so it had to be done to save their skins. What he did know is, that for the first time in nearly a year of confinement he felt alive with adrenalin and the fear of excitement stirred inside him. Was it right, was it wrong, he did not know. What he did know is that he would go and whatever will be, let it come. Zoe hugged him tightly and couldn't stop thanking him for his help. She knew that he would.

When Jacques left the cottage with all his things packed, his horse Arc couldn't take the entire load, so had no choice but to also take Jeanne's mare. When he decided this he smiled and thought of what she would be like when she came back and found him gone and remembered how he looked up to the stable roof asking her to forgive him. He looked at Lilly, Rebecca's mare, which was stabled next to Jeanne's horse but decided to leave her be. Once Arc, Arthur and Jeanne's horse were ready and loaded, Jacques turned his head towards the cottage and gave it one last look. It was the place he had shared with Jeanne and he would never forget her. "Are you ready Zoe?" Nodding that she was, Jacques clipped Arc and both galloped off to Mousehole.

After a thoughtful but easy jaunt, they entered the shrouded woods a mile before the town to make camp as Jacques wanted Zoe out of sight in a safe and secure position. He would shortly, before it gets too late, go to the harbour area to find the Moonshine and that scallywag Prideaux before they set sail. He wanted some answers and answers he will get no matter what it takes. Jacques had, lucky for Zoe, quietly kept Prideaux informed of his whereabouts, just in case. There was no time to waste so unloading all he could, he made sure Zoe was alright. He then went over his plan of action and his further intentions so Zoe knew everything that was going to happen. He would be back before or just after nightfall and then, with a kiss from Zoe, rode off at a fast pace. Arc seemed to know that he was back in the game and had an energy of a refreshed stallion. Jacques had not felt this renewed power from Arc or himself in a long time. "Good boy Arc," he shouted, "Good boy." Arc's sharp ears flicked up with new adrenalin at Jacque's words of encouragement.

Jacques gave the stable boy at the open town stable a penny to look after his beloved Arc. Jacques had no weapons as this was forbidden while in close detention.

However, now he had broken that oath he needed them more than ever. As he walked to the dock area his eyes were darting left and right in search of something or someone that could harm him. He noticed the Moonshine was still docked and being loaded at the far end of the harbour. As he looked to his right he saw the Harbour Inn and so quickly dapped inside to take a look. It was nearing noon but knew that devious Prideaux liked his drink but on looking about saw that he wasn't there. Only one place therefore he could be and that was on the ship itself.

With his collar pulled neatly back and walking with pure upright confidence he quickly found the ship's gangplank. Acting like a superior officer he strode boldly up towards the main deck.

The ship was very busy getting the last loads on board and only a couple of low ranking ensigns were in his way once he got on deck. Talking with an assertive French accent he asked to be taken immediately to another low ranker, a sub lieutenant by the name of Prideaux on matters relating to the French crown. Jacques then waved a piece of paper and waited with his head held high as if any small wait was a burden and somehow non loyal. ''Yes Sir, please follow me, I believe he is in his bunk below.'' ''Thank you young man, that's what we like, efficiency.''

''Johan, I don't give two monkeys about who or what, I want to know how, why and what the bloody hell is going on here. Tell me all Johan, tell me all.'' ''Johan sat back on his bunk with a hangover he longed to go away and now, of all people, he had to explain his actions without fault to Jacques, who he knew was a man of hard means. "Jacques, I thought you were dead." "What do you mean, dead." "The man who grabbed me said he would do to me what he was to do to you and the girl traitor if I did not do exactly what he said."

"What man? Tell me everything this man said and how he said it and then you can describe him in detail." "Jacques, this man promised he would kill me." "Johan, you have got yourself and others like Zoe and me in deep trouble here. Your double crossing action has got you into this mess and I promise you this, if you do not tell me all, I will have no choice but to kill you myself." Johan didn't know if Jacques was serious but backed down and did as was told. He had nothing to lose. Jacques quietly took everything in on what was said and, more importantly, tried to put it all together. Jacques paid particular attention to the words the unknown man had said to Johan on what he should do when he took Zoe and pointed out the place where Jacques was living at Marazion. He was told that once he had done his signal, he was to leave the area immediately and let her go in alone. Jacques, for some reason, went a little cold as he recalled back in his mind the time he actually met Zoe that morning, when both of them had heard a weird, eerie scream coming from afar, over at the cliff tops edge. Johan rubbed his face up and down with the palm of his hands trying to make sense of the trouble he was in. Jacques was sitting opposite watching him in silence.

"What do I do now Jacques?" "You do nothing and carry on your duties as normal. I will do all I can to protect you and find this man of danger, now let me have a pistol and blade." Johan got up and rummaged around the bunk to get the weapons asked. Once Johan had handed Jacques the somewhat old pistol and blade they sat back down as Jacques wanted to say some final words of heed.''

''Right Johan, now lets us shake hands and I will see you in two weeks and do not forget the sign.'' Johan nodded and put his hand out. Jacques then suggested that Johan now quickly see him off the ship with dignity and calm as if their meeting had been good for all and Country. Their boldness and common step will show people around who are busy loading the ship to see nothing but just two men in boring discussion which, is of no concern to them. Walking briskly off the ship, Jacques headed straight to the open stables to get Arc.

Jacques entered the forest the way he and Zoe had done so before, that was the rule and tied Arc next to Arthur, Zoe's big black and white patched stallion. Jacques noticed with ease how the two horses were becoming friends with each other. Zoe had lit a small fire in a little hollow out of sight and was sitting gazing into the flames with bottle and pipe. As Jacques got closer to the fire Zoe turned her head and smiled without voice. ''Are you alright Zoe?'' ''Yes, I am alright thank you Jacques, just deep in thought in trying to work out how I got myself into this terrible mess.'' ''Well, a mess it is that's for sure but let's not think too much about why at this moment but more about what are we going to about it. I think once we are a little safer we will then have the time to work out what the bloody hell is going on.'' ''Did, you see Prideaux?'' ''Yes, I did, that scoundrel and he looked shocked to see me saying he thought I should be dead, and you.'' ''He said what?'' ''Dead, killed, both of us.'' Jacques, your words are worrying me.'' ''Pour me a drink and I will tell all.'' Jacques noticed that Zoe had prepared their bed for the night with a cover over the top should it rain. Although they had some food, both were not hungry. A stiff drink is what they needed.

Settling down by the fire Jacques showed Zoe the pistol he got from Johan and the working of it. He then proceeded to reload ready for immediate fire and laid it down between them. Zoe listened with intent on what Jacques had gained from Prideaux and mingled with the conversation as she saw fit as Jacques let the discussion run both ways. Jacques kept rubbing his chin with the unknown situation and was trying to keep to the known facts without assumptions.

As time moved on, Jacques was now getting a little tipsy as was Zoe. However, Jacques felt safe in the woods, at least for tonight and told Zoe so. She seemed to relax hearing at last some positive words spoken rather than the doom and gloom of fear and dread.

Jacques went over again in his mind the simple fact that someone had killed, at long range and in cold blood, Zoe's childhood sweetheart and lover, Jon. That was in France and then months later that probable somebody had made a lot of effort to reach across the sea to Cornwall to get Johan and Zoe and then trace them to him. Why and how did he or they do that? Johan had said he had never ever seen the man before in his life.

Night time had fallen and the forest lay dark with a sense of uneasy calm. Jacques brought the horses in closer to their bed and made them settle. Their straps were to remain tight and in place and everything that wasn't needed on the ground was packed away ready to ride in an instance.

As they lay down together under the blanket, Zoe nestled into his strong body and said, ''Jacques, I'm getting really worried.'' ''It will be alright Zoe, all will be alright.'' She then gently got hold of his hand and put it in between her breasts and kissed him. Jacques responded as he had done many times before and she helped him undo her blouse and take her inner skirt off. ''Jacques, how long do we have to stay here?'' 'Until the Moonshine docks again which Johan said would be two weeks as from today.

We can do it Zoe but we need to be patient and not rush, people will be out looking for us. When Johan returns, we can then get away safely without being seen.'' ''Jacques, she whispered, why don't we go back to my safe house in Falmouth with my lovely friend Sarah?'

Chapter 35

It had been four long days of nursing the sniper back to life. Sarah inwardly hated this duty of care and the old couple downstairs were simply useless. The sniper, now sitting up in bed, was eating like a pig and drinking like a fish. Sarah had been his sole maid and nurse and had done well. The upper right arm joint had been completely crushed and torn from the shoulder but by some miracle, the blood and bone had fused together causing minimum blood loss. Sarah was totally bemused by this.

Apart from mass bruising and trauma, she had also kept the fever under control. But the main job was to get the torn gangrene arm fully away from the shoulder blade and sear all things together. The red hot poker, sharp knife and her unskilled hand had done the job well. Sarah, in her travels, had seen this done on an ankle to an injured colleague and had memorised what had been done. It was all to do with hygiene, keeping the wound and tools clean at all times as the surgery progressed. Speed was also of the essence. The sniper had been given much alcohol but still had passed out when Sarah applied the hot poker searing the skin, muscles and bone at the shoulder. With the now severed arm in her hands, Sarah went downstairs and quickly discarded it onto the main fire below. Sarah threw it on with utter disdain as someone would throw a log and then used the poker to mix it in with the flames. Although she didn't like playing the wet nurse she had carried out the operation to the best of her ability. In the back of her mind, she also knew that by doing what she had just done would give her more kudos from Peter the Frenchman and may well increase her purse. Now the sniper was getting better, now she would get him to talk and talk he would, one way or the other. He now owed her his very life and she would use this to get what she wanted and that was information.

Sarah brought the chair closer to his bed side and listened to his story. While she was looking at him she found that he was somehow different. Whatever has happened, be it true or false, he had changed. His once arrogant, hard and ruthless way of living life had gone being replaced with a humbleness of sincerity. She found this new softer manner totally repulsive to what a man should be. Also, not only had his right upper body shrivelled, but his private parts also had. She noticed this when she stripped him down on the first night. He had also aged. What a loser she thought. However, she played the game well and listened with quiet intent and made notes. She would get all the information she could, like a she woman wanting water in the desert.

''I have money Sarah, lots of it, hid away in a secret place.'' This took Sarah by surprise as he was just mumbling on about something or other and then said this out of the blue. ''Why do you say that'', she asked. With a tender voice he replied, ''Sarah, 'I know you, and I know that for my life, I will give you it all.'' ''Don't be silly, you silly fool, we are in this together, now carry on with the story and don't leave anything out.'' ''Sarah, I am not being silly and I mean what I say, I have lived a life of killing and been paid handsomely for it but no more, something has changed inside. I know not what, but I have and I say again, you can have it all, it is also here in Cornwall.'' This made Sarah's ears crop up. ''In Cornwall, you say?'' ''Yes, it is here in Falmouth.'' ''Where exactly is it in Falmouth?'' ''Sarah, I will tell you when you promise to let me live a new life without sin.'' ''But you are a walking cripple with nothing.'' ''I am glad, now I can see things as they really are from a cripples point of view, real life, like a wounded dog on the dirty streets." "But do you not want to go back to our great France with all that money and live and eat above others?" "Sarah, I have done most of my killing, sometimes of innocent people, for pure self gain in England and here in Cornwall. I feel this is where I must stay and pay back in love and repentance for what I have taken from them." Sarah looked at him in astonishment as she believed what he had just said was the truth.

After getting all she wanted, Sarah went downstairs to talk with the old couple. She told them to look after the sniper as best they could and also keep an eye on number twenty five, her cottage opposite. Sarah briefly mentioned her friend Zoe and not to be at all disturbed if she turns up some time while she was away. She would return in a few days as now she had to go and meet someone from France, the true people's Country of the righteous way. They kissed her hands and with sweet grace bade her good will.

Once safe inside her cottage, she read the message again.

Sarah,
Meet Cove, Thursday usual time.
Stay at Plume.
Love Peter.xxx

She had better get a move on but first though she had better write a message for Zoe, just in case the bitch returns. She had also to go over all in her mind what the sniper had said. Peter liked the information steady and in a calm procedure to visualise events as they happened. What he would make of the butterflies on a rifle scope lens and the black lion with deep golden eyes and fangs as large and sharp as cut throat razors only knows. He would probably think that she and the sniper had gone raving mad but that is what the sniper had said and that's what she will pass on. She would leave for the Plume and Feathers at Portscatho this afternoon and then amend the notes she had taken. The little cove she had to get to at the witching hour of midnight, she found really spooky. It was also a dangerous long walk from the Inn and could only be got to by foot due to the steep jagged rocks and gulley's. Peter much liked this rendezvous point as it was remote, out of the way and on the edge of nowhere. It was important to him that a quick escape could be made by sea and tide at the very hint of any trouble.

After eating a few spoons of the stew she had made the day before, she then doused the fire and made haste.

She had been to the Plume a few times before and just didn't like it at all. But, they paid the Inn keeper and also laid a nice room but she still didn't like it. It was totally out of the way and the men drank like tramps and urchins.

After tying her horse up, Sarah entered the Plume from the stable backyard. The Inn keeper's wife greeted her well but Sarah felt suspicion in her manner. ''Have you my room.'' ''Yes, all is ready, please follow me, do you want a hand with your things my dear?'' ''No thank you, I will be fine.'' The lady escorted Sarah the short walk to her room which was set back from the main drinking and near the stables where her horse was tied. Sarah asked if it would be alright if food could be sent to her room as she was very busy. ''I am sure that would be fine my dear, we serve at eight o clock is that alright for you?" "Yes, that's fine, thank you."

When the lady had gone Sarah rested herself on the bed and thought about what and how she would say things to Peter.

After eating her dinner Sarah went out down the back way to the stables to make sure her horse was well. She quickly felt that the air had chilled and noticed the clouds were low and no stars could be seen. She would have to wrap up warm tonight. The good thing about her room was that she could move in and out without anyone seeing. They were all in the front bar getting drunk and laughing at stupid man jokes. She would rest up one more hour and set off.

As she had thought, the way down to the cove was slippery and wet. She had to be careful and the darkness and cold chill were not helping. Bloody midnight she thought, why does he always have to choose bloody midnight to meet? After half an hour of tense walking down the wet grass slope the ground changed to sharp rocks but bit by bit she was getting there. She aimed to get to the small manned rowing boat which would be tied around a protruding rock, deep in a gully under the cliff. Step by step she got closer and when about ten yards away she saw a man's head bobbing up and down. He also saw her and so quickly called the code word. She acknowledged and then carried on towards him. "Good evening my lady, here take my hand, it's quite choppy, I will help you in." "Thank you my good man." Sarah tried to get in gracefully but the movement of the sea with the boat swaying up and down just wasn't to be. The young seaman was going to laugh as he could see and hear her struggle and curse aloud. However, after many undignified attempts to get on board and settled, she managed to plonk her bottom down on the cross plank. ''Are you ready my Lady,'' the seaman asked. ''Yes, can we just get on with it.'' With that, the young man unhooked the rope from the rock and heaved strongly on the oars. With the initial surge of forward motion, Sarah who hadn't taken a proper hold and also with soaking wet bottom slipped backwards off the cross plank straight onto her backside to the bottom of the boat. With both legs splayed in the air and showing all her underwear the sailor couldn't help himself. ''Don't laugh, you young idiot, help me up.''

The small unlit French galleon was around the next cove about half a mile out to sea. The captain dare not bring the ship any closer to shore as that was too risky. It also gave him a quick and clear exit, just in case.

As the small boat attached itself to the ship's side Sarah got on board and with a face like thunder, Peter the Frenchman greeted her. ''You look well Sarah,'' he said, with a big grin. ''Don't be so bloody stupid Peter, why we have to meet at these way out of the way places and at midnight is beyond me.'' ''Sarah, my dear, it is for your safety we do this, now let's go down in the warmth of my cabin and we can talk.''

Sarah and Peter got to the cabin and after initial discussion and dinks, they started the meeting. Sarah went on to give a thorough and detailed brief on all the information she had gained. Peter was very happy with her work and so as a reward gave her one hundred guineas cash bonus on and above her normal pay. She would now stash that away in her safe treasure chest as she had done many times. She loved money and would use it all, with lavish, when her time comes. The meeting had gone well but had lasted for two hours and when both had agreed on their next moves the meeting finished. Peter escorted her to the main deck and after kissing her cheek helped her to get into the small boat. Sarah got back to her room at the Plume just before the sun was rising. She was exhausted and needed sleep

Sitting down in the chair, one thing kept nagging at her as it just didn't make sense. She had always thought that when she told Peter about the massive cat with sharp fangs and what he had done to the sniper Peter, he would just ridicule her and laugh at its stupidity. But he did neither of these and to her surprise just sat there silent, stony faced without a trace of emotion.

H also suggested that the good work done by his team has laid the foundation for them to push forward. But Peter, then coldly advised her that although he much appreciated the sniper's work, he did not need his services anymore. He was an invalid and invalids have no room in his team and would also save a lot of money in non payment of his last service. Zoe too, although of unknown whereabouts at this precise moment, didn't interest him either as she had also done her bit, the traitorous bitch. The likely hood is that she would return at some point to Sarah's house in Falmouth and, with a bit of luck, with Jacques too. He suggested that Sarah do what she wants to Zoe and the Sniper as they are surplus to his needs. Jacques would now be the main line of interest as was his contact Johan, the sub officer on board the ship Moonshine. The old couple was still of use as was the safe house they dwell in. Peter said he felt good but Sarah noticed he had a very serious ashen face, more than she had ever seen before. Peter also felt he was close to the target and said that once he had one or two extra pieces of information he will meet with their employer. He would also immediately deploy more men to help catch that traitor Jacques. Two of them would live at the old couple's place, in wait.

Sarah, having tired from all this thinking got up from the chair and took off her wet clothes. She dried herself off, got into bed and pulled the blankets up. Looking up at the cold ceiling, in the quiet darkness of her room, she couldn't help but visualise back to the very moment when she was at the door, leaving the cabin. It was when she looked back and saw him in very deep thought, stroking his chin with a look of real worry. This disturbed her much.

Chapter 36

"So what do you think Mother?" "I think it's better than the others we have seen, quite nice actually," Jeanne replied. Both Mother and daughter had hitched up Lilly to the little gig and were house hunting in Helston. Approval had been given to Jeanne to retire with an agreed smaller pension but a larger capital payout for her services rendered.

Lady Street is a small area of houses at the bottom of town but with nice views over the trees and hills to Porthleven. It was also importantly only a short walk from the main street and the Inns, especially the Blue Anchor.

The little cottage was tucked away just off the road with a small front garden but a large back one. There was also, very importantly, enough room in the back yard to secure a few horses and a gig. It was a little tight but very doable. The cottage itself also had a pretty front gate and a more sturdy rear gate. Jeanne didn't want much anymore, she never really did.

In her youth Jeanne, was a very pretty lady and had always been practical with a simple no nonsense approach to life. Indeed, that's what Joshua's Father, John, saw in her when Richard, her husband, was killed and why she was asked to replace him.

The little cottage had two bedrooms, a nice large front room and the scrub area was adequate. The granite walls looked well-built and the windows were of iron and glass. The whole place had been well looked after and Jeanne felt very comfortable most of all it fitted her budget to buy and own outright. She had stipulated to the auctioneer that she must own the freehold and not lease hold. The man's eyes flustered when she had said this as all his sales were leased or rented with the freehold being held by rich yeoman men, not women. "Are you sure you want to live here Mother?" ", I am sure my love; it feels nice and fits most if not all of my wishes. Now before we meet and discuss our lower buying price with the auctioneer tomorrow why don't we book into the Red Lion and have a relaxed evening." "How about the Blue Anchor, I prefer their cider." "O you naughty thing; what say we book the Red Lion, stable Lilly and then walk down to the Blue." They both laughed at the plan of action and walked out of Jeanne's soon to be little freehold cottage.

Sitting in the snug bar they could hear the one man banjo singer singing his merry tunes from the main bar area. The atmosphere was one of daily merriment from workers who have had a little too much. "Wasn't it nice of Joshua to call the new baby Richard after your Father." Jeanne raised her wine glass to celebrate saying, "Here's to Little Richard,". Rebecca clinked her glass and said, "Thank you Mother, but what if it's a girl?" "O, I never thought of that." They both giggled and drank back in celebration anyhow.

"Mother, I am worried about Joshua." "Why my dear, he said everything was going fine." "He would say that but I know him. When he took the promotion to run Cornwall for George Kernow, after Hosking's got the boot, I think he felt it would not be that difficult and his inner niceness would get him through." "Rebecca, every time I hear that name Hosking it sends shivers right through me. For some reason, I still cannot get out of my mind the time when we were escaping from France and how he survived without scratch or pain from the boat explosion while I and Joshua's Father were still in it. Sorry Rebecca, I digress, what were you saying?" "I am saying I think Joshua needs to harden up and be more ruthless. He seems to be trying to please everyone all the time and can feel he is struggling. It seems that he is afraid of making a mistake where beforehand he would just make a decision, based on his gut feeling, and get on with it." "Hmmm, I know what you mean Rebecca, but he is now responsible for other people's welfare not just himself now, he also worries about you and little Richard." "I know Mother, but I feel if he keeps diddling around like an endearing office manager, he could get hurt." "So what do you suggest?" "I don't know." "Well, maybe you should talk with him clearly on what you are feeling because if you are right and he does get hurt, then the very people he is most protective of, will lose that very protection."

Joshua was now at the Sennen Farm sitting down talking with Bull in the farm's big open front room. The farm itself had been vacant for nearly two months now which in terms of security was a no, no. It was in a strategic position and needed people living in it for that coastal line's protection.

"Joshua are you alright?" "Well that depends on how you look at it but I am fine thank you Bull, why say you that." "We are friends Joshua and with full respect and if you don't mind, the men have been talking and feel you have changed somewhat since we first met you." "What do you mean Bull?" "Don't get the wrong idea Joshua. I really do believe you are the right man for the job and I am, like you, determined to protect our good Cornish people but your decisions lately have become, shall we say, a little fuddled." "Fuddled?" "Yes Joshua, fuddled."

Joshua could not help but chuckle at this observation and was going to argue that Bull be quiet and do as told but he knew that this man in front of him was a good and trusted friend. Bull delicately but honestly went over a few things comparing how Joshua would have done things differently before his promotion. Joshua listened in silence as he knew deep down that he had changed and that, through ego or lack of confidence, had become what Bull is saying. He had taken his eye off the ball with all the various paperwork and meetings as well as being Kernow's chief pen pusher in the South West.

Both sitting opposite each other Joshua, in deep thought, scratched his chin with his thumb and forefinger. ''As I said Joshua, my men noticed the change and brought it to my attention a while ago. We mean nothing by it only that we want to help you if you require us.'' Joshua watched as Bull was speaking and could feel in his voice that this man was genuine and that his men were concerned. He decided to come clean with the respect back.

''Thank you Bull, I must admit it is true what you and your men say. I am finding things difficult at this moment. I cannot believe that Henry Hosking managed all of this with calm and good manner. I thought taking on his position would be easy as he had portrayed it.'' ''Joshua, don't be too hard on yourself. Hosking's only ever thought about him and also didn't run a cell as you are doing. All he ever did was pop up now and again, make blanket type remarks and then relied heavily on you and me to get things done. In fact, when I think about it, what exactly did he do? '' ''It is true as you say Bull, trying to manage the cell as I do and all of Cornwall at the same time has in truth stretched me to the limit.'' Joshua then stopped talking and went into thought and Bull, in respect, let Joshua be silent for a while and then offered him a nip of brandy. "Here you go Joshua, have a little nip." After a few minutes more of silence, Bull said, "Joshua, you said it yourself, relieve yourself of running this team or running Cornwall, one of the two, you can't do both." "You are right Bull, then we need to recruit a team leader and quickly."

Joshua went over the situation of the cottage they were in and how it being empty and unguarded was vulnerable to attack and needed to be sorted. Also with Jacques having vanished and Jeanne gone to retire in Helston, the cottage at Marazion needed to be sorted too. Both places are essential for the Cornish South West protection plan. Joshua also mentioned about Henry Hosking's escape and then sat back, breathed a heavy sigh and said, "Bull how much time have you, would you like a pipe and a smoke, I think it's time to change." "I have all day Joshua and thank you, I will at that." The two men felt very at ease with each other as both knew the Cornish depended on their loyalty together

Bull sat back with a feeling of renewed confidence and then looked through the window out over the open fields up to the forests yonder. He also noticed two beautiful black and gold coloured butterflies sitting still on the window ledge. He looked at Joshua to say about the Cornish colour of the butterflies outside but as he turned his head back to the window saw both of them fly away towards the trees. Bull smiled to himself thinking how lovely nature is.

Zareb had been lying deep down in the dark under growth in the trees with his bright yellow and black eyes watching the Sennen Farm for hours. His black coat blended well in the dark tree line. He had left the dark moor of Bodmin two hours before the midnight moon and bounded westwards across the countryside without stop. Once nestled down in position his body never moved and his steely eyes lay fixed on the farm's cottage. After many, many hours of stillness, he saw the two black and gold butterflies fly off from the window and head towards him. They flew into the tree line and when over his head circled twice and then flew away eastwards. Zareb understood and so eased his body up as it was time to return to Zelahnor.

Chapter 37

Christine was sitting learning to speak with the squirrels. While Ruby was being held in Christine's small open palm close to her face they chatted away with each another. When Ruby asked a question and Christine got the answer wrong the little squirrel would shake her head to and fro and give a squeaky giggle. Christine would chuckle back and try again.

It was now dark with the stars shining above when the door of the shack opened and Zareb slowly entered. As always he went directly to Christine and rubbed his massive head on her before anyone else. Ruby would have none of it and squeaked as if to say, get off you big brute. Christine cuddled his massive head and kissed his big nose with love. "He loves you above anyone, you know that Christine," Zelahnor said lovingly."

With that Zareb moved over to where Zelahnor was sitting. The two black and gold butterflies were already with her sitting on her shoulder whispering in her ear. Zoar was out with Deborah on the moor. All the other animals, including Zoar's cubs, which were getting bigger by the day, we're in the shack. "Christine, my beautiful child of light and love, Zareb wishes to talk but he is very hungry." "Then I will make Zareb some nice food for when he has finished and also will fluff up his bed as he must be very tired." "That's lovely my precious sweet." Zareb licked his lips in wait. "Well my lovely Zareb, you are very brave, tell all that you have seen." Zareb did as was asked and everything he said, fitted well with what the two butterflies had already reported. Zelahnor kissed his nose and said "Very well done Zareb, now go and eat and then rest your tired body my beauty." Zelahnor now knew what she had to do. It was the time to inform the other three Princesses. She walked out onto the darken moor and when fifty yards away from the shack, called out to the sky. The cold silent night heard her and took her plea across the large bleak moor way away up to the hills and trees afar.

Within five minutes three peregrine falcons flew swiftly to her and as she raised her arm they each rested. Their claws were deadly sharp but each had folded them back so as not to scratch the one who loved and protected them. They were gentle like new born babies with their Mother. Zelahnor kissed each one and then talked with them and with their keen eyes and sharp minds they listened intently. When Zelahnor had finished speaking, she gently kissed each one again and said, ''Go now my beautiful birds of this night's sky, fly with love and speed, I will await each of your return. All three flew off in turn but in different directions. One went North by North East, one North by North West and one East.

As Zelahnor watched the birds fly away, Deborah and Zoar were just coming back from their outside activities. When they saw her they went straight to her side and hugged her with utter love. Zelahnor kissed them both and suggested that they all go in to have something to eat and some lovely nettle tea. Zelahnor suggested they go on ahead of her as wanted to look up into the night sky. As she gazed above she could feel that the stars were looking down at her with love and understanding. Thank you,'' she said.

When all three had entered the shack, Christine, Deborah and Zoar cuddled each other tightly. While Zelahnor had been out, Christine had been busy making things ready and so all enjoyed the warm tea of nettles and food.

When all had had their fill, Zelahnor looked at the two girls with a smile of love and warmth. They then all held hands and started to sing a beautiful soft ballad to the love of the good Cornish people, to the deep sea that surrounds them and to the earth that feeds them. Once the beautiful ballad had finished, Zelahnor, Deborah and Christine needed to say nothing more and hugged each other tightly. They all knew, and all were so very happy and joyous.

Chapter 38

As the sniper lay in his bed he looked up at the ceiling with thoughts of his past and the things he had done. His left hand went to his empty shoulder socket in which his whole arm had been severed by that beast. He threw the blanket aside and got up to look in the mirror.

Getting to his feet for the first time in a long while he found things very unsteady. Once his balance had corrected itself he walked over to the mirror and standing close took a long look at his near naked reflection.

He found he had lost weight but in the right places. His shoulder, which he thought would be completely red with dangly sinews and full of puss, was the complete opposite. It was the same colour as the rest of his body fully healed and sealed with no pain at all. His face, which he had seen the day after the attack had smoothed out and was younger looking although he was in need of a shave. He stood back a little, pulled himself up straight with his shoulders back and looked again. His chest and torso looked well as were his legs but he couldn't get over the view of having no right arm. It just wasn't there.

He put some clothes on and decided to go down stairs to ask the old couple for some hot water for a bath and also a razor blade. He was starting to get his strength back and felt it was now the time to get up and start his new life.

As he wearily and slowly got down the stairs the old couple were amazed at how well he looked. He didn't seem aged anymore and the colour had come back to his cheeks. Out of politeness and respect, they didn't say anything about his absent right arm. Both got up and dutiful did what was politely asked of them. As they went out to the scrub area the sniper sat down in a seat and waited for their call.

When they got out of the sniper's earshot the old man said, "Did you hear how he talked with us my dear?" "Yes I did, it's very strange, what do you think." "Well, to be truthful, I found it rather nice and comforting but a little off putting as we both know what he is like." "Maybe the injury has affected him." "You may well be right my dear wife but we must be careful to keep our guard." "Alright, my dear, maybe we should tell Sarah when she returns, what do you think?" "Hmmm, I think we say nothing and go about our quiet ways as we have always done, say nothing and hear nothing."

When the bath was filled and the soap and razor ready, the old lady went to tell the sniper. He had dozed off but as she spoke he opened his eyes. "Your bath and things are ready now," she said. "Thank you, my dear lady, you have been most kind to me and I thank you for this." She didn't respond but again was confused at his kindness and loving tone towards her.

As he fumbled his body into the hot water he felt an over whelming sense of calm and ease. The water soothed his mind and he just lay there taking the senses of life's beauty deep into his mind. However, he again found it strange that he had only one arm and the left one at that as he was right handed. His right hand had always been his payment in life, it paid for all his daily wants. When he killed with his deathly right hand trigger finger, he got paid. Shaking his head out of these dour thoughts he quickly got back to thinking of his new life and so began to scrub his body all over to rid himself of the past gone.

When he had finished he decided not to ask the old couple to empty the water and clean the bath but instead he would clean up and not put them to any trouble. When he had dried himself and put his clothes back on he went upstairs to his bedroom thanking them both on his way through.

The old lady got up and went to the scrub area expecting at least thirty minutes of work to clean up after him. However, she found it as clean as it was before he went in. So after standing confused for a few seconds she went back in and told her husband, who just shrugged his shoulder with no answer.

Feeling refreshed and alive the sniper went again down the stairs but this time he went out into the back garden to get some natural light and rest. As he sat there with the sun above, his mind was becoming ever stronger and thought, yes, he would do what his inner conscious was now calling him to do. He also thought about what people have called him all these many years. They all called him the sniper or snipe for short but his real name was Ricardo and he wasn't French as they all thought, he was Italian. He was born and brought up in a little village called Pinerolo near the French border. His parents were poor and had both died early of consumption. He was regarded as a scrag end kid with no future and so decided to join the Army becoming a superb marksman, at long distance. When he left the services his ability for quiet killing became known to the rich and he never disappointed. They had paid him well, especially the French with their big ego's and hatred of anything English, specifically their Queen.

Sarah was standing at the back door silently watching him from behind. She stood there thinking how she would kill him and get him out of the way. He was now useless and as Peter the Frenchman put it, a waste of space. She would think on it for now and then walked over to him. "Hello Snipe, how are you?" He looked up startled at the voice as he had not heard anyone approach and now seeing Sarah by his side surprised him as she has not been here for a few days. For some reason, he felt fidgety at her presence but never the less was very polite in his response. "I am feeling much better thank you Sarah, how are you?"

Sarah noticed he was indeed looking very well. His ageing had somehow reversed itself and his eyes were bright and alive. The only thing she did see that was the same was his loss of arm but he had folded and fastened his tunic sleeve tight across his chest and it looked very smart.

They chatted a brief while and then Sarah made her excuses to leave him in peace to enjoy the fresh air and promised to come back later tonight and make him his favourite supper of rabbit stew with big dumplings. "Thank you Sarah, you are most kind, I shall look forward to it." "I will bring it up on tray specially and you can have it in bed."

Sarah went back into the house and spoke to the old couple and after nodding their agreement saw her out of the front door. Ricardo was still in the garden thinking on Sarah's visit as he knew her well, very well. He decided, for some reason, to check on his horse which was stabling in the field directly behind the garden fence.

Getting back into her own house, Sarah made ready. She quickly stoked the fire and hung the big pot of water over the spit. She then went into the scrub area to find the little box hidden away behind the wall and on taking out a portion of the deadly nightly shade, both root and flower, she smiled.

As she was busily stirring the stew her mind went on to the traitors, Zoe and Jacques. After what she had been told by the sniper she thought that Zoe would have returned by now with or without Jacques. But, it is what it is and would deal with them after she had dealt with the useless Sniper.

As the day grew older the sniper had retired to his bedroom but not before thanking the old couple for their kindness and hospitality.

At around eight o clock, Sarah knocked and walked straight in through the back door with a large pot of stew in hand and found the old couple sitting together talking. Putting the stew pot on the table the old couple got the bowls and bread ready. ''Thank you Sarah, me and my husband do love a nice stew.'' With a sweet voice, Sarah replied, ''My pleasure, I enjoyed making it for you; it makes me feel nice inside too. Now both of you take what you will and I will then take a bowl up for our wounded colleague, bless him.''

The old couple took their share and Sarah, with the snipers filled bowl on the tray went upstairs. As she got a few steps from the top she bent forward and put the tray down on the landing floor and taking out the small sachet emptied its contents into the stew. After carefully stirring it in, making sure not to disturb her lovely fluffy dumplings, she stood up and composed herself. Feeling a real sense of excitement and power she walked on and without knocking entered the sniper's bedroom.

In her best girly voice of innocence she said, "Good evening Snipe, your favourite food is made ready for you. "Good evening Sarah, thank you, I am looking forward to it and sat himself up ready." Sarah moved to his bed and laid the tray on his lap. "Would you like me to feed you," she said. "No, I am fine thank you but please could you put the napkin around me, if you don't mind, I am still getting used to only having one arm," Sarah, did as asked with noted gentleness but once again, she couldn't help but notice and wonder at his new polite and considerate way of talking. "Now," she said, "I will go down and keep the old couple company while you enjoy your meal in peace, I will be back in a while to tuck you in and take the dish away." "Thank you, you are most kind." Sarah had absolutely no intention of coming back at all, not for this soon to be dead one armed useless prat. How she lured people to her traps of death made her most proud.

When Sarah closed the door behind her, Ricardo looked at the dish of stew. Smelling delicious and himself being very hungry he quickly picked up the spoon and as he did, he started bursting for a wee. He tried to hold it in but there was no way and he didn't want to spoil the meal by getting half way through and then was forced to get up, so grudgingly using his left hand he slid the tray to one side and got out of bed and walked to the pee pot in the corner.

Downstairs, Sarah made her goodbyes and said she would be back tomorrow to fetch the pot and dishes. "Thank you Sarah, the stew is very nice." Sarah smiled and nodded her head but didn't reply and shut the door rather sharply."

As Ricardo peed in the pot with a feeling of great relief, three butterflies in the corner of the window ledge flapped their wings at the twenty aged fly's which were all waiting by their side. The fly's, who have all lived their lives to the full, understood the butterfly's message and flew straight to the bowl of rabbit stew. Ricardo saw the fly's in the corner of his eye but thought nothing of it and just carried on.

Ricardo, in just his pants, finished his peeing and got back into bed. Gently sliding the tray back into position with his one hand he picked up the spoon. It was then that the three butterflies flew around his face which made him stop in mid tracks. With spoon in his left hand, he reacted by trying to wave them away with his right, but he had no right arm. So he put the spoon into the bowl and as he did, saw with concern, a lot of flies floating on top of the stew, all dead.

This was the second time that butterflies had got into his life at critical moments. He looked down again at the stew and with care and calm moved the spoon around and sifted a little food up with a few dead flies mixed in. He lifted the spoon to his nose and smelt. There was a strange odour but what it was he couldn't tell. He put the spoon back into the stew and raised it again to his nose. This time, he began to smell more gently over a longer period. After a minute or so of doing this an ever so light fruit berry fragrance started to come through. Being a man of death he knew only one odour that smelt of berry fruit and strong enough to come through all the herbs, meat and dumplings, 'Deadly Night Shade.' The bitch he thought. He put the spoon back in the stew and started to gently touch each fly in turn for a sign of life. He counted them one by one and got to twenty and none moved as all of them were dead.

He looked around for the butterflies but, they had flown out of the small opened top window. He sat still in his bed with utter confusion trying to work out what best to do. He could ignore all and just eat the stew set in front of him, flies and all, and most likely be dead within minutes. He looked at his right shoulder and the emptiness of an arm that should be attached and thought, yes, eat it, eat it all, why not. But then thought why someone would do this to him, why, he thought. Not only why but who. Then he realised that when you are so full of your own ego and self-worth, you miss things, and with deep thought, he looked back and put himself into his employer's position, Peter the Frenchman. What would he do if an expensive employee had become useless and getting in the way through injury of the team's success? With those cold thoughts, the dawn of reality came into his brain. He had also, through his own self righteousness and confidence, forgotten the deadly ways in which Sarah works and the very blind fact that she too works for that bastard Peter, the Frenchman. He then laughed aloud at his naivety and near fatal error.

He then got serious and took stock. He looked up to the heavens and said in a most humble way, ''Whoever you are, wherever you are, thank you for looking after me. I know deep inside what you have wished of me all my life but I have been too afraid to do it, afraid of being looked at as a weakling and feeling ashamed of leading a simple caring life like my good Mother and Father.''

His only thought now was to get away and quickly before Sarah got back. Getting dressed and his things together he went to the corner of the room and knelt down. Gently prizing the floorboard up, he reached down and withdrew his cash tin and on opening it up he checked his life savings and was grateful he had saved when he could. There was enough to do what he now knew for sure what he wanted to do.

With all things packed he walked out and down the stairs. On reaching the bottom he nodded to the old couple and walked out the back door without a word. He went through the garden out into the open field where he called his horse. When the loyal animal came to him Ricardo jumped on his bare back and rode away to his new life. He was going to set up a night shelter and food charity for the village poor at wherever the Lord took him. Forty three lives he had taken from this earth and so forty three poor lives he would help for the rest of his life in repentance and, he felt good.

Chapter 39

Peter and Alfred, the Spaniard, were awaiting the presence of sub officer, Johan Prideaux. The Moonshine had docked over a week ago in the port of Brest thirty miles south west of Morlaix and, Prideaux had been trailed ever since.

Since the time the ship had docked, Prideaux had been in most of the Inns about the port drinking much wine and, whoring. Being a young middle aged sub officer made him think he was a good catch for the girls. He was single and had no children so he could do what he wants. As he was sleeping soundly one early morning with another unknown woman next to him, the door to his room opened and three burly men walked in carrying pick handles.

One of the men stayed by the door as the other two went by the bed. The young whore awoke and looking terrified was quietly told to be quiet, say nothing and get out which she duly did. Prideaux was oblivious to it all and stayed fast asleep. They poked him with the pick handles and when he too awoke was informed, "Prideaux, get dressed, you are to come with us, some people want to talk with you." Blurry eyed and with a hangover he got the picture and thought, O dear what has he done, what has he done wrong now and who the bloody hell wants to talk with him at this time of the morning. Giving no resistance, Prideaux was taken out and put into the carriage and the men said nothing. Their job was simply to bring him to Morlaix for questioning.

Prideaux just sat nervously thinking that all had been good, these last days, he had been happy and hurt no one so what was all this about. It was that bloody Zoe, that's what it is and that bloody nutter who banged him over the head in the latrine at Mousehole. It can't be he thought, someone has got something wrong and he will talk to his Captain about it, yes that's what he will do, talk with his captain as soon as he could about all this.

Around mid-day and being held with his arms behind his back he stood outside a door at the back of the Morlaix Inn. One of the guards knocked and was told to enter and when he came out told the two men holding Prideaux to take him in and sit down. ''Thank you gentlemen,'' Peter said, ''You may leave us now but please don't go too far.''

''Good afternoon Johan, do you know who we are?'' The Spaniard, sitting next to Peter sat quiet and listened. Their questioning was as always very good and knew that they would get what they wanted one way or another. Prideaux did not need to hold back, he had done nothing wrong and gave all that was asked. ''Just one last question and then we are done, when do you sail for Mousehole?'' ''We sail at high tide tomorrow night.'' ''Thank you Johan, you have been very helpful and will inform you're good Captain, you may even get a promotion.'' With total surprise, Johan said, ''The Captain of the Moonshine is coming here?'' ''Yes, did you not know that, we do apologise, your Captain is on route as we talk.'' Indeed, this was true as Peter had sent a secret message a few days back to ask, under the Crown's security provisions, that he was to make himself known this very day at five o clock and, the message was answered to the positive.

Johan confirmed to Peter and Alfred what they had thought was going to happen. It was the timing and location which they did not know, but now they did. Prideaux had done what they thought he would and apart from him doing one more thing, would be of no more use. The information had fitted well and with some minor adjustments, their plan of action would work. It was now time to let Johan go back to Brest, to drink and whore as he did best and then await the Captain's arrival. They would ask him, with some personal reward if wanted, for his assistance to defend the Glorious crown of our good King Louis X1V, his loyal Princes, and to help rid France of its traitors. Things were looking good.

Chapter 40

It had been well over a week now since Zoe and Jacques had first slept together in the woods, a few miles outside of the port town of Mousehole. Their minimum food supply had run out quickly within only a few days. Zoe wanted to return to Falmouth to her good friends Sarah's place so both could get warmed and cleaned but Jacques suggested they should wait a while longer before doing anything.

Arc, Arthur and Jeanne's horse were laid deeper into the forest and seemed to be doing well off the grass and leaves. Jacques however was starving and so laid traps in the night to catch a rabbit. Zoe said again that if they go to Sarah's house then this entire trapping and silent living lark would be over and done with. Jacques was starting to be tempted to do as Zoe asked but, after catching his first rabbit, knew that leaving the safety of the forest at this time before the Moonshine's next docking would be wrong.

He had to explain to Zoe in simple terms that this was not a game, it was serious. While they had been in the forest no one had come near or seen them, they were safe. Leaving the forest, to a warm house in Falmouth, would induce risk, a risk they need not take and for her to please understand his experience in survival. They had already lasted twelve days and only now need last until the day after tomorrow when they would both meet Johan and the Moonshine and get away. Both lying under the blanket Zoe asked, "When we get away what will we do Jacques, will you stay with me?" "Zoe, my sweetness, for some reason our lives have always intertwined, even though hundreds of miles had lay between us. You loved

Jon and I loved Jeanne. However, for reasons I know not, these have been taken away from us through maybe our treasonable ways." "Jacques, don't say that we were not traitors." "Jacques lowered his voice and in a sympathetic guilt conscious tone said, "Yes we were Zoe." Zoe started to sob while Jacques just stared up at the big trees around their little camp. He thought of Jeanne but knew that life was gone and asked the heavens to look after her. "Zoe, what we have done, is done and the clock cannot be turned back, we will get through this and when we get to France we will flee and find a remote place to live and I will not leave you, I promise." Zoe cuddled in closer to him and although they had dearly loved others in their past lives, they had now to love and look after each other for their very own lives depended on it. "I promise you also Jacques, Zoe replied."

Jacques also cuddled Zoe a little tighter in response to her promise to him and said, "Right, now let us both get to sleep as we have only more one full day here and must get ourselves prepared for our new lives in France.

Chapter 41

"So Peter, do you think the Captain will abide by what we agreed?" "I believe he most definitely will, he has all to lose and all to gain, his very work and way of life depends on his cooperating with us. He may not be under direct orders of our wondrous Navy, but he is a merchant of the sea to our great Country. If he does not cooperate he will not only lose his ship, he will lose his head." They both laughed out loud at their successful ways of manipulating people with or without the power or authority, it was all the same to them. Some lies mixed with truths equals enough doubt to get what they want.

On leaving their room and going down to the bar area they both turned their heads to the front door as a message boy came running into the Morlaix Inn, heading directly toward their table. When the boy got to the table he stood still and upright as he had been trained but was still puffing and panting after running all the way from the town's message office. Then bowing his head said, "Excuse me please but I have a message for Monsieur Peter." "That's me, thank you boy." As the young boy handed over the message he was told to go to the corner and wait as a reply may be needed. Peter eased himself back and opened it knowing the hand writing to be Sarah's.

Peter,
Snipe is gone to the Lord.
Z & J not returned.
Love Sarah. xxx

After reading the short message Peter smiled inwardly with content and then handed it over to Alfred to read.

When he too had read it Alfred looked up at Peter and said, "So, the Snipe is no more, that's sad, job well done I think." "I think you are quite right, and on this news, I think we deserve a good drink my friend," "She is good that one Peter, very good, I wonder how she did it?" "I have no idea and don't care, all I know is that he is dead as we wanted, out of the way completely, and that is good news."

What they didn't know is that Sarah had lied to save her own skin as she had no idea where he had gone. When she went up to his bedroom she expected to see him lying in his bed, dead as a door nail, and then she would scream like a terrified girl, knowing not what to do. However, what she saw was the bedroom cold and vacant and the plate of stew empty and washed cleaned on the tray with a note under the spoon.

Sarah,
I am finished with this way of life.
One day you may see the light.
Love Ricardo. x

'Finished and may see the bloody light,' what is this man doing, what is he on. She also noted his real name. Ricardo, that's not French either she thought. Did he eat the stew or not? If he did he would be dead, here in the bed and if he did not, why not. She had used the deadly nightshade to kill three times before. One was a stupid old lady and two were strong young men and all had died within the hour of eating. She tried to work things out but stopped herself from assuming and thought the positive in that he was now gone, that's it, that's all that mattered. She didn't care either way so long as they didn't get to know, and they wouldn't because she wouldn't tell them. However, as ordered, she had to message Peter telling him straight away when the deed of killing him had been done. She decided to add the honest truth and mention that also Zoe and Jacques had not returned which should take away any heat of deep thought on the snipe. Clever little thing she thought to herself.

Peter called to the boy over in the corner and asked him to fetch note paper and scribe as he wanted to reply to Sarah.

As the message boy went to fetch things, Alfred said, "What about Zoe and Jacques not returning to Falmouth?" Peter, with a fresh glass of cognac in hand, was calm in his answer. "Well, we both thought they would do, that is true, which would have made things a lot easier for us both. But now we have Prideaux and the Captain, and also our own men aboard the Moonshine, I am sure we will get them both in one swoop. The way Prideaux talked about the traitors I do feel it is really their only route out at this time. Anyway, we will soon know my friend as it won't be long now before the ship will be at Mousehole ready for docking

The Moonshine, through turbulent seas, had indeed crossed the channel and arrived at the mouth of Mousehole the very next evening but due to customs, the ship could not dock till the morning tide. So with the anchors down all waited on board for sun up. Once the ship had docked Peter's men, went over the plan once again and then got themselves into position. They had kept a low profile and posed as a team of builders on their way to discuss the harbour expansion at nearby Penzance. Only the Captain knew who they were.

Prideaux had not slept at all well these last two nights and was very anxious on what to do for the best. He knew that Jacques, and possibly Zoe, would soon turn up and so had stayed in his cabin thinking things over. One thing Jacques had said was not to divulge their secret signal to anyone. If he raised his right hand and scratched his chin would mean that all was well and for Jacques and Zoe to come aboard. If he used his left hand that would mean danger is about and for them to get away. He started biting his thumb nail with nerves in trying to work it out. If he did the right hand signal both Jacques and Zoe would be captured and, if he did the left hand, they could get away. He could then plead his innocence in that he had acted accordingly as ordered as no one else knew the signal except Jacques. He decided that whatever he did he would do it after a stiff cognac to calm his nerves. He owed neither party anything it was purely down to his gut feeling and living for the rest of his life knowing he had betrayed a friend or he had been loyal to others he knew not. On the other side of the coin, he owed Jacques nothing.

Jacques had left the forest late that evening and after tying his horse to a tree not too far out from the town walked in casually, getting to the harbour at midnight. The town was empty apart from the taverns in which he could hear loud singing coming from within. Staying back in the shadows he looked across to the harbour area but the Moonshine wasn't docked as he thought it would be. Then looking further out saw it anchored just out from the walls of the harbour, presumably waiting for customs checks and high tide. This means the ship should dock early morning. He smiled with an inner feeling of relief, turned himself about and headed back to his horse and Zoe. They must get themselves prepared and ready.

Zoe smiled and hugged Jacques with the good news. "At last," she said. "Yes, this day we are away," Jacques replied and started to pack most things there and then ready for a quick off. Jacques suggested they get there around midday when the harbour would be at its busiest with the loading and unloading of cargo and prayed that Johan would be there.

As the early morning grew into late morning, Zoe and Jacques were now ready to leave the safety of the forest. It was only a short ride in and Jacques did not want to be exposed for longer than necessary. Leaving Jeanne's horse behind, Zoe jumped on her stallion, Arthur, and Jacques did the same on his own trusted stead, Arc.

They paid the stable boy to look after both horses knowing they had no intentions of coming back and then offering his arm out to Zoe walked off as good husbands and wives do with Zoe on his left. When the harbour came into view they stopped by a corner of a building and waited. They were now at a point of no return and seeing the Moonshine on the dock they looked for Johan.

Johan had made a decision. Right or wrong his mind was made but then kept saying quietly, may it be the right one. Leaving his simple cabin he walked up on deck and went to the ship's side and leaned on the railing looking across the harbour for Jacques. He put both his hands tight around the wooden rail and held his body completely still. When he catches sight of Jacques, and Jacques him, the hand he puts up to his face must be decisive and clear for Jacques to understand the message given.

After looking around a few times over the dock area they both sighted one another. Zoe saw him too and squeezed Jacque's arm tighter. Johan looked around to see if anybody was watching and when he felt comfortable that no one was turned his head back and looked straight at Jacque's face. After a few seconds of complete stillness, Johan then lifted his left arm and rubbed the left side of his temple as like easing the pain of a hangover and then ever, ever so slowly turned his head from side to side. Johan had decided, for better or worse, to help his friend with the truth that things were not good, and for him to get away. Hopefully, Johan could worm his way out of any questions that came his way on why Jacques and Zoe did not come forward to the ship.

"O no," Jacques said aloud, and then just as he tried to turn himself and Zoe about to get away he felt the pistol in his back. "Stay where you are," the man said with a deep voice and with strong hands, took hold of his shoulder. The trap had been set and Jacques and Zoe had walked straight into it. Without fear or hesitation, Jacques whipped his head back and pushed his body against the strong hand holding his shoulder while twisting his body to the right at the same time. In the same flowing motion, his right elbow thumped into the man's head. Jacques had practised this technique many times in training. As his initial defensive movement finished Jacques continued the flow by dropping his body to the ground while his left, now released from Zoe's arm, pulled out his pistol. However, the man's orders were very simple, to take both persons dead or alive, no matter. The man, taken by total surprise at Jacque's instant defence movement had hesitated ever so slightly before pulling the trigger. But Jacque's backward twisting motion had moved the pistol barrel and the shot deflected to the left. With both men now falling back onto each other Zoe, standing still in utter confusion took the full hit. Jacques didn't get off free as the hot ball had clipped his left side. Zoë screamed with pain as the shot pierced her body. Horrified, she looked down and could see blood gushing out from the front right side of her stomach. She put both her hands on the entry hole to stop the flow but dizziness quickly came and she fell to the ground.

Johan saw it all happen as he stood aboard the Moonshine so quickly got himself away back into his cabin. He wanted nothing to do with it, nothing.

Jacques was in complete survival mode and nothing would stop him. His actions of escape continued. He flattened the man's back onto the ground and then rolled himself around keeping the man tight to his own body as he could. Jacques then managed to nudge his own pistol into the man's gut and pulled the trigger. In an instant and without any wait after firing, Jacques released his hold and sprinted away as fast as he could, leaving both Zoe and the man on the floor dying.

As the commotion escalated so did the onlookers, all fearing that a riot was about to take place. But then after Jacques had run away and things had become quieter with only the two bodies on the floor, people started to creep forward.

The small team of men posing as builders and who had come over with the Moonshine on behalf of their employer, Peter the Frenchman, were not fazed in the least. They had considered Jacque's possible actions as he had not been successful in his profession by being a wimp and therefore took precautions. Hence once they were in their positions all had to be in sight of one another for support back up should it be needed. When they saw Jacques go into defence and escape mode the other men immediately quit their covert roles and ran to help. Although Jacques was quick at what he did, it did not deter the younger and fitter men of the team chasing after him up the street.

With all the commotion going on the constable of the small town was sitting easy at his desk by his sea view window when he heard the firing and shouting. It was his job to keep the peace and make sure Mousehole runs quietly so got up to see what was going on. He was now on new orders coming from the top with easier lines of communication in place. He knew not from who but things had changed in that any unrest, smuggling, theft or matters of the town's security, no matter how small or trivial, had to be reported without delay.

Joshua's open and frank meeting with Bull made him see things more clearly and so had reverted back to his old more positive self. His new orders sent to all the towns and villages within his total protection of authority, were not in any way dismissed and must be acted on with urgency. This new approach had gained him vital information. True, some were a waste of time and some stupid but that didn't matter, he was getting to grips with the ways and means of his territory. Names were especially useful. This is what he had been lacking, information, and had also sent word to the other two cells in Cornwall on this approach.

When news came in that a firing of pistols had taken place in the harbour town of Mousehole and that two people, one seriously wounded and one dead, were possibly French in origin, Joshua's eyes lit up and instantly went into action.

Chapter 42

"Let this day be a lesson to all Frenchman who betray their Country for their own gain. Traitors and Hypocrites who ignore and slander the very good and honest nature of our people will never go unpunished. Let us therefore rid our good Country of these poisoned locusts to protect our good citizens who without fear or moan, fight and protect our beloved France and our most gracious King, Louis X1V."

With a roaring cheer from all aboard the Moonshine, the Captain then nodded and the guillotine blade was released from its catch and, with sheer ice cold precision, swooped down and severed Johan Prideaux's head clean off.

The Captain then bowed his head and started to walk back to his cabin. "What shall we do with the body?" a man shouted. The Captain stopped in his tracks, turned himself about and shouted back with authority, "Throw both head and body to the sharks, away from this fine ship and crew." With that, another cheer went up.

It was early next morning and although the Moonshine was now far out at sea it had not got away from the harbour without delay and suspicion. As the furore of the previous day's shooting had quietened, the authorities had taken over the area to find out what had exactly happened. Also, the two people lying on the ground who had been shot had been taken to the back room of the Smugglers Inn.

The woman who had been shot was in a critical condition and so a physician was called but the man was dead and so nothing could be done except call the local priest to do his work. On checking their clothes and pockets things became evident that these two people were not Cornish. They had French under clothes and most of their personal belongings were French related, such as jewellery, monies and some writings. The constable, on putting two and two together, realised these people could have come from the one French ship in the port called the Moonshine. Without further ado, he ordered the Harbour Master to impound the said ship until he had further orders to the contrary. The Captain of the Moonshine, on being informed of the order of impound was not happy but had no jurisdiction to argue and simply had to abide. All loading and unloading were forbidden.

Jacques had run for his life up the street heading directly for the town's open stable yard where he could get Arc and flee. However, the three men chasing were quicker and stronger and were gaining ground on him. Normal people passing by were trying to get out of the way of these thugs. One of the chasers then stopped, took aim and fired. The hot ball hit Jacques in the leg which made him stumble forward to the ground. The two other men who were still running at pace then quickly jumped on him and dragged him aside. The people around saw what was happening but again did not want to be involved. Once Jacques was held firmly they got his arms behind his back and hand cuffed him. Jacques could do nothing; he was trapped like a broken rabbit. With one of the men's feet on his head and his body held face down to the filthy ground the man spoke up, ''You run fast, you traitor, but not fast enough.''

After patting their mate on the back for firing a good shot they dragged Jacques like a rag doll up the street into a side alley, out of sight. There they gagged him and waited as one of the men went to fetch the horses. With all the noise and commotion that had gone on, there was no way they could safely walk back through the open town to the ship lying at the dockside. They also didn't have much time so there was only one option and that was to use the planned back up route of escape. When the four horses came by the two men kicked Jacques up off the ground. As they pushed him to a horse he fell down due to the shot wound but that was simply of no concern to the three men and was told to get up. When he did as told all three then grabbed him and threw him on a horse like a sack of potatoes and strapped him down tightly. When the tying down was done they all mounted their horses and galloped off at pace. They were off to a secluded cove just over the next rocky inlet where a fifth team member was hiding the small boat of sail. Their aim was to get Jacques off the Cornish coast and meet the Moonshine in deeper seas.

As the Moonshine had been impounded pending a search, the men with Jacques in the small boat decided that to wait where they were so close to Mousehole was just too risky. They all agreed that a local search party would be made and sent out to find them, so with haste they set sail out into the safety of the open ocean to wait it out.

It would not be until the next high tide that the Moonshine would be allowed to weigh its anchor. The authorities had checked over the ship with fine detail and questioned the Captain and the crew but found nothing. Only one person not to be questioned was Johan Prideaux, who was locked and gagged in a secret cavity way down in the ship's hold.

The constable of the town was also very much aware that the ships loaded cargo of fresh pilchards was gained from the hard work of the locals who had yet to be paid. It was a double edged sword and only after Joshua had arrived that the order was given for the ship's release. Once the ship had weighed anchor it had taken many hours before she was in clear and deep enough water away from the Cornish coast to shoot the flares up. The men in the small sail boat, cold and drifting aimlessly, saw the flares in the sky and turned the small sail to meet her out in the deep open sea.

When the small sailing vessel bumped into the Moonshine the ropes were thrown down and all the men climbed up aboard. Jacques was escorted to the ship's physician and after a little treatment was then taken away and thrown in the brig. It was then, with the Captain now happy having got his man that he gave the order for the traitor Prideaux to be brought up and executed. Johan was also whipped before having his head sliced off in front of a delighted crew. After Johan's decapitated body was thrown into the sea, the Captain then shouted for full sail so as to waste no more time sailing to Brest. Once there, he could then rid the Moonshine of the other traitor called Jacques and get his cash reward.

Chapter 43

Before the Moonshine had departed from the dockside at Mousehole, Joshua had arrived at pace on his trusted steed, Harry. "Good to see you Joshua, thank you for coming." "No, thank you Constable, very interesting message, what have we got?" Joshua went with the Constable to the front room of The Smugglers and was given an in depth briefing on what had happened.

Joshua took control and started to manage as he saw best. The first thing he wanted to see was the two people who had been shot. The Constable led the way to an old room at the very back of the Inn. On entering Joshua noted that a physician was working on one of the two people. The other was simply covered over in a white sheet. Joshua went to the physician's side and after acknowledging one another turned to look at the patient.

He was stunned with utter shock and stood open mouthed at the woman he knew as Zoe, the very woman who had helped save Jeanne from that nasty Philip de Albret and his pup Bouchier. Of all the people it could have been. Zoe, why he thought, and what the bloody hell was she doing here? Joshua noted how at peace she looked and although unconscious her breathing was steady. Joshua looked at the physician and asked his opinion of her state. "I am sorry to say that the lead ball is still in her lower abdomen and I am reluctant to remove it due to her being so weak." "And her chances of survival are?" "Not good, I am afraid, probably two to three days at the most, if that."

Joshua nodded at the clear appraisal and then went over to the table in the corner where the other person's body

273

was lying. His mind was racing, if that was Zoe, then the other person must be Jacques. It made sense, it all fitted, that's why he left Marazion so quickly. Getting to the body he lifted back the cover sheet and stared at a person's face he simply did not recognise at all. It was that of a younger man who was physical in body and had light hair. With full respect to the family of whoever this man was Joshua gently replaced the sheet back over him.

Both Joshua and the Constable then went out of the room to the front of the Inn to talk. Joshua wrote messages to be dispatched immediately, one to Doctor Smith and one to his man, Bull. He needed to get Zoe away quickly to a safer place that he knew. He also knew it would be many hours before Smith and Bull would arrive but at least it gave him time to think, walk about and give sanction to the Constable and his men to search the Moonshine.

It wasn't till much later that Bull and the Doctor eventually showed up and, after Joshua explained the situation, Doctor Smith went in to take over from the present physician with one objective in mind, to keep her alive. Bull and a couple of his men were to make good and organise getting Zoe to the safe cottage at Marazion. Joshua was only thinking a week ago that he would sell the cottage at Marazion due to Jeanne retiring and move all to Sennen. However, this was the second time Marazion had become useful due to its closer location to Mousehole or Penzance so maybe he should close and sell the Sennen Farm instead. Whatever he chooses now was not the right time to do it.

Joshua wanted to be in the cottage as quick as he could but it needed to be warmed up first as insisted by Doctor Smith. The place had been empty for a few days now since Jeanne had left, wanting to get away from it all and get on with her new life. Rebecca was at the cottage in Gunwalloe and Jeanne was living in a hotel in Helston called the Seven Stars, waiting to move into her new little cottage she had just purchased in Lady Street.

So it was up to Joshua to get there and sort things but before he left the town he wanted to make sure that all was being done as he had asked. Meeting the Constable again later that afternoon they went over what had been done and what was needed to be done. The Constable assured him that the Moonshine had been thoroughly checked over and was clean and really nothing could be gained from keeping it in the dock. However, one piece of news had come in from one of the town's open field stable boys in that two stallions had been left overnight and the owners have not returned and the boy is afraid of what to do.

Joshua thought about his timings for the rest of the day but felt he needed to take a look. "Two stallions you say." "Yes, that's what the boy said." Where is the field?" "It's the one as you come into the town on the right." Joshua thought about it for a while and said, "Well, I do have to get going but this sounds very interesting and it wouldn't take long, I could have a look on my way out, would you have time to escort me?" "Yes of course Joshua, with pleasure." "That's good, thank you, then let's get going."

When they reached the field they saw the little boy waving his hands at them so went directly to him. The boy said what had happened and then escorted them to the covered night shelter just off the way. Getting up close to the two horses Joshua didn't recognise the first one but definitely knew the second, it was Arc, Jacque's trusted steed. Both horses were saddled ready to go and what seemed like fully loaded saddle bags too. Joshua thanked the little boy and said he could be excused then rummaged through the bags attached to Arc. Joshua pulled out all sorts of things that people would take on a journey such as underwear, shirts, socks and also some gunpowder and shot. This was indeed Jacque's things. Putting all things back he then went over to the other horse and did the same. This time it was all women's things relating very close as being from no other than Zoe. It had to be, there was no other logical answer.

Joshua suggested that both horses go with him for now and asked they be tied to his own horse, Harry. He really did need to get to the cottage and prepare things for the injured Zoe's arrival. "Thank you for your help Constable, you've done good work, please carry on with a full search of the area but please be careful as the man who I think is at large here is very capable and armed." "Thank you Joshua, we will get on with it with urgency."

Joshua rode off with the two horses tied behind. He also decided to get word to Rebecca at Gunwalloe to ask that she come as quickly as possible to the cottage at Marazion as he needs her help.

All had gone to plan and Zoe had been safely taken away from Mousehole and was now in a warm bed being cared for by Rebecca. Doctor Smith had done what he could for Zoe but had to agree with the previous Physician that she did not have long and he could do no more for her. "Are you sure Doctor, are you sure?" Joshua asked. "Yes Joshua, I am sure." The Doctor then asked to be relieved from her care so he could carry on his practice.

Sitting down with Bull, Joshua said, "I don't like this at all, it seems that while I have been dithering around Cornwall trying to manage all things, a plot has been going on right under my nose." "Joshua, a plot or plots are always going on around here; it's what we do about it that counts." "Bull, I would like you to send your best man with messages to our Bedruthan and Mevagissey friends. I will also write to Kernow, he will be particularly interested in the person with have here." As they were talking a knock on the door came with a message from the Constable. A lone horse has been found tied to a tree in the small forest on the outskirts of Mousehole. Joshua asked Bull if he could sort this and report back. Joshua left now to his own thoughts, got up and went to make some tea for both himself and Rebecca.

As he entered the bedroom with the tea tray in hand Rebecca turned to him and said, "Joshua, I am glad you have come she keeps mumbling but I cannot understand." "What sort of things is she mumbling." "That's what I said Joshua, I can't understand, I suggest you get ink and paper quickly." With that, Joshua went out and fetched all as asked and then could scribble things down as he heard them.

It was now well past the midnight hour as Zoë drifted in and out of consciousness. When she murmured something, Joshua scribbled it down and if it didn't make sense, which was most of the time, they would answer back in reflection what they thought they heard as for Zoe to repeat.

The words that kept getting mostly repeated from Zoe were names such as Jon, Jacques and Sarah. Joshua picked up on the name Sarah as she would always add the word 'friend.' With Zoe being a French woman and not Cornish, Joshua picked up on this and so started the slow process of finding who this woman was, who knew Zoe close enough as to be called a friend.

It wasn't until the early morning that Joshua pieced together with methodical repetition the words spoken in a mumbled way from Zoe. Rebecca had said a few times to let Zoe be and Joshua understood her reasons for saying so but he had no choice. Zoe's breathing was now very shallow and he knew she was in the dying process and it was only a matter of time, so with respect to Zoe and Rebecca, Joshua got up and left the room.

Leaving Rebecca alone with Zoe, Joshua went into the main living area and threw a few logs on the fire. Sitting down in the candle light he went over the notes and scribbles he had written down.

'Jon, love of her life. Jacques, help, help me, Sarah, friend, my friend, Prideaux, Arthur, Sarah, Drakena Redge, twenty five, Falmouth, Albret, Bouchier.'

Some of the notes made sense and some did not but what took his eye was the address of Sarah. Every time Joshua asked for the name of the road where she lived, Zoe kept mumbling Drakena Redge which wasn't an English name but he had the town Falmouth and a number so that was good. Joshua started to yawn and so laid the paper on his lap, put his head back in the comfy chair and quietly went to sleep.

It wasn't until much later that morning that he felt someone nudging his arm. ''Joshua, Joshua,'' Rebecca said with a quiet voice. ''Yes my love, I am awake, what is it?''

"She has gone," she replied with sadness. "I am truly sorry Rebecca, I truly am." With that, he took Rebecca's hand and moved her close so they could cuddle each other with love. "Did you say a prayer for her my love." "Yes, I held her hand while she was going and asked the Lord to forgive all that she had done wrong and that he take her soul" "That's good Rebecca, she is also now with the love of her life, Jon, as she kept calling him, and that we have to be thankful."

Joshua held Rebecca for a long time then got up and put her in his place. He laid the blanket back over to keep her snug and for her to sleep on as he went in to see Zoe.

Pulling the sheet back from her face he noted her eyes were closed and she was without any more pain. He would now need to get the doctor back to process the body. He would also need to get word to Kernow that Zoe has passed away and find out what should be done with a women's body who is of French blood and of unknown address and, had one time been a danger to the Cornish people.

It wasn't long after that Bull entered and leaving Rebecca to sleep, both went outside to the horse Bull had got from the forest. "Yes Joshua, it's Jeanne's and it seemed very glad to see me." "Well I never, she will be pleased." "I also looked around the area for anything else which could be of interest and found a small burnt out fire as if someone had stayed for a short while." "Well done Bull, let's walk Arc over to Jeanne's horse in the stable; I am sure they will have missed each other. By the way Bull, I must tell you the sad news that Zoe died early this morning." "I am sorry Joshua but I have my own feelings about traitors who want to harm us Cornish, be it women or men." "I know Bull but I thought you should know." With horses reunited, Joshua lightened the conversation, "Bull, how well do you know Falmouth?" "Quite well, I have relatives there and drink in the Masons, why do you ask?" Joshua showed Bull his scribbles on the note paper and said, "It's the Drakena address that bothers me." Bull took the paper of scribbles and started to repeat the word Drakena over and over, 'Drakena, Drakana, Dradeana,' but it didn't make sense. He then closed his eyes and spoke them again softly aloud but this time stretching the words while Joshua looked at him strangely, then he got it. "It's not Drakena Redge Joshua, it's Dracaena Ridge, up on the slopes as you go into Falmouth on the left. They were built five years ago and I remember there was uproar from the gentry as the houses were sold with no ground rent for the first time ever." "Really, that's good. So now we need to get some men over there as quickly as we can to give covert surveillance. But Bull, I have learnt dearly from this close observation work, as you know with Rebecca getting hurt, so this time before we go charging in, we need to know who owns Twenty five, which legal Company administered the contracts and more importantly trace any census reports on the occupants."

"By the way Joshua, on a different note, have you any news on that bloody Hosking's?" "None, have heard nothing. I have put messages out with facial sketches of both him and Jacques to all port authorities in Cornwall and have heard nothing. It seems they have just vanished from the Earth." "I don't like it Joshua." "Neither do I Bull, we must be alert. Now let us haste to Falmouth and sort this so called good friend of Zoe's out."

Chapter 44

Henry was struggling that was for sure but he had no other choice. He had weighed it all up from all sides of the argument and kept coming back to the same conclusion. The plan he had devised was risky but, if it could be done, he would get what his heart and life desires. He knew he had secret information that could be very useful to certain people who had the resources he needed and if they were willing to trade, then he would give them all he knew. He had nothing to lose. If he wanted Jeanne, he had to. If he wanted that bastard Jacques wiped out, he had to and if he wanted to stay alive without further savagery to his head, he had to.

Getting away from the asylum was the first step to start his mission. His mind was made up. They had thrown him on the rubbish tip and knew he was nothing to them anymore, nothing. 'Well, they can all kiss my backside,' he said aloud and started to laugh at the very thought of it.

He had watched for many days the routine of the medics and guards and noted their weak spot was around two in the morning. He also noted to his surprise that not one of them was armed except with pathetic clip boards.

Indeed the break out went as planned and he did not hold back by taking silly prisoners but swiftly wiping them out and then taking all, money, horses and food, enough to get where he wanted to go. They were simply not expecting anything like it and were very ill prepared. Once away he headed north to Bristol. He knew that when they got wind of his escape they would all expect him to go to Truro or somewhere in the south west. When

282

he reached Bristol his plan was to then change direction and ride to the very end of west Wales and catch the next ship to the busy port of Brest, Southern West France. Yes, that's what he would do.

All had gone well and he was now in his room sitting in a chair in a secluded Inn close to the town of Morlaix. He had been there for many days gaining good information from the local people. He then picked up the hand mirror to look at his head as he felt a trickle of fluid run down his face. What those bastards had done to him was nothing less than pure brutality. Picking up his cloth he then wiped away at the hole to dry the area once again. The wound itself was healing and the fluid escape was lessening by the day. His hair was also growing back and the large cavalier style hat helped much. Henry started to relax and sparked his pipe alight. His drinking habit had also improved but he still liked a strong brandy when he felt like it and so picked up the glass and gulped the large one back in one.

He would be going to the Chateau tomorrow after sending messages to say he had secret information which may prove useful. He had then waited in vain for more than two days thinking most of the time his messages were falling on deaf ears. But then on the third day, he received a reply stating that the very good Lady Antoinette is curious and would indeed like to meet. It was now or never, he thought. He would tell all and leave nothing out, he had nothing to lose. He heard constant rumours about this lady and the word is she was a ruthless bitch and wants revenge for her uncle's death to inherit the Chateau and the wealth that goes with it. This is exactly what he wanted to hear as he had what she wanted and he would give it to her, he didn't care, he will do what it takes to get what he wants, so trade it will be.

Arriving at the Chateau at the desired time, two men came out to meet him. They apologised but needed to search him first before he entered the building. Once they were happy he was clean the butler escorted Hosking into the library where he was to await Lady Antoinette's presence. He was nervous but tried not to let it show. After a few minutes of silence, the door opened and in she walked. Henry got up, bowed and said, ''Good morning my Lady.'' ''Good Mr Hosking's, please, call me Antoinette, and if you don't mind I will call you Henry as I think we may need to talk with a little more freedom of ease.'' Henry smiled and for some reason liked her gait and manner.

As they sat down opposite each they waited for the tea and biscuits to be served. ''I have asked for tea as I think you English like it for some reason.'' ''Thank you Antoinette, yes we do, but if you have a little cognac to go with it that would be nice too.'' Antoinette smiled and rang the bell. She was weighing him up and after her initial apprehension was now beginning to like his demeanour too.

When they were left on their own, Antoinette spoke, ''So tell me Henry, you say you have some information that may be useful which is good, but before you say anything, I think it would be wise for you to explain exactly why and what brings you here?'' ''Thank you my lady, I was hoping you would allow that and can assure you that what I say is the truth and trust you will in turn tell me why you find it of interest to meet me. Antoinette nodded her head but had heard men say this before and so was wary.

As Henry went into detail about his life and why he was there, she listened with intent and as the conversation went on, Antoinette herself opened up many times. Both parties had nothing to lose in talking and all to gain. As time went on Antoinette was intrigued and getting very interested in this man and suggested she order some food and more tea.

Although both were getting on well, each had fear of saying too much until Antoinette suggested as much. It was then that they both started to open up more freely going further into depth on particular issues and subjects. This refreshing approach gave a clearer insight into each other's ways and means and was also the fuse to a mutual friendly alliance.

"Henry, your timing in coming here is good as I have the important guest as I described coming here to see me in two days to further discuss this meeting of ours." "It would be good to meet him too but maybe we should all meet on a more neutral ground." "What's this Henry, you don't trust me, after all I have revealed to you this day?" Henry smiled but replied, "It's not you my lady Antoinette, I assure you, but I also have revealed much of myself this day, it's just a precaution." Antoinette smiled back, "Of course Henry, I'm sorry, I think it would be good for you to meet him." It wasn't till late afternoon that they both said their farewells.

With the butler called and showing Henry out, Antoinette sat back down in the comfy chair and smiled at the mirror hanging on the centre right of the main wall. Then after a few seconds had passed she heard the three light taps come from behind the mirror.

After nodding her head at the mirror where the three taps had come from, the secret door then opened and in stepped the Prince with a gleeful smile saying, ''Well done my dear, well done indeed.''

On sitting down in the still warm seat that Henry had been sat in, the Prince got himself comfortable as Antoinette said, ''So what do you think my Prince?'' ''I think it is a blessing come to us.'' ''I think that too, did you hear much?'' ''Yes, I heard and saw it all, the two way mirror and new sound holes work excellently.'' ''So, what are the next steps, my Prince.'' ''You have the message from The Frenchman, let me see it again.''

My Lady,
Good news, we have found the one you wish.
Will arrive Chateau Thursday morning.
Peter.

The Prince read the message twice in silence and weighed up its short contents.

''The Frenchman states that he has the person we want. I now have much doubt that this is correct after listening to our visitor this very day.'' ''So what are we to do?'' ''That is the question my dear Antoinette, that is the very question.'' With that, both fell silent.

The Prince handed the message back to Antoinette, and said, ''By the way, I am pleased to say that I have received yesterday a formal signed letter from my Father, our good King, confirming our increased status and worth, subject to us doing what he asks.'' ''That's really good my Prince, then the Chateau and titles will soon be mine.'' ''Yes, it will, but we must be mindful my little minx, my Father is no fool and if we happen to bring the wrong person, it may be our heads and not theirs on the block." They both laughed at the silliness of such thoughts.

After a brief pause of consideration the Prince continued, "I say it is of no small coincidence but a divine message from above that this Henry has come to us at this very moment. I think therefore we should arrange to meet him again before the meeting with the Frenchman, this coming Thursday."

Once again both fell silent. "Please pour me a drink would you my sweet Antoinette, I am in deep thought and wish to push further deeper." Antoinette got up and did as asked.

Taking a large sip of the best cognac, the Prince closed his eyes and then slowly reopened them with a new brightness of thought. "We are now getting very close to our rightful inheritance and feel this Henry man is our angel and key" "What do mean my Prince." "I mean, when we next meet him, we must be candid, frank and open. He has come at the precise time to help us in our hour of most need. We shall also find what he needs from us too." "As you heard him say himself, my Prince, he did many times mention the words, being thrown to the wolves, revenge, hatred and love." "And he has my sympathy, as I know them all very well. We shall work out a plan together to confirm or not if the Frenchman has indeed got the person we want." "And what if Peter hasn't got the right person and Henry has the information we need?" "Then Henry, our sent saviour, as I believe him to be, will release his knowledge to us and lead us to them.

It then would also become very clear that we have been fooled and led down the garden path by two crooks that have been out to swindle and cheat us from the very start. Should we find this to be the case then they will get my full vengeance. They know too much and we cannot have any fear of future blackmailing or suspicion hanging over our new lives of importance and wealth, so we will have to kill them both quickly and without trace. Not only then will we rid ourselves of two treacherous heathens but we will keep their massive bounty to ourselves in the process. Either way my dear we will soon know the truth and I will now send orders to my loyal guardsmen to get here quickly to aid us.''

Feeling the inner power of his authority, the Prince smiled broadly, puffed his chest and sat back with an aloofness of proud superiority. He then, with utter self-confidence said, ''Now, let us no more talk over these simple details, go on up to bed and make ready.'' ''My Prince, are you sure, it is still only early in the day.'' ''My dear Countess of Morlaix, I have a good feeling about this Henry person and am in a jolly feel. Time is of no concern to a man with a manly prowess like mine whom now wishes to show and make good his woman.'' Antoinette giggled at his so manly talk. ''Now on you go upstairs and I will be with you in a little while.'' As Antoinette closed the door behind her, the Prince felt into his jacket pocket and retrieved the small capsule, given to him by his old alchemist, then poured the substance into the brandy and drank the mixture down.

Chapter 45

It was late in the day when the Moonshine started to make her way into the dock at Brest harbour. Peter and Alfred were waiting by the window in a quiet room above the Harbour Inn. Although the ship had been delayed from exiting at Mousehole the wind had been kind so the delay was hours, not days. Peter had considered this possibility due to the situation that may occur when getting Jacques and Zoe onto the ship and out of Cornwall. They watched through the window at the progress of the ship but would not meet the Captain until darkness when all was quiet.

As mid evening approached and the moon had been shining in the night for two hours they heard the knock on the door.

After shaking hands they warmly invited the Captain to come on in and sit down. ''Would you like a drink,'' Peter asked. ''Yes I would, a large rum would do me well.'' The Captain had the seat looking out of the window and could see his ship the Moonshine standing proudly in the harbour against the full moon above. Once the drinks were poured they started the discussion.

The Captain went over in detail what had happened when they docked at Mousehole and how before exit his ship had been impounded and searched. ''Did you get Zoe and the traitor man Jacques,'' the Frenchman added, after getting a little anxious of waiting. ''We got the traitor but not Zoe, she was killed in a scuffle when your men went to snatch him.'' They couldn't have cared less for the bitch but were joyous on hearing that their main target had been caught. ''Where is he?'' ''He is in the brig in the

Moonshine, locked and chained." "And what about your sub lieutenant, Johan Prideaux, where is he?" "He is with the sharks as he rightly deserves, the traitor." "Well done Captain, you have done well and the people of France are very thankful." "Thank you too, so what of my reward?" "Yes, of course, we have it here, but first, we would like to see Jacques."

With the ship's cargo now unloaded most of the crew of the Moonshine had gone on shore leave and getting drunk in the local Inns so the ship was very quiet.

The Captain with a lantern in hand guided both Peter and Alfred down and down into the eerie depths of the ship. As they walked along the lower deck the Captain stopped and lifted the lantern to his right side where there was a large metal cage. "Here he is," as he shone the light on to a man sitting with his head down and his hands stretched up above his body, chained towards the back of the brig.

"Oi you, put your head up," the Captain shouted. Jacques didn't respond and sat motionless. Peter then said, "That's alright Captain, please could you open the door as I wish to go in," "Are you sure?" "Yes, I am sure, he is chained isn't he?" "Yes, he is." "Well then please open the door, I would like to talk with him."

Peter went into the cage but Alfred the Spaniard kept back outside along with the Captain. Peter went forward with caution then put out his hand under Jacque's chin and lifted his head up. What he saw was a man with eyes fully closed but was trying with difficulty to open them to see who or what was touching him. As their eyes met Peter took a step back in some form of defence as he could see the venom of hatred coming from the man's crystal, cold blue eyes. "My name is Peter, I am here to help you, are you the one called Jacques?"The prisoner didn't say anything but dropped his head back down. Once again Peter went over what he had just said and done but this time louder with more sincerity. After a few seconds of silence, he heard a small groan of a response saying, "I am." "That's good Jacques, then we will now take you away from this wet dungeon to somewhere which is more warm and dry as we need to talk."

As Peter walked out of the cage the Captain relocked the door. "Alright Captain, we are happy, let us now conclude our arrangement and gift you your well earned reward." When all was completed and the Captain's cash reward was handed over, Peter and Alfred walked off the Moonshine with an assured confidence and back to the Inn.

This time though they didn't go to their room but went to the bar to celebrate their victory with the finest cognac and maybe, just maybe, a whore to boot. It had been a long and difficult mission but they had succeeded. Now they only need to get the man Jacques back to Morlaix where they could question him further in preparation for their meeting at the Chateau. Thoughts of Zoe, Prideaux and one of their young men being killed didn't enter into minds at all. They were cold and ruthless and soon they were to be cold, ruthless and very rich.

Chapter 46

"Cup of tea Jacques or would you like something a little stronger?" The three of them were now in Peter's room at the Morlaix Inn. Jacques was shackled, arms bound behind his back and sitting on the floor with his back against the wall.

"Come on Jacques, what will it be, tea or cognac?" Jacques just kept quiet and looked down at his bare feet in disgrace to himself. Peter got up from his chair and walked over to the prisoner and lifting Jacque's head up with the blade of his knife said, in a more threatening manner, "what is it to be then?" Jacques stared into Peter's eyes and said simply "Cognac." "Good, now that wasn't so hard was it."

As Peter set the bottle back on to the table, Alfred then went over and picked Jacques up and helped him to the table to sit with them both. It was time to talk. Jacques had been here before, being questioned by ruthless people for their own gain. He had got away with it a couple of times in the past but somehow knew that he wouldn't this time. He was trying to work out who these two people were holding him captive, but his experience told him to be patient and they would reveal. He also knew that if he told the truth he may get, just may, get a chance.

Peter and Alfred were to meet the Lady of Morlaix in the morning and so it was extremely important to have all the information prior to that meet. They had all day and night if needed and would not rush. Now all were seated around the table, Alfred picked up the glass of cognac and put it to Jacque's lips to drink as they did not untie him. "How's the leg Jacques, it looked like you were hobbling?" "I believe it to be infected." "I thought I could smell something, O well, not to worry, we will get someone to have a quick look at it as soon as we can." "Thank you, that would be good."

"So, tell us Jacques, where are you from?" "Before I answer, please could you tell me if Zoe is here?" "She is not I am afraid, she is dead, killed in the scuffle with a pistol shot when you fought off one of my men in Mousehole." Jacque's head dropped down in total sadness. 'O my lord what have I done, what have I done,' he thought to himself.

After letting Jacques take a few minutes of Zoe's death to soak in, Peter asked the same question again, "So Jacques where are you from in France?"

Jacques breathed in deeply and raised his head and said, "I am from a small village called Pontivy, South of Brittany and I am not French, I am a Breton of the old Cornish." Peter was in a confident position and wanted all he could get from this man, the more information he could get, the more his reward. A Breton you say, of the Cornish, are you sure on that?" Jacque's head rose a little further, in the truth of pride on what he had just disclosed. He had never, ever, before mentioned this to anyone in his life, bar one person, his beloved Jeanne. "Yes I am sure; our people of the village are all of Cornish descent and have been for hundreds of years. My parents and their parents before were proud of this." "So why then did you betray the Cornish?" "Very simple, money, that's why, the very greed of money. I have worked in the service of the French, loyal like you are, for a long time and they were happy with my work. The money was fair and my work area had always been in France or

Countries close to, and never against the Cornish. One day a man with the high status of a Count, called Philip de Albret, knowing of my work and our people's good knowledge of the land of Cornwall, came to the village and offered me a huge amount of money for one mission. For the first time in my life, I had a chance to be rich in one hit, if successful. I knew with this one last job, I would have enough money to improve me and my poor parent's lives forever." Jacques realised what he had just said was true to its core and how his parents would feel the utmost shame that their brave loving Son had betrayed their old Cornish roots for money. Jacque's head went down in the shame of it all.

Peter didn't bat an eyelid at this sob story. He looked at Alfred while Jacque's head was bowed and smiled with a knowing confidence at the information being gained from the traitor in front of them.

They went over and over on what Jacques had done in the past and questioned him relentlessly without peace all day. Jacques didn't hold back on anything and answered all he was asked. As the day drew on, both sides of the table were more relaxed with each other, just what Peter wanted and all was becoming very clear. One thing Jacques did not and would not ever mention was the name of Jeanne. O Jeanne, he thought, how precious are you to me now.

"So then, after you betrayed the Cornish people by infecting their water supply in Mousehole, you then turned about and betrayed Philip Albret, the very man who was going to pay you the large amount of money. Why did you do this Jacques, it doesn't make sense at all." "Because, because," Jacques started to stutter a little here as he would not bring the name Jeanne into anything, it was the only decent thing left for him to do. "Because of Love, that's what." "Love, what the bloody hell has love got to do it?" "I tell you the truth, it was because of a love between me and a woman who I had once been told was dead and then found that she was alive." Peter and Alfred struggled with this motive and shrugged their shoulders at the sheer utter weakness of the man in front of them. They were expecting something more sinister and manly. "Love, you say, and what was the name of this so called love?" "The Lady was called Zoe."

That night, after a very long day, Peter said to Alfred, "Well my friend, it took quite a time and money but we have him and feel good that once we hand him over, we will get our five thousand Guinea reward." "And how much do we get out of doing this?" Peter had quietly, along the way, been doing his sums and workings out as he knew Alfred would ask this question sooner or later. "If we take all the monies spent, plus the monies saved on the Sniper and taking out Sarah's fees, I believe we will come out of with at least three thousand five hundred between us, we're back in the money Alfred." "About time Peter my friend, my funds have been running a little low." "That reminds me Alfred, I must send a message to Sarah tonight to inform her that our mission is now complete and she should return for her full payment." They clicked their glasses in a job well done.

Chapter 47

Seven, eight, nine, ten, he said to himself, as he finished his press ups. He then stood up straight and touched his toes then stretched his arms back up above the head. Joshua had always liked to keep his body flexible as best he could but over the last several months he hadn't bothered. But his mindset was changing and when time permitted started to do this discipline every morning before breakfast.

It was early in the morning and he needed to be at twenty five Dracaena Ridge in an hour. They were going in.

Joshua had taken up residence in a back room of the Chain Locker Inn by the quay side in Falmouth. It was ideal for relaying information quickly as required while carrying out surveillance of the cottage where one Sarah, so called friend of Zoe, lived.

Joshua had done his homework on the buildings concerned and had all the information sent to him for analysis. Most of the cottages at Dracaena were bought by local people who had put down a small deposit and then got a loan to pay the balance of the freehold which made perfect sense to Joshua. Number twenty five was bought outright in cash which is rare but not that unusual until Joshua started to check who bought it, who managed the paperwork and who witnessed the legal transaction. This is when his feeling of suspicion arose as there was none of it, only a single piece of paper confirming the sale and ownership and this was direct from the builders themselves. Joshua had visited their offices in Truro and talked with their legal team. They said it was not unusual for some rich people to do this and as long as they paid them in full, they were quite happy to relinquish title and deeds to the said buyer. However, what was a little strange, that on this occasion the man who paid them was not the owner but a proxy on behalf of one Peter La Frau, who wanted to use it as a holiday home, and was from the Netherlands. The man paid in cash and supplied address and signature of proxy. On drilling down it came apparent that he also bought number twenty four across the street.

Bull was due to arrive any minute with the carriage to take them both to Dracaena to manage the entry of the house, by force if needed. The constable of the jail had been informed and a room was made available. Bull had previously informed Joshua that the surveillance was not going too well as the terrace road with its walls and fences was just too tight and therefore they could not get the position to sit and watch for any length of time. It had been a case of watch and move, watch and move which produced very little information. It was then that Joshua took the reins and after getting the signed authority from the sheriff to enter the building, he would now stop the surveillance and act. He then heard the knocking on the door and a voice shout, "Joshua, are you ready?" "I am coming now Bull."

Sarah had been thinking deeply about the Sniper and the no show of the traitor bitch, Zoe. She found that quite odd as Zoe had said she would definitely return. Also, she had not heard from Peter and as the days went by she was getting more anxious as to what to do, something didn't feel right. If she did nothing but sit and wait she could be there forever and maybe be caught in something she had not prepared for. She decided to clean the house out completely of all signs of her work activity and wait one further week. She found a dry safe place to bury her money far away from the cottage and if she heard nothing after seven days she would leave the house, get the money and get to France.

With the cottage surrounded and being advised that a lone woman of middle age and no others had been seen in there, Joshua and Bull went up to the back door and knocked.

Sarah heard the knocking so got up and peeped through the side window. On seeing two men of stout figure her inner tenses were raised and knew she had to play the game, and play she would, as she had done many times. "What do you want," she shouted. "Please open the door we would like to talk with you." "Why, where are you from?" "Just open the door, we mean you no harm." Sarah's tone and actions of being a sad and lonely heartbroken woman had started.

As Sarah opened the door Joshua was taking no chances and, as planned, swiftly handcuffed her while Bull and his men searched the place thoroughly. Sarah was then taken away for questioning at the local jail.

Over and over Joshua questioned Sarah on her life and her relationship with Zoe. She however, was not fazed by this man and answered all he asked in an unknowing way to everything. She described how she met a woman on a ship from Brest sailing to Falmouth and that they had made friends with each other. Zoe had nowhere to live and so offered her a bed. Everything that Joshua asked she had an answer, in the shape of either being badly treated by being thrown out of her home in France by her nasty husband, or of her late Mother's wishes to look after her in the house that she fully believed her Mother owned outright. At every opportunity Sarah sobbed like some hurt frail woman who was being victimised and knew nothing of what these men wanted. When asked again about the unknown foreigner who legally owns the house she just kept saying, that's not true my Mother owns it like a loyal little daughter, naive to the big wide world, would.

It was around noon that Bull came in and informed Joshua that the house had been fully searched and was clean with no incriminating evidence found. "What you say Joshua?" "I say we pull your men out, rest and prepare the same for tomorrow at twenty four." "What about the woman" "She has told nothing of any wrong. She also keeps crying all the time and keeps going to go to the toilet. If she is in on something, which I think she is, then she is only a pawn but there is something wrong here, it is all not stacking up, I can feel it but we will not find what it is with her sat here. So, I am letting her go in a short while, like a rabbit out of the trap, and would like you to track without being seen to find out where she flees and don't stop her." "I fully understand Joshua and have just the person for the job"

As the hour passed Joshua did indeed let her go as he had advised Bull. He asked if she wanted a carriage to take her back to her house but she wanted to walk. Joshua thanked her for her cooperation and apologised, like a gentleman would, for any inconvenience that may have been caused.

Sarah thought of going back to the house to warn the old couple at number twenty four that something was up and for them to get away. But thought no, they would have to look after themselves, stupid old goats.

As always she thought of number one, herself, it was the only way to survive. She needed to get away and get away fast and knew she could be followed but better that than the noose. First, she went to the quay side asking porters about the ships lying in or around the dock and if any are sailing this day to France or any Country, it didn't matter. After many times of asking she was told that a small twin mast schooner at the end of the dock which carried messages and light goods was to sail on the tide early this evening. Their destination was the town of Roscoff in France, very close to where she wanted to go anyway. She looked quietly up to the heavens and thanked them for their help.

Then finding and pleading with the ship's officer that she had to get back to France as a matter of urgency to be by her dying Mother's side before she passed away to the Lord. The Captain, who was a kind man and worn down by this lady's heartbreak and sobs of hurt, agreed, but she could take no luggage or steeds, just her person, nothing else. She would also have to pay the fee in full when boarding one hour before sail. Sarah, with tearful thanks, needed only to get her money and wait.

A few hours after Joshua had given orders for Sarah to be trailed one of Bull's people reported to him on what she had seen. She had done a good job and Bull was proud of her work and knew himself that watching people without being seen is not easy. After thanking her for a job well done, Bull went discreetly over to the harbour master to enquire on the small two mast schooner and, once the facts were known, headed off to the Chain Locker where Joshua was staying.

"Roscoff, you say," Joshua said. "That's what the harbour master said and also showed me the paperwork to prove things." Joshua thought about the location of where Sarah was heading. He got the map out and thought once again that this location is very close to the town of Morlaix and the place of one Philip de Albret. This is all just too close for comfort. Joshua then acted on his suspicions.

"Alright Bull, this is what we will do. Let the little rabbit Sarah, or whatever her real name is go to Roscoff. I will get message to Kernow to track her from there. He has contacts in many places which I know not." "What are you thinking Joshua?" "Well, all the evidence suggests coming from or close to the town of Morlaix, our very last place of operation and it feels just all too close for comfort." "Revenge?" "It's possible, I don't know but I think it wise to raise our alert status to amber until we know more, which just maybe after we enter number twenty four tomorrow. Bull, please could you dispatch two of your good men to protect Jeanne."

Chapter 48

Dear Peter,
Due to important matters meeting deferred to Friday noon.
Thank you.
Antoinette - STB Countess of Morlaix.

Peter threw the message at Alfred to read and said, ''Bloody woman, does she not know what we have done here?'' ''It doesn't matter Peter, it is only one day.'' ''Maybe so Alfred, but one day is another day with the traitor here, I wanted all this sorted by tomorrow.'' So, with quiet reluctance and a short period to calm, Peter accepted the twenty four hour delay. Then with Alfred and the traitor Jacques, hands still cuffed but now moved to the front of his body, played cards and waited for the long day to pass.

If truth the delay wasn't Antoinette's at all but on the direct orders of the Prince. He, after many hours of talking with Hosking and hearing first hand his true testimonies and facts was completely spell bound with intrigue. They had somewhat become akin to each other, like brothers both. The Prince, as with Henry, had too been badly spurned in life and felt a deep mutual affection knowing full well how much it hurts inside.
You never get over that inner feeling of betrayal, never. They both wanted the same things in life that should have rightly been theirs anyway, only now they would do it together. And so it was then, that the Prince asked Antoinette to send a message to Peter the Frenchman to delay the meeting. Both the Prince and Henry wanted to spend more time with each other to create a plan of attack with a timed strategy to achieve their goals. It soon

became clear they would need an increase in men and resources so the Prince sent messages for others in his support network to make ready. As part of the initial plan, they went over how they would manage the meeting on Friday with Peter and the Spaniard, who calls himself Alfred, and the persons or person with them. The Prince clapped his hands with joy and delight at the very thought of it.

At the Morlaix Inn, after a very long trying day night fell and as Jacques, the traitor, slept at the table shackled, Peter and Alfred got to bed. With all the candles blown out the silence of the night soon came as they drifted off to sleep.

It was around seven the next morning that Peter heard the tapping on the door and a whispering, voice, 'Peter, Peter.' Getting up he gently walked to the door noticing that both other men were still at rest but Jacques, with his head resting on his arms across the table had started to move a little.

With pistol ready in hand he unlocked the door and opened it ajar. "Sarah, what are you doing here, I only just sent the message two nights ago, did you get it?" "Peter, let me in, I have been travelling along while and haven't stopped." "Is anyone with you?" "No, I come alone." "Then come in we can talk in the back room."

Sarah sat down and became very relieved she had made it. "Did you get my message," Peter said again." "No, I did not." "Then please tell me what is going on." After a while of talking, Peter went for the cider jug to quench both their thirsts. Sarah then carried on with her briefing while Peter listened with much interest.

"So you see Peter, I just had no choice, I had to escape while I could." "I agree Sarah and you have done well." Sarah took a small drink of cider to refresh her inner body and give her a little boost and waited in silence for Peter's advice. As Peter was also quietly thinking, Sarah interrupted his thoughts by asking, "Peter, who was that man at the table when I came in?" "I will tell all Sarah in a little while once I have sorted out in my mind if anything needs to be done or changed on the information you have given me." "Tell me again Sarah, how easy did you feel it was on how you got away." "What do mean?" "I mean as I say, how easy was it?" "Well, very easy actually but that was only because the small ship was sailing that very day." "I'm not on about the ship, I am on about getting away after being questioned in the jail by the man you called Joshua." "That was very easy, they just let me go." "Hmmm, he said aloud." "What are you thinking, they trailed me?" "It's what I would have done, and that's the very point." Again, Peter pondered as Sarah started to sob quietly. "Don't start that with me Sarah, I know you too well." "Peter, you are so hard on me."

"Alright," he said, in a decisive confident tone, "It doesn't matter either way whether they know or not, they have no time in which to do anything as after this very afternoon we will all be dispersed and the traitor handed over. When the meeting is finished we will split the money and ride off into hiding as done before." "I get my five hundred Guinea's, yes." "Yes Sarah, you get five hundred as agreed and once all has died down and things have been forgotten, we will then all meet up at our rendezvous point in one year to the very date."

Peter then added, "So the only thing that has changed as far as I can see, is nothing except you Sarah are coming with us to the Chateau." "What time are we due there Peter?" "At twelve noon my dear, which is only a few hours from now, and Sarah, may I suggest you get yourself cleaned up a little as you are looking rather bedraggled?" "Peter, I know the way I look, I have been up all night getting here, you know that." "Alright Sarah, I know, I am not having a go it's just an observation and once you are freshened I will introduce you to the traitor, called Jacques. I think then it would be good if you, Alfred and I sat down to quickly recap and get our stories straight for the Lady Antoinette. There can be no hesitations or doubts whatsoever in the meeting and If you are uncertain about anything, no matter what, this will be the time to ask. Our carriage leaves here at eleven thirty."

Peeking out the window they saw the carriage arrive and with everything ready they went down the stairs and out the back. When all four were safely aboard they set off on the short journey to the Chateau. Sarah was sitting opposite the traitor and felt very uncomfortable as he kept looking at her with those icy blue eyes. Peter and Alfred said almost nothing all the way except when they got to the Chateau gates and noticed for the first time they were being guarded which felt a little odd. "What do you make of that Peter?" Alfred asked. "I say it is good, she is taking precautions on this day which I find reassuring." As they rolled through the gates the guards put their hands up in a form of a salute and understanding but didn't stop them. Peter, in respect to them, put his hand up too. Getting to the front entrance the carriage stopped and the driver climbed down to open the doors then within a few seconds five armed guards appeared with one going direct to Peter to talk.

"Yes we do, he is in the carriage on the right side, shackled and chained," Peter replied. "So there is just one person?" "Yes, just one, I will explain all to the Lady." "Fine, we will look after him while you all meet." "That would be good but be careful he is very dangerous." "What about the other two?" "They will come with me, they are friends."

As Jacques was led away, the three of them started to walk to the main front doors. "Sorry, Sir," the main guard said aloud, "But we need to search you all before you enter, precautions you know." Alfred and Sarah looked at Peter for what to do but he nodded to them in the understanding of the guard's duties. Due to Sarah being a lady the guard called one of his colleagues to fetch a woman to search her. Each was found to have pistols and daggers on their beings and so all were swiftly taken from them, under strict orders. "Thank you all for your patience, you can pick them all up on your leave." Peter was somewhat impressed with the guard's skills of body search and courteous manner. Now, without any personal weapons, the three were led into the lobby to await further instructions.

Sitting in the calm library room, Antoinette, the Prince and Henry Hosking were sipping tea when the main guardsman came in to explain the situation. "That's very good, are all your men in place as we have practised," the Prince asked. "Yes my Lord." "And just the one man you say?" "Yes my Lord." "Please describe him." The guard did as told and then was ordered to leave them to get ready. "Well Henry, you were right all along, well done my brother." "Thank you my Prince." The Prince then turned to Antoinette and asked if she was ready and with an inner confidence said, "I am ready." "Good then let us all get into position."

After what seemed like a long twenty minute wait for the three visitors the guard came back into the lobby and said, "My apologies for the delay, please could you all follow me?" They were led to a quiet anteroom off from the library with a large table and many seats around. The guard pointed to the side where the three should sit to face the many pictures hanging on the walls and the mirror. "Please take a seat the Lady will be with you shortly." As the guard left the room, Peter said, "Now don't forget, let me do the talking, I don't want to be here any longer than necessary, agreed?" Alfred sitting to his left and Sarah to the right both said, "Agreed." Sarah then said, "This place gives me the creeps." As Sarah spoke those very last words the door opened and in walked Antoinette with two guardsmen, one of which was holding her pet poodle. "Please don't get up, and I apologise for the delay," she said. On sitting herself down facing the three visitors she took the poodle from the guard and laid it on her lap. The guards then walked towards the door, turned around and stood to watch over them." Now, before we start, would we all like some tea?"

Now, with the strained formalities over and the tea poured, Antoinette opened, "So Peter, what have you got for me?" Peter introduced his colleagues and went over all they had done and, as there was a lot to discuss, he kept things direct and to the point and Antoinette listened and sipped her tea. Sarah didn't like her one bit but kept her composure as she only had to bear it a short while but she could feel was not quite right.

''That's so good Peter, well done to you all. Now, where is this traitor who is responsible for my uncle and my so dear husband's deaths which may I add have broken my heart both?'' This was the one little weak point of Peter's work, he knew the traitor Jacques was instrumental in the death of her uncle Philip Albret, but couldn't really find anything to connect him with the other murder. However, he was sure it wouldn't matter as she would accept Jacques as the main person in both killings. ''He is here my Lady but before we ask your guards to bring him in, you do have the money we agreed?'' ''Yes, of course Peter, I am a lady of honour and it is what we agreed.'' ''Thank you, please then could we ask your guards to fetch him in as he is outside being held by them.'' Antoinette looked up towards the door and nodded her head for one of them to action.

As they were waiting for the prisoner, Antoinette broke the silence, ''So Sarah, ''How long have you worked for Peter?'' Sarah didn't want to speak to this woman but she put on her graceful face and said, ''Only recent my Lady, not long at all.'' ''Well, let me say, you have done well.'' ''Thank you my Lady.'' With that, the door swung open and Jacques was brought in by two other guards and put roughly down into a chair. The first thing Antoinette noticed was his rugged good looks and icy blue eyes. She then said, ''Please ensure you chain him secure and then move back.'' Once they had done what the Lady asked they moved around to the back wall with pistols at the ready. There were now four heavily armed guards in the room. Peter noticed this and started to feel intimidated as the room was now filled with more guards than he liked and all very close too.

The Prince and Henry were watching and listening through the two way mirror in a secret chamber and when they saw the man named Jacques enter and put into a seat, the Prince said, "Is that the man Henry?" Yes, that is him my Prince, the pawn is here." "Very well I shall meet you back in the main library as planned." The Prince got up and went out of the secret chamber through the Library and around to the main front Lobby. All the guards were there waiting for him as ordered and once he had got them into position they stood in silence, ready for the anteroom door to open. Henry, still in the secret side chamber, kept looking through the two way mirror at the four visitors but his eyes were transfixed with a burning hatred of Jacques.

"Are you the man called Jacques," Antoinette said. Jacques didn't answer, he was like a worn out rat that had been saved from a drowning. His clothes were tattered, his face swollen and he stunk. "What is that smell she said aloud to all." "It's the shot wound on his leg it has become infected and puss ridden," Peter replied. Antoinette tried again in a more careful way and got a slow nodding of the head and a groaned 'yes," like from a man who was simply finished.

With that, she turned to face the three people in front of her and said, "Well Peter, it seems that our contract is finished. You may all leave now and get your reward from my butler who is waiting in the lobby for you." "Thank you my Lady, it has been a pleasure working for you and if we can be of any assistance in the future please ask." The three of them got up, bowed their heads and walked to the door. Peter took the lead and went first then a very relieved Sarah with the Spaniard last. The guards followed closely behind.

The Prince was standing furthest away across from the door in the large lobby area and saw them come out. He waved to Peter as if to say I am the one you want. Peter noticed him straight away and so walked boldly across the lobby floor towards him while Sarah and Alfred followed.

Just as the Spaniard had come out of the anteroom doorway an unseen guard from the side quickly pounced. With strong hands around Alfred's head pushed his chin up and with a sharp blade slit his throat deep. Hearing the noise of a scuffle behind them, Peter and Sarah stopped in their tracks and looked back in shock and horror as all the guards in the lobby raised their ready cocked pistols at them both.

It was then that the man who Peter had thought was the butler and who was holding the money bag of their reward said aloud for all to hear, ''Now, you two scoundrels, you dare bring me a puppet and disrespect a loyal household to the King when the real killer is still at large, you are nothing but thieves and rogues. Guards take them down before I lose my temper and have their throats slit too.'' The Prince then turned and calmly walked back through the lobby into the library without saying a further word.

As the Prince went into the Library and closed the door behind he saw Hosking's and with a smile said, ''Henry this is so exciting.'' ''Would you like a drink my Prince before we see the traitor'' ''Yes please my brother, you have saved me a lot of money this day, and my prestige will be of the highest when we return to my Father with that Cornish Witch, the true killer of the French.'' ''Have you mind yet for sail my Prince?'' ''Yes, all has been arranged, we set sail tomorrow night from the small inlet off Plouescat, heading as we agreed, to the Dark Cove near Tintagel."

After they both swished their cognacs down, they went to the ante chamber and as they boldly entered, Antoinette, the guards and the prisoner looked up. When seated the Prince asked the guards if the traitor was chained down good. On hearing he was, they were then ordered to wait outside.

Jacques could not believe that of all people, Hosking was now sitting in front of him with a smirk of self satisfaction written all over his body. "You two know each I think, is that right Jacques," the Prince asked with a certain pride of knowing. Jacques didn't respond as if he hadn't heard the question but just stared at Hosking with pure venom. He then couldn't help himself say in a low gravelly voice, "You bastard Hosking's, you bastard, I knew it was you, it had to be you, you bloody bastard." "So you two do know each other," the Prince said laughingly aloud.

Henry too with a smirk of pride all over his face didn't react to Jacque's angry remarks, instead, he just simply replied by saying in a very vindictive voice, "Would you like to know how Jeanne is?" On hearing his true love's name, Jacque's eyes opened further with dread but kept his mouth shut. Henry continued, "Well, let me tell you Jacques you little traitor, she will be mine very soon, all mine, and I will bed her good." Jacques immediately lunged forward to get at Henry Hosking's throat and strangle him to death with his bare hands but the chains were tight and couldn't move from the chair. "Now now Jacques let's not fight, we have some questions to ask first," the Prince said.

Antoinette stayed quiet and watched Jacque's every move as the Prince continued. ''Jacques, what you know of the name Zelahnor?'' As soon as the Prince spoke the name the lamps began to flicker and the poodle, sitting snug on Antoinette's lap, jumped up and hid under the table. Jacques was silent but again looked at Henry straight in the eyes knowing now how far he had gone to betray the Cornish. ''Tell me Jacques, what do you know of her?'' Jacques sealed his lips tight and went cold with fear as he dare not speak the name or reveal anything of the oldest myth in his Breton Cornish blood. He had done wrong in the past, he knew that, but now he could do right by staying silent and let his parents and ancestors be once more proud. The Prince called two of the guards in to make him talk but Jacques would not speak and took the punishment with a renewed inner strength of doing right. Antoinette and Henry looked on with relish at the pain being given.

The Prince waited quietly for the traitor to speak but knew he would not. The name Zelahnor had spooked him. So he told the guards to stop the beating and take the traitor away to the dungeons and throw him in a cell next to the other two traitors. As the guards walked out of the ante room holding the prisoner by his arms, Jacques saw the large fresh pool of blood on the floor and two servants on their knees cleaning it up. Jacque's mind went quickly to his captives, Peter, Alfred and Sarah and which one of them had got it. While the door was just closing behind them two small moths flew out past his head, through the lobby to the main front door and then out to the open forest ahead.

The guards held the prisoner in front as they walked down and down the steep steps to the dungeons below.

Jacques could not help but think that this is where he had walked nearly a year ago with Joshua to free his lovely Jeanne who was being held captive by the very nasty de Albret. As they got to the bottom they turned right to where the dungeon was located and the guard sat. Still holding Jacque's arms tight the main guardsman said with sternness, "Open up a cell for a traitor." "Another one?" the sitting guard said, but then quickly did as was told and got off the seat. It was then that Jacques realised and knew which dungeon it would be.

When the cell door was opened Jacques walked calmly to its entrance and stood still facing inwards. The guards then took off Jacque's wrist cuffs from behind his back and then kicked him hard forward. The cell door was then closed and locked without further word. Feeling alone he shuffled deeper into the cell and laid down his body on the very bed that his beautiful Jeanne had laid and closed his eyes. After a few minutes of earthly silence, he opened his eyes and looked up into the dark of the cold wet cell. With his mind and body calmed, he whispered aloud, 'O Jeanne, the love of my very life, I lie here now where you once lay, let them bring what they will, I am content.'

Chapter 49

It was four in the morning and the baby badger was sitting on Christine's lap and tenderly nursing the cut paw. "Now, this won't hurt you my little sweet," she said, while ever so gently wiping the little wound clean. While Christine was nursing the badger, Deborah was sitting next to her with a small squirrel in her hands that had tummy pains, and so was feeding it a herbal solution to ease things. While both were nursing the young animals they were also singing tunes in harmony of love and happiness. The fire was roaring and the butterflies were flying all around in the joy of life.

The three growing up pups of Zoar were playfully trying to mimic their Father and uncle's ways of protection. One was laid by the door and one each by the feet of both the girls. Solar, their Mother was lying down watching all with love.

Zareb was outside lurking in the shadows of the dark night guarding the shack when his ears pricked up. It was then he saw Zelahnor and his brother Zoar coming back home.

Zelahnor had been all night away by Tintagel, deep down on the rugged rocks in a quiet hidden cove where the sea, land and air meet. This hidden cove in Tintagel is the place where Zelahnor most feels she can talk to all creatures. For hours she had stood still in the surf with arms out stretched and the water of the sea up to her waist. Zoar had also laid in watch lying unseen in the cove close behind. Zelahnor, looking across the massive blue ocean with the reflection of the full moon shining down, could now talk with all her sea and land animals, mammals, sisters and the birds above. It was not until two in the morning that all the parties she had talked with agreed the course of action that they must take due to the very seriousness of the situation and what was to come. Therefore, the letter would be written to Joshua and be delivered by two white tailed eagles next morning. She thanked them all dearly for their protection and love of the Cornish.

Zareb rose up to greet Zelahnor and Zoar at the entrance to the shack. Zoar rubbed his huge shoulders with his brother and then went inside and kissed all his sons and wife, Solar. Then after greeting both girls he laid his body by the fire to rest in readiness for what was to come. Zelahnor sat down with Christine and Deborah and held hands in quiet love.

It was then that Zelahnor asked Christine, "My child of the light, you have something on your mind you wish to ask?" "Yes, I do." "You have no need my darling let me answer these for you, your Father is called Jacques and he is living in France and he loves you very much as Deborah's Father loves her." Deborah smiled at the loving thought of her lost parent.

"Is my Father well, as I feel he is not." "O my sweet bunch of honey, how you are growing in the senses of life. No, he is not well in body at this moment this is true, but he is strong in mind, and he himself will be well." "Did he love my Mother?" "Yes, he loved and loves your Mother very much and she loved him with both having a true endearing affection for each other. And yes, to answer your one last question Christine, your Father is of the Cornish blood and true to the old ways of the ancient, that is why you and Deborah have been chosen to serve and love." "That makes me so happy," Christine said. "And me," Deborah echoed. They all hugged each other tightly as the butterflies danced in joy.

As day moved into night the two girls slept with the cubs tucked up snug and Solar slept close by as she always did.

It was then in the quiet early hours that Zelahnor took pen to parchment and wrote to Joshua as had been agreed with all whilst at Tintagel cove. When finished she wrapped it tight and went out in the dark night of the moor to wait. It didn't take more than two or three minutes before the white tailed eagles came gliding down to her side. Thanking them for their time she fixed the message to the female and then kissed them both wishing them safe speed. The female flew off first followed by her gallant male.

Zelahnor went back into the shack and kissed the sleeping girl's cheeks and tucked them up. It was now time to talk with Zoar and his brother as time was now short and they needed to get sorted and moving. She called them across by the warmth of the fire and quietly listened to her gentle tones of action. When all things were said they purred their understanding of what they were to do and bowed their heads with loyalty. Zelahnor hugged them both in love and farewell and opened the door as they both ran out at speed onto the cold dark, bleak moor.

Zelahnor looked at Zoar and Zareb run from the shack until both were out of sight and with a heavy heart closed the door and walked to where the children and puppies lay sleeping. She gently laid her body down between them and cuddled them all. Solar felt some sadness so also moved in close and rested her body with them. As they all quietly slept like a family of chicks in a nest, the butterflies flew from the roof and rafters to lay down with them covering all like a silk blanket of coloured warmth.

As the eagles soared high over the high cliffs of Gunwalloe they sighted Joshua's cottage below. After circling many times the male decided it was time to rest and keep out of sight and so guided his wife to a tree a few hundred yards away to wait for the early sun to rise. When the darkness had drifted to light was when the male saw Joshua come out of the cottage and walk to the nearby wood shed. It was then they acted and flew like arrows in the early sun straight to the doorway which Joshua had left open for his return.

As Joshua was walking back with a few logs under his arm thinking of the day ahead, he stopped in his tracks at the very sight of these two beautiful birds standing in his path in the open doorway. They looked at him and he looked at them. It was Joshua who talked first as if it were the most natural thing to do, "Good morning, and what are you two doing here?" The eagles bent their heads forward as if to say good morning back and then the male, with his sharp bill, pulled at the message wrapped around his wife's leg. Joshua saw what he was doing and looked on in sheer and utter bewilderment. As the message came loose the male with the message in his beak walked the few feet to Joshua and dropped it by his feet. Joshua bent down and picked it up and on the outside it read very clearly the name, Joshua. Joshua shook his head but then just naturally said, "Thank you, thank you very much, I think I understand." With that, the two birds flew off high towards the sun and back to the moor.

Still shaking his head in disbelief at what had just occurred he walked on in and sat by the fire to read the message. It was then that Rebecca came through the scullery door and asked who he had been talking to. "You wouldn't believe it Rebecca even if I told you." "Try me," she said. "Alright, I will, two white tailed eagles giving me a message." "And what message may that be?" "This one here which I am just about to read." Rebecca, unlike Joshua fully believed it all.

While Rebecca was still standing watching, Joshua unrolled the small parchment, it read.

Joshua.
'La Faye' - Enemy Galleon
Dark Cove east of Gull rock.
Seize Monday as the sun rises.
Traitor of known hurt and harm aboard.
Believe in the way Joshua.

Joshua shook his head again in disbelief at the information the message contained and given to him at the back door of his cottage by two white tailed eagles. He gave the message to Rebecca to read and after doing so calmly looked up and asked with pure simplicity, "So Joshua, what are you going to do?"

Chapter 50

The 'La Faye,' with canons loaded was trying its best to get as close as it could to the hidden inlet as the Prince did not want to waste valuable time using slow rowing boats of long distance to get to shore. It was now the Sunday night, two days after the message was sent to Joshua by the white tailed eagles. The sun had set an hour ago and the Captain was watching closely all around in getting the ship as close as he dare. As the ship eased itself forward with the ebb and flow of the tide the Captain decided that was enough and shouted, "Down Anchor!" "Well done Captain, well done indeed" the Prince said. "Thank you my Prince,"

The sea was calm but the Captain could feel a storm ahead. With the anchor down and ship steady they started to make haste in getting men, horses and stores ashore. In all, there were seven people, the Prince, Antoinette, Hosking and four of the Prince's body guards. All were fully armed to the teeth and clothed with chain link armour. The Prince called them his 'Troop of the French Revenge,' which made him feel like some sort of Joan of Arc. His posture and the shouting of orders made him also feel like a general in the midst of battle, overcoming all odds. With the troop came five very large Bull Mastiffs of French breed and each weighing two hundred pounds with deadly reputations. They could kill anyone or anything with one bite of their massive powerful jaws. One of the horses carried a small wheeled cage with room to imprison one person and, once caught, to be dragged back like an animal for all to see. "My Prince, you are so brave, "Antoinette said, "Thank you my dear, now get behind as I will lead this attack as a brave Prince of the French should." "Are you ready my brother Henry?" "I am my Prince," he replied. When all was ready they set off with the Captain of the guard by his side leading them all due east. The French Bull Mastiffs couldn't wait as they knew something was up and were ready with fangs gnashing.

The distance was about ten miles as the crow flies which should take about two hours. They were to move directly through Slaughter Bridge and enter the edge of the moor west by north west. Once there they shall call her name aloud through the still of night and when she comes they will attack her and all who follow her without mercy. They had to be back on ship no later than five tomorrow morning with the prisoner Witch caged.

Zoar and his brother reached the dense forest at the western edge of the moor in which they protect and waiting for their arrival were all the other animals of fight and mane. All had come without any hesitation in the purity of love for their Zelahnor. Zoar talked with them all from snakes, badgers, foxes, wild dogs and ponies. Even little squirrels came to help as did the birds of prey. They all listened with intent at what Zoar was saying as they all wanted to do their best for him. It was agreed that the enemy force which is coming to attack Zelahnor will walk through the forest to get onto the open moorland. Therefore, it was up to the little ones to do what they could inside the forest of trees. The larger animals and creatures would stay out on the edge of the moor waiting for the enemy to come through.

It was just before the midnight hour and the moon was high that the Prince and his armed Troop entered the forest from the west. As they got a little deeper in the forest the Prince suggested that the dogs be brought forward to take the lead and so the Bull Mastiffs, on long leashes and snarling with a want to kill, went ahead and started to lead them through.

It was then that the snakes on the ground and the owls in the trees slithered and swooped into the enemy. The horses started to get very anxious and jerked their heads to and fro and up and down while kicking out their legs. The Mastiffs were also trying to bite the snakes and the owls which were all around them but all were too quick for their big jaws and carried on harassing. With all that was going on the Troop did not stop and pushed on through the forest. It was not until they were at the forest end and about to set foot on the moor itself that they saw the two massive black beasts standing twenty yards in front of them with their jaws wide open roaring with anger.

The five French Mastiffs strained on their leashes to get at them and simply being unable to hold back their powerful strength they broke free and attacked Zoar and Zareb head on. It was savage as all animals ferociously bit and tore at each other. Zoar and Zareb fought courageously but it was no good as the Mastiffs were terrifyingly brutal. Then the wild dogs of the moor which have been lying in wait in two packs often attacked the savage mastiffs from either flank in a pincer movement and turned the advantage. The horses of the French troop, seeing all the war of blood before them, reared in terror and threw their riders to the ground. The horses, stricken with panic and not being able to go forward or to the side to escape ran back through the forest they had all just come. The Prince and all the troops people now on the ground and bruised from their falls dashed back to the safety of the forest's edge and then turned and fired their pistols. Now it was the birds of the sky's turn as more than twenty eagles and their falcon brothers, with talons sharp and fast speed, swooped down from the air at all angles to tear at the French enemy who wanted to hurt their beautiful Princess of the Moor. Then all the badgers and foxes were doing their loyal duty too by bravely running through the dense undergrowth and biting as many legs and feet as they could. Reloading and firing another salvo of shot, the main guardsman moved to the Prince's side and said, ''My Prince we must go back now, this is carnage, something is very wrong here, we must withdraw.'' The Prince looked at the guard but as he did an eagle swooped again and slashed his forehead deep. ''My Prince, we must go back.'' All the people of the French troop were now bleeding from either bites from the undergrowth or slashed from the air.

The roaring of the fight between the French Mastiffs and Zelahnor's loyal animals of the moor was now quiet as all the mastiffs lay dead. It was then that the black beasts and wild dogs of the moor, bleeding heavily from shot and the mastiff's fangs and claws, turned their attention to the French attackers lying at the forest's edge.

For a third time the guard repeated his words but this time he grabbed the Prince's tunic and dragged him backwards. The Prince was in some sort of trance and could not believe what was happening as it wasn't meant to be like this. The guard realising that the Prince was not right raised his voice for all to retreat, back into the safety of the forest.

Once they were far enough back they stopped running and fell to the ground. The seven of them were exhausted and totally confused on what to do next so the guard spoke up and suggested, while they were all still alive, that they go back to the safety of the ship and rethink this through. The Prince suggested, with favour of more money, that the four guards go back and fight for them and get the bitch they so dearly wanted, while he, the lady Antoinette and Hosking wait here out of harm's way. The main guard looked at his three fighting mates and all shook their heads in refusal. "You are nothing but cowards," "Sir, we are not cowards we are soldiers but this is wrong, we cannot fight animals of the night and things we cannot see. You saw it with your own eyes, not one human in sight just bloody wild animals everywhere." With that, the rain and wind picked up with a vengeance. "Sir, I suggest we go back."

It had been two days since Zoar and his brother Zareb had left the warmth and love of Zelahnor to go and defend the moor and the old Cornish way of life. But now as the sun rose on the early Monday morning they were back. Slowly and limping badly from the French Mastiffs' savage attack they released the catch on the front door and entered the shack. Solar got up and went straight to her husband's side and started to lick his deep wounds. Zareb was also badly injured and so Christine and Deborah tended to him with ointments of herbs and love. Zelahnor thanked the skies and heavens for their safe return and sang an old ballad of soft sweet voice. Christine and Deborah joined in and the butterflies fluttered and danced all around with love and happiness at their return.

It wasn't until nearly five in the morning that the Prince and his French troop reached the cliffs above the inlet of Dark Cove. When all were together sitting down the guard fired the red flare up into the dark morning sky and then waited and watched for the same from the waiting ship out at sea. When the reply came they all scrambled down to await the two small boats to take them away.

By the time they had all struggled down the deep rocks two rowing boats had been dispatched from the ship and were only a few minutes away. The Prince ordered that the four guards go in one boat and he, Antoinette and Henry will go in the other. As the two boats steadied themselves against the rocks all persons got in as planned. Then as they were being rowed back to the 'La Faye,' the sea below started to swell in strength and height. The rowers had to pull hard and started to struggle to keep the boats going in the direction they wanted. The first boat, which had the four guards on board eventually, reached the ship first, but then they had helped the rowers with their oars through the now rough sea. The second boat was way behind and struggling as no one was helping the two rowers in their efforts to cope with the bulging swells and high wind. In fact both Antoinette and the Prince thought how pathetic the rowers were. The Prince leaned forward closer to Antoinette and said, ''These rowers are like my four so called guardsmen totally useless When we get back on board I shall tell the Captain of the cowardice of all four and have them shot, no one does not do what I say do, I am Prince.'' ''You are quite right my brave Prince, but have them guillotined instead as it is much more exciting, they are pathetic and weak people just like these stupid bloody rowers.'' ''It shall be done as you wish my lovely Countess of Morlaix. Then we shall go back with better men and more supplies and cage that evil Cornish Witch who calls herself bloody Zelahnor.''

The Prince had just finished his last words of defiance when he heard Hosking's shout in a very loud voice. "Look, did you see that," pointing to the deep blue sea. "See what," the Prince replied. "I thought I saw something move under the swells." "Don't worry my brother, we are nearly there now, calm yourself down, we shall all have a large brandy very soon." Indeed his was right as after a few more heavy laden pulls of the oars the boat touched the ship. As the rope ladder was thrown down Henry caught it and without the slightest care to anyone but himself got the grip and scaled his body up.

As soon as Henry's feet had left the small boat it was then that the great Sperm Whale came up from the depths of the rough sea and smashed his full body weight into the small boat. The boat went up in the air and split into two sending the persons aboard flying out and into the sea. Following close behind the Sperm whale attack were two adult Bull Sharks who ever so slowly rose from the very darkness of the deep ocean. The two rowers started to swim to the rope ladder still hanging from the ship's side but the Prince and Antoinette stayed where they were shouting at everyone to come and help them. The two bull sharks left the rowers alone and went directly for Antoinette and the Prince and once upon them opened their jaws and grabbed both by the legs and dragged them down to the bottom of the ocean.

The Bull sharks agreed mission, once the air of life had gone from the two bodies, was to stay deep to the sea floor and take their lifeless forms far away from the Cornish shores back to the land of whence they came where they can do no more harm to anyone or anything. Once there, they were to be released close to their land and let the tide and currents take them home.

The Captain of the ship saw it all and was amazed at what he just witnessed. He had never seen anything like it. The two rowers of the small boat were still in the sea but made it to the ship's ladder and hastily helped each other up. Hosking, also saw all and although he had many cuts and bruises was alive and safe on board the 'La Faye,' unlike the other two. The Captain, feeling very nervous at what had just happened did not want to wait any longer around these shores and so shouted, ''Weigh Anchor and set Full Sail.''

Joshua, with the very insistence from Rebecca that he takes the message by the white tailed eagles seriously, got things organised.

It was now sun rise on the Monday morning and Joshua and Bull were each aboard two ships of the line which were waiting behind Gull Rock, out of sight. They had arrived only a few hours ago but Joshua had the foresight to send a single two man team to hide in and upon the cliffs shoreline at an angle where they could see both La Faye and Joshua.

The hidden two man team looked through their long range scopes and saw seven people get into two small rowing boats. Nothing was amiss with this as their main target was the La Faye which was anchored and remained steady. It was when they had seen the massive sperm whale and sharks that activated high tension. Then when they saw the crew of the La Faye running around in haste and weigh anchor they had to make a decision. They looked at each and both agreed that the signal be given to Joshua and Bull and so uncovered the bright oil lantern with dark background three times

On seeing the signal from his team on the shoreline Joshua acknowledged and sent the same signal to Bull who was on the other ship preparing for attack. Then, on orders from both Joshua and Bull, the Captains of the two ships of the line with sails already raised slipped anchors and took the wind. Both ships caught the current which was in their favour and sailed around the Gull each appearing from different sides. And then in line abreast both headed directly to the inlet of Dark Cove to trap or destroy the enemy ship. The lookout high in the crow's nest aboard the La Faye caught sight of the two ships of the line with Cornish flags flying coming at them and started to shout, "Ennemi, Ennemi." The Captain of the 'La Faye' looked over to the direction where his lookout was pointing then rushed to the ship's side to look through his scope. On seeing two powerful galleons of the Cornish closing in, said to himself, "O my dear Lord."

Once the 'La Faye' was in full view the two ships of the line steadied and then orders were given to fire salvo of canon.

The two salvos of canon ball went flying past front, stern and above the 'La Faye' to show warning of intent. All the crew of the La Faye stopped what they were doing and looked in stunned silence at their Captain. He was standing on the top deck but knew he couldn't go backwards, forwards or sideward, nor could he outgun them, it would be suicide.

He had no choice, there was just no choice and so with utter shame on his face, he looked at his lieutenant standing by his side and with an acceptance of defeat, nodded on what to do. The Lieutenant fully understood what the Captain wanted him to do as he also knew they were trapped and so replied lowly, "Aye, Aye Captain." He then turned, stood tall, and shouted the order, "Raise the White Flag."

The End

Love to my Mum & Dad

Printed in Great Britain
by Amazon

26833607R00185